TOPIARY – A NOVEL

TOPIARY – A NOVEL

by

A. Stephen Engel

The Oliver Arts & Open Press
http://www.oliveropenpress.com

Library of Congress Cataloguing-in-Publication Data
Engel, A. Stephen, 1965-
Topiary–A Novel by A. Stephen Engel

ISBN 978-0-9819891-3-6

The Oliver Arts & Open Press
2578 Broadway, Suite #102
New York, NY 10025
http://www.oliveropenpress.com

DEDICATION

For Bonita
And, in order of importance (more or less)
Burt, Glenda, Mara, John, Phyllis

A Preface
"Call me Plantman"

Or Tammuz, or the Trickster, or El Loco or Le Mat or the Fool. The Green Man has many names. In jolly England, long before Jesus stole Easter, Green George–the Fool dressed in leaves–was celebrated as Spring. Because, after the terrible death of Winter, despite all evidence to the contrary, Spring does return: The Fool believes this. As son and lover of the Moon, this Madman or Lunatic was, long before Jesus, the archetypal embodiment of the original Death and Resurrection, after three dark lunar days.

Call him–literally–Dionysus, who does the Saturday night fever-dance of drunken fertility. He brings the wine, he brings the dance–"he is the wine, he is the dance."

On every continent of the ancient pagan world–Asia, Africa, Europe, the Americas–the Green Man was Earth's beloved Clown. He walked over cliffs while playing his flute. He carried on his back, and in his groin, a bag containing all the seeds of every thing that grows. Flowers, ferns, trees, grains, nuts, fruits, and their coming and going on the seasonal Wheel: The Green Man was the energy-surge of all vegetal life, and as such the

Holy Fool was the Holy Food of all animal life.

After death, the souls of Mayan men and women must carry bundles of all the genitals of a lifetime's lovers. This bag of penises and vaginas is heavy and burdensome, but once arrived in the Underworld, the more sex organs the better! The newly arrived dead soul flings them at the World Tree–a Fig Tree–to dislodge its fruits, the food of the Afterlife. Thus sex, death, and vegetation enact our mortal energy-exchange with the gods. I knew once a real-life Mexican god of rain and fertility. He was always stoned. A freelance gardener in Tucson, he loved to stand with a hose for hours watering desert yards and dusty bushes–on somebody else's water bill; or when really drunk, he'd spray piss all over your front door or living room carpet; or when horny sneak around at all hours impregnating barrio women–every child his garden blossom, he supplied all the seeds.

Yes, that's our boy. But those were simpler days.

Topiary's Plantman incarnates in the City of the Near Future as Keeper and Protector of office greenery. He waters and trims and tries to sustain the sad life of "corporate flora" in the cubicles of tall, huge, busy, dead buildings where only money lives. As in the Grail myths, the entire planet is Wasteland. On a dying planet, the pure knight searches for the Holy Grail, which in this case is The Missing Girl. (Grail and Grrrl throughout Western literature are variants of the same thing.) Plantman, a man of his own nature, in his daily life and work encounters "trials," which are the collisions of a death-binge culture where creatures are born alive but only into manufactured terms. Each character and situation here is a condensed saga, a handful of seeds. Plantman's terrain compacts the modern techno-dilemma in its recurrent mythic guise: The University of Vigor & Ambition; The Hall of Hoaxes, with its resident Giant Hoax; The Indian Museum; The Museum of Women. Within the city's cynical parody of "culture," real agony occurs: The Possessed Man (a brilliant update of Thoreau's Desperate Multitude) is neither good nor bad. He is terrified, alone–even among friends and family. Though he works to support his family, he is not sure, exactly, what he *does.* According to his Job Description, he "Administrates Creative Product Strategies." Lucky to have a job, doomed to Kafka's prediction, he's reached his final rung. He knows he hasn't the energy to kill, the visceral burning to climb further. The remaining energies of life will be directed toward hanging to the rung on which his life precariously clings–a long, grim struggle to maintain his place on the limitless ladder to the sky. He can barely see the people at bottom, but he would need a powerful telescope even to glimpse the Movers and Shakers at the Top.

Before incarnating as Savior of Greenery, Plantman worked at the Ad Agency: "What was I doing, me and my false words? De-generative lingua-phobia. Overexposure to corrupt grammar of 'the sell.'" In his journey around the vertical ice-cube trays composing the high-rise city, Plantman is more or less androgynous, able to sense the doomed bio-romantic stasis of women who once twined naked with him under a rhythmic Moon. Women office workers, the Datists, work for a world of male world-managers: "Computers sucked girl juice dry from cunt to womb. Terrible brightness of the afternoon (or was it night?) under florescent suns. What is a girl's desire in the world of men?"

Plantman's empathy with every life form and human type–like his plants, struggling to stay alive in synthetic space and mechanical time–is real but helpless. His "condition"–terminal anemia–signals the energy fluid of Life itself dying from the biophobia of the World–a world in which The Death Squad, a "weekly documentary for the war-juiced public," is the favorite hit network TV "live-action series."

> The Death Squad ventured into neglected quarters of The City, retrieving corpses (many a corpse corpsed under suspicious circumstances). Questioned nosy neighbors, investigated scenes, chauffeured corpses to the morgue. Live autopsies exposed live audience to the gruesome-gruesome.
>
> "The dead, the indigent dead, accumulate with a rapidity that taxes The City's ability to process the remains," the Celebrity Commentator explained.
>
> The Death Squad consisted of two cops in a car and the ambulance van–a hearse, really, labeled "ambulance" out of respect for the paramedics, known in the trade and show vernacular as "Reapers." The Commentator and Cameraman rode back of the van with Night's retrievals.
>
> The Commentator spoke of faces. Past night's faces under burlap blankets reemerged in dreams. Death Squad: cleaning agents plucked dead cells from Metropolis. Decrepit sections of The City; smegma spread. Crimes to be solved, reports filed. Black ink ball point. Triplicate.

Uh-huh, yeah. Now the commercial.

Engel's narrative is discontinuous, but this is more than some kind of Post Modern strategy. The archetypal world is cyclical, not linear, and its story is one of seasonal appearances and disappearances. Heroes, demons, mazes, and epiphanies pop up, are deleted, then reappear in a quantum peek-a-boo process throughout human/historic time (story time) even though they are not of that time.

It's a smart trope (and Tropism) to orient this bio-data toward the larger energy source of myth and cosmic agenda, just as the earth's vegetal realm is oriented towards the sun and moon cycles.

Plantman carries water, does what he can to nourish the material roots and blooms of vegetal life-forms in the humanoid city. Engel has created not a far-fetched Future, but he has held the mirror up to the present. The human spirit, isolated in its unnatural cubicle from the primal juices of planetary life, is Wilting unto Death, and we all feel it.

Plantman is sick. Red blood going pale. Green blood growing thin and desert dry. The planet is sick with poison and deranged consciousness, and the rejuvenation skills of millions of evolutionary years are failing. Like every life form on the over-manufactured planet, Plantman is alone with his mythic destiny. Carrying a bag of fading cells, he must look for The Missing Girl in this classic scenario: In search of the Only Real Magic which can refresh and fertilize Earth–while he also seeks his own resurrection from impending Death.

He will journey out of the City, westward to the Desert where, at an oasis, the Missing Girl comes cyclically to renew herself by eating the Fruit of the Tree of Life. To rebirth herself, like this ancient scarred Earth, into the dream of another Generation.

> "How do you know She will come?"
>
> "She always comes. She will remain nineteen, the age at which I introduced her to the fruit, always and forever."

If you pass Plantman on the highway, with that bag of seeds over his shoulder, trudging drunkenly Westward–he's headed toward that oasis. Always and forever. – Barbara Mor, 2008.

Mor is author of *The great Cosmic Mother: Rediscovering the Religion of the Earth* (1991).

Overture: Call Me Plantman

Call me Plantman.

Summer The War suddenly, not unexpected. For weeks The Nation's Uniformed Young amassed The Enemy border. Pump of Young like sperm into the vicious Rogue Regime. Carnage ignited a galaxy of screens, monitors. 24/7.

Escape?

Persona: Plantman, Keeper Protector The City's office green. Grim fluorescent light can be, will be, serene.

I watered, trimmed, dusted corporate flora. Green Man at large. Horticultural Technician. Indoor Landscaper of potted plants. Verdure The City. Complex unruly. Sprout, contort, evolve. Snake-like struggle to?

The Light.

Anchored in cylinders of soil. Dirt. Same thing (for instance: "He soiled his pants; she dirtied her diapers" etc.). Plants too are data. Input/output.

Me, my Self displaced. Fiction a New Self. Watering can, scissors, agon. Deep daydreams the war.

Plantman and his room-mates, Music and BEING.

Rise with dawn, Green Man, Plantman, vigorous magician!

They waited for me. Potted oases of The City. Florescent days accrued–a past! To study and transform. The City was work to be done as if into a girl. Real life living, coming to a cubicle near you. Watering can, feather duster, scissors. Adjustable Topiary Techniques apron.

In Search Of: Ivy in window sills creeping up walls. Ficus, Fiddle-leaf Fig. Song of India in Executive Suites. Pothos, Dieffenbachia, Kentia Palm for workers' cubicles. Dead leaves guidelines for care. Pluck 'em, chuck 'em.

"All plants are created," veteran technicians claimed.

How true. Fundamental problem keeping life alive in the steel-and-concrete City.

Too late to exchange all this? For military green? Experience, not merely imagine, enemy fire? Lose Self permanently always? Gone? Exotic Time-passes, options.

Imagine a camouflaged Self. Exhaustive wrenching of the will. Muscles of Being: weary, relaxed, a fist unclenched.

Release the Me I bore more than a quarter century.

Voice of The Nation

Awakened midnight nobody home. Alone against the music of the Angry Young.

Kid outside screamed poems into a mike. Squat amp dragged behind him on a wagon. Surrounding friends clapped stomped cacophonous. Launched his dithyrambs against The City. Cannonades of sing-song bass.

Josh razed Jericho with song.

"Turn off the NOISE and tune in The VOICE of The Nation."

That ad from somewhere I remember. Subway maybe. Turned on the stereo. Fight noise with noise. Lonely like I've never. Unbearable rip. Inside. Alone me in the midnight.

Tried to reach The VOICE myself. Dialed, the line was jammed. WSOS after midnight. The VOICE beseeched by the Sleepless of The Nation.

Cassette recorder/radio on my bookshelf. Little block of gizmo purchased student days to record the lectures of Great Men and listen to the music of my day. Provides Flamenco for the run, now. Listen to Flamenco when I run.

Stole fresh batteries from my room-mate, raised the volume.

The VOICE said to the Sleepless of The Nation: "Voices that command, command. I overwhelm you with my immanence if I'm not real who is? My words redeem you, you can't penetrate my words I pump them into you like bullets you don't hear them high frequency like dog whistles raise primordial spooks to haunt your creepy skulls do what I dream you to do, and THEN you will be loved. You harden in pockets of darkness like old gum, oh shadows, you are doubts articulated you are puppets."

I said to the recorder: "Call me Plantman, the Indoor Horticultural Technician. I nurture gardens in the sky, bring water, fertilizer and impeccable grooming to The City's indoor flora. The workers anticipate my coming. Cramped in stalls and cubicles at nose-pinching altitudes, hunched over keyboards, the workers turn from radioactive memoranda to witness photosynthesis."

A caller identified himself as Brown, author of Wild Card. The VOICE commanded him to speak.

Brown said: "My book is a mirror in which each reader sees his own story therefore each reader is writing while reading. I worked on it seven years."

The VOICE said: "Yeah, so?"

Brown said: "So I awoke one morning and found myself STILL unknown. . . writers trying to repossess lost time. . . type in darkness, thousands of them, tippety-tap-tap-tap. . . trying to define The Nation, it is beyond them, they are alone and frightened. . . ."

The VOICE said: "I'm losing you, Brown. You're fading."

Brown said: ". . . the lights out there, bright lights must be humanized, my words will humanize the lights. . .the page is a dead land. . . still water. . . so many sentences secreted hourly, The Nation is immense. . . writers are jostled in the street, they must create space for themselves. . . they colonize the page with words. . . ."

The VOICE said: "Brown Brown Brown is fading. . . fading. . . fading. . . Poof!"

The VOICE said: "What heart pounds in the beer-gut of The Nation, waiting to be born? I am Vesuvius I am the core, I am The Beast crouched clawing through the womb: I thrum I resonate I'm hemorrhaging! Bathe in my syllables I devastate you."

I said to the recorder: "Plantman ascends towering mausoleums to make concrete bloom."

I said to the recorder: "I'm practically a Folk Hero. Like Johnny Appleseed. Imagine those corporate hives if nothing grew. If all they saw or smelled was carpet and Formica, flashing screens. . . they'd go mad. Mad. Mad. Insane. Plantman keeps their plants alive. Their Pothos and Aboricolum; their corn plants, silver leafs, and Marginata; their Spathyfilum, spider plants and Ficus. My labors allow workers hundreds of feet above the earth to sit under the shade of a potted fig tree and discuss favorite colors or whisper secrets. Who knows what banality lurks in the hearts of men? The fig tree knows. . . ."

I said to the recorder, "Over two hundred horticultural technicians work for Topiary Techniques. Largest indoor landscaping outfit in The Nation. Clients range from small businesses to major corporations. There can be anywhere from five to five hundred plants at a site and the technician on whose route that site is situated is responsible for every damn one of them.

"Technician's mission keep the flora on his route alive and young. When a plant dies or becomes unsightly, the client is entitled to a replacement. The technician must fill out a form in triplicate and hand-deliver it to the Dispatcher, who must sign it and send it to the Men-In-The-Nursery, who release the replacement to the Delivery Men, who place the new plant on a Topiary Techniques delivery truck and ferry it to its new home. All this costs time and money, 'cause the company supplies replacements gratis. Every client is entitled to unlimited replacements so long as:

"a) the moribund plant was originally purchased from Topiary Techniques

"b) the Topiary Techniques Maintenance Staff–we technicians–are retained for weekly visits to the site.

"The client corporation is entitled to have healthy green life always on its premises and nary an old brown leaf or jaundiced stem."

Threw on a pair of jeans, shut off the stereo; clipped the radio/recorder to my belt, went up to the roof. Paced under the idiot moon. Shocked-faced moon, eyes wide, mouth wanting. Voyeur moon can't get enough. More drama more sex more murder more violence man to man or machine to man killing, killing. Libidinous Moon gets off like a prison guard. Watch us kill and be killed. Panopticon moon knows all, sees all. Who's sleeping who's awake. Who's bad good naughty nice. Be dastardly exciting, be his thrills. MAN in the moon. THE MAN is IN the moon. THE MAN owns the moon, like everything else.

Not a moon pleaser, I, though not Moon-Man-Mad like many I've known. Piss off, Mr. Moon MAN, Mr. MAN in the moon. How much? How much did YOU pay for the moon? Or did YOU just take it, like everything else, by force?

Stacks and stacks of lighted windows teased with possibilities. Sky irrelevant; stars lacked wattage. Out in The City the core, where life is. Out there the center of the world.

City's Sleepless awake by choice. Night their milieu. Imagine: rooms of bodies cosmeticized by colored lights and artificial fog, secret corridors of beauty, pleasure, music. Places people gather to be better than themselves. Better than human, more than.

"Ten million lives in The City and I'm not living any one of them," I said to the machine.

Coming home the subway packed I feared sticking people with the nozzle of my bucket protruding like the barrel of a gun. Old man lugged his life into the car. Frail old man. Accent indiscernible. Dolls and imitation cell phones hawked from a wet shopping bag.

"Ring ring. Phone three dollar. Wee wee. Pee-pee two dollar."

He squeezed the buttocks of the Pee-pee, a boy figurine with knickers rolled to its knees. Water jetted from its stubby shlong. Accidents happen: Pee-pee over-shot its mark, soaking the tie and tabloid of a stranger. Stranger struck the vendor.

Air-borne Pee-pee knocked hot coffee from a woman's hand. She kicked the vendor's bag. Stranger pummeled the old man to the floor. Ripped shopping bag bled dolls and phones. Passengers stomped on them like eggs. The vendor pressed a phone to each gray cheek, as if to call for help, and wept.

Was this a job for Plantman? Avenge the poor fool, who was probably senile, and peddling without a license? No. Plantman's energies reserved solely for the maintenance of flora.

Looked up and beyond the wretched scene, above the newspapers and sunglasses and wet heads, to an advertisement for a cologne called "EARN." Wedding party in the park. Entire scene tattooed to a curvaceous bottle of cologne. Caption read, "EARN the moment. Forever."

"My copy," I said aloud, plucking tension-strings of overwrought riders, bunch of nervous wrecks (me too, I suppose if not for the booze). "I wrote that line. That's my work."

Before I gave my life to LIFE, I was a copy-writer for THE ADVERTISING COMPANY (and before THAT, a Salesman, in yet another life. . .).

Often during "work-life," traveling my route, I turn from the panicked masses and observe advertisements on the sides of passing buses, on billboards, in rows of magazines that form accidental colorful collages in smoke-shops and kiosks. The advertisements feature models in scenarios of work, courtship, celebration, the pursuit of death in powerful machines. But really they're doing nothing, the models, but looking beautiful, and still, and firmly planted at the center of the world.

The most beautiful thing imaginable is to do nothing. Bliss of stasis. Stop time directly where you stand. Center of the world. A horticultural technician is always doing. To foster growth is to provoke decay. Always a struggle against replacement.

I said: "Plantman was underground, preparing to ascend. Trains roared past like dragons."

Caller identified himself as "Light-Catcher," said: "For years I traveled The Nation. I photographed everything. Great men and events as well as the desultory dramas of common lives. The cities and their artifacts, the young who are young no longer, everything that fades I captured. Now I am old and confined to my studio, my walls plastered with images of The Nation, every square-foot dense with faces and machines. It occurs to me: The Light-Catcher did not record The Nation, he created it. The Nation was conceived in my camera and born out of my darkroom like Athena from her daddy's brow."

The VOICE said: "Nonsense. You didn't create ME. You don't even know what The VOICE looks like. I could be anyone, even YOU."

Light-Catcher said: "But I have seen The Nation, it is HERE. In my apartment. Studio. Whatever."

The VOICE said: "Listen to me: once I had a bellyache I had a bellyache I dreamed The Nation. Go to sleep, Light-Snatcher–"

"–Light-Catcher."

"Whatever. Go to sleep! You are not well."

Mouthing an imaginary coil harp, I sang the Plantman theme song to the stars:

"Boing boing a-boing boing boing boing
Boing, boing a-boing boing boing boing
Ohhhhhhhhhhhhhhhhhhhhhhhh
Plantman has his scissors and bucket,
Plantman waters all that's green,
Folks say Plantman 'don't-give-a-fuck-it,'
Cause after five he's never seen.
Boing boing a-boing boing boing boing
Boing boing a-boing boing boing boing."

Uncle Joe, whom I planned to visit Sunday, lived in The City Home for Adults. They let the old people out into the park twice a day, morning and late afternoon.

The old people are guarded from the general population. When I visit I get close enough to study the intricate etchings on their faces–Death's Rococo graffiti–and to listen. The old people are vague, obsessed with their own mismanaged lives. They offer fragments about jobs blown, lovers lost, festering emotional wounds. They speak of objects. Things they'd touched. People caressed who no longer exist.

The old people are ghost radios. They spook me.

The guards flash me nasty looks for venturing so close, even to my Uncle Joe. They have their hands full, keeping teenage boys from beating the old people to death. Children play in the park. Their mothers prevent them from bothering the old people and god forbid contracting Time. Senescence contagion.

The VOICE said, "Oh hollow notions you are beer cans you are filter-less I reify you."

I said to the recorder: "In a canvass bag marked with the emblem of Topiary Techniques, Plantman carries the tools of his trade: one four-gallon watering can, (commonly referred to as a 'bucket.'); one pair stainless steel scissors for trimming and shaping; one feather-duster for brushing dust motes, skin particles, nail-clippings and other impurities from the leaves; fertilizer; insecticide; and various other necessities.

"Plantman has enemies: mealy bug, spider mite, scales, and all manner of insects and diseases that attack the vegetation of The City. He doesn't hesitate to poison. With his enemies he is ruthless. The potted, green 'Citizens' worship him as Godman."

A caller identified herself as "The Missing Girl." Said: "You know who I am. Years ago my face graced the covers of The Nation's magazines. I was the Missing Girl, poster child for The Nation's lost children. Had I been abducted? Killed? You never knew. I've been around. But never where I was supposed to be. I'm married now; my husband is a pilot in The War; he drops bombs on The Nation's enemies, many of whom happen to be children, missing now and never to be found, but I forgive him. Not long ago, before they sent him off to fight The Enemy, I traveled with my husband to the Museum of Ghosts.

"There was an exhibit titled, 'Before She Was Missed.' They'd transplanted my old room like London Bridge, moved all my possessions from the old house to this museum in the middle of The Nation. They put on a skit for the visitors with a teenage actress playing the young me. A ten-minute domestic drama of no account really, but interesting in its implications. My parents, older but vital still, played themselves.

"'Sometimes I feel her presence,' my mother sobbed. 'She touches me but I can't see her.'

"'Objects disappear and reappear suddenly, without explanation,' added my father. 'Trinkets that were the favorites of our little girl.'

"They recognized me in the audience but said nothing. Kept their cool. Times are hard in The Nation, and The Missing Girl Exhibit appeared to be the most lucrative in the museum.

"Before we left, I walked onto the set, opened the drawer to my old night-table and took out a pack of cherry life-savers I'd purchased in another life. I gave one to my husband and took one for myself. It tasted like virginity and dust. This is my body, I said as I popped it into his mouth, and this is my blood. We sipped the sugary grape drink the museum offered as refreshment."

The VOICE said: "So what are you telling me, sister? You're telling me that YOU are THE Missing Girl?"

The Alleged Missing Girl faltered.

"Well, I am Missing. Or was. For a, for quite a while. Missing a long time."

"No, Honey, you weren't missing," said the VOICE. "In order to be missing, one must be missed. YOU, girlfriend, were merely LOST."

The VOICE said, "Oh Orphan of The Nation: your parents, erstwhile consumers, were consumed. Monsters leapt out of the television and ate them. Nnnnnnext!"

I said to the recorder: "The Ad Agency is a labyrinth shaped not unlike a brain. Convolutions of cerebrum. Hundreds upon hundreds of upholstered 6 by 8 foot partitions; maze of cubicles where artists, copywriters, and concept men work day and night to define the products of The Nation.

"Only one plant at the Ad Agency is the property of Topiary Techniques; the rest are cacti. The bucket grows heavy as Plantman trudges from cubicle to cubicle only to find gaunt ad-men laboring beside the squat, spiked dessert plants to whom Plantman is indifferent.

"Tacked to the partitions are advertisements dating back over a century. The clothes and artifacts change with the decades, but the youth and beauty of the models remain constant: sylphs and dandies posed like glyphs on Pharaoh's tomb.

"Plantman recalls his earliest experiences with Desire. He hums jingles long forgotten, craves snack foods, toiletries and baubles of his youth. This is TEMPTATION.

"The plant he seeks is the Tree of Life, for which, according to the memo in his pocket, there can be no replacement. Plantman is certain to find it at the center of the maze."

The VOICE said: "Listen to my echo machine: Ha!"

"Ha," spawned digital generations. "Ha ha ha ha ha ha ha ha ha ha ha ha ha ha ha ha ha hahahahahahahahahahah."

The VOICE was daring us to rise from our mattresses and pull our plugs.

The secretary in the Real Estate office was alone and beautiful. She'd been smoking hashish, the office reeked.

"Just you and me, today, Plantman. The Bossman go bye-bye," she laughed. "Bye-bye, Bossman."

I hesitated. I was afraid.

In the Fashion House a designer mourned the spathyphilum on her desk.

"She's sick today. She's suppurating. I didn't know plants oozed like that. What does it mean?" she asked.

"Jeepers. I don't know."

"What do you mean you don't know? You're paid to know. She's slouching like a junkie. Make her stop!"

I wished I were dead.

The VOICE said: "You are sick and weary, you are filthy! Even the Night steals from your bed, she cuckolds you."

Monday, rather than attain the center, I will wear alien clothes. I will carry my bucket into elevators and ascend to space stations where ivy grows and workers toil parallel to clouds.

Plantman, as much as any advertisement for eternal being, is a vital illusion.

The VOICE said: "You are clay dolls animated by my fictions. I release you I abandon you bereft of my spirit you are vacuums. Inhale, exhale; gather yourselves and go. For Dawn comes even to The Sleepless."

Communication Breakdown Pain

Cannot know.

Cannot do.

Cannot relate.

Cannot define.

Cannot place.

Cannot nowhere.

Cannot no one.

Cannot nothing.

Cannot true.

Cannot be.

Cannot Cannot

Cannot

Say

II.
Music and BEING

The Apartment

Twenty-nine is no longer young. Not old, two-thirds life ahead–possibly. But alas, beyond the market age bracket of the eighteen-to-twenty-fours. Let them pass. We are huge, despite unmarketable advanced degrees, dollars blown on our 'afraid to work with our hands.'

Look at me. There. In the mirror. Cleansed and dapper. Green-and-yellow Topiary Techniques t-shirt; blue jeans; green-and-black sneakers. Ready to go. Ready to go. Ready to go.

BEING already in the kitchen, sipping coffee he'd picked up at the corner bakery. Sticky buns, muffins and The City News. BEING was a big man, not a fat one. A soft man. Big soft man-boy, BEING. I offered coffee I was brewing but he had his cup, preferring the bakery blend, extra sweet. He craved sweet morning foods and The Bakery Girl who worked the cash register.

Comics. Headlines. The War and its progress; murder trials; this person does this gets into trouble; that person does that gets into trouble.

"So what about this guy killed his parents?" I said.

"I've thought about it. Often," said BEING.

"But this guy was a regular successful Joe Citizen. 'Administrator of Creative Product Strategies' of Something-And-Such Associates. Had a wife and kids."

"So what happened?"

"What it says. Went out and whacked his folks. With a tuna fish."

"He killed them with a sandwich?"

"Poisoned. He poisoned them. Doesn't say anything about a sandwich, actually. Or tuna. Could have been sushi. Bad sushi. An accident maybe."

"People are fucked," said BEING. "Eating raw fish like that. Just asking for it. Food poisoning. Hepatitis. Whatever."

He read comics, I the clock.

"I have a gig," he said.

"Yeah?"

"Next week. Here in the neighborhood."

Freelance factotum for Starlight, "Caterer and Facilitators to the Stars." They called him occasionally as extra staff: food services, production. Film, television. BEING prepared and served. BEING would work every day, if he could, among The Stars, but there was not always work among Stars to be had. His was a pair of Starlight's extra hands. He hoped to break into the business full.

"Television show," said BEING. "Taping should last weeks."

Meanwhile the phone. Loud cough, flick of Music's Zippo.

"Yello," then silence. Then Music screamed, "Don't you talk to me like that, fucker! I've got guts. I've got guts!"

Slammed the receiver.

Five-foot eight 250 pounds of Music built for roof work, construction, not to lead his band to fame. "Puppets of Weltschmerz." Hard, loud music for the Angry Young. Music huge in boxer shorts and t-shirt, poured coffee, tossed his butt into the swampy sink.

"It's gonna be one hot fucker, one hot fucker on that roof," said Music, facing a day of smearing hot tar on asphalt for his blazing father under blazing Sun.

"Been down to the bakery, BEING? Ask that girl out?"

"I don't know. . . ."

Music patted BEING's shoulder.

"We gotta get you laid. What we gotta do. We gotta get BEING laid. Too long, if ever. Ever been laid, BEING?"

“Damn, Music! Stop,” with conviction.

“How old, BEING? Twenty-eight?” asked Music.

“October. I’ll be twenty-seven all Summer.”

“We gotta dip that stick, BEING. Gotta dip that stick.”

“Piss off, Music.”

Back to my room. Collect my gear. Breathe. Assay the Day.

BEING

Cakes don’t change. Plastic wrappers. “Real” cream filling. BEING. His television, milk and pastries. Adolescent twenty-seven. Soda, smoke, snacks. Like ten years gone had never been.

Passive, floating, shuffled by Time. Sixteen. New body shapes new clothing. Tunes. His room. Door locked. Illicit herb burned in a dirty-water bong.

Loitering at the Mall, buying, driving, posing. Movies, pizza, boon companions.

“Won’t last forever,” Guidance Counselor warned.

Aptitude test discovered aptitude.

College: “Media studies.”

Four-year extension of childhood that was campus life. New friends, scenery, same old television box of noise and diatribe, sports and speeches. Cream-filled cakes. Time away from Mother. Grade point average "C" for confusion.

Graduation. Masterful display of stealth and cunning; black gowns so they can sneak up from behind. Gates of Knowledge opened, Alma Mater tossed him out. Gates slammed shut.

Classified Ad hook-up with Music. Apartment in The City. Young men asserting to The Nation. The Nation asserted back.

Work paid well. Not constant. "Caterer and Facilitator to The Stars."

Building a career watching television, eating cream-filled cakes. Smoke and video construct. Locked cabinet in Time they called "The Day."

Things change, BEING remains. Cream-filled cakes. Celebrities, Stars.

(Young men, not kids. Time is Now. Look differently on BEING. Remember ambitious me work-toward-an-end. The end. I understand inertia knuckle-twist to spine, BEING. Now, now. I forgive, I understand.)

Voices from Home. Father, past seventy, fought the war of his generation, made himself millions. Work, cunning, investment. Called to ask "What work? what job?"

"Television? What kind? Writer, actor. . .?"

"Production assistant. Celebrities. Stars. Work is slow. I have to build. Whenever there's shooting in The City, they recommend me," said BEING. "My name."

Father sent money. His only son. No choice but to believe. Faith in BEING. Still young, a kid. Plenty of time to make of himself. Something.

Mother fretted about her son's ability to yield.

"Your sister goes to The Graduate School. Why not you? Young. Become a lawyer."

"I want entertainment. To be in entertainment."

"As what, a waiter, serving fancy people fancy drinks?"

"I'm a production assistant. Lots of things. Catering. I build sets, help with equipment."

"BEING... BEING..."

"Leave me alone I'm doing fine."

Dirty old bong. Crinkle-crush of wrapper. Comforting, cream-filled cakes.

BEING in Love

Love. Love. Love.

The Bakery Girl and big, soft man-child BEING.

Morning The Bakery sweet muffins and coffee.

Said she "Wouldn't mind, you know, were he to ask."

BEING left his bong, showered, combed. Destination bakery.

"Wanna go eat and maybe a movie?" asked BEING.

She said, "Sure."

Soon The Bakery Girl regular in the apartment. Not stun-drop beautiful, not Magazine. Hip-Heavy, soft, like BEING. Harem girl allure. Love in BEING's room. The Bakery Girl partial to men and women. BEING her first man in a year.

Daily meeting at Life Cafe, across from make-up trailers and wardrobe stations of The Stars.

Apartment, cigarettes, beer; chips, smoke, cakes. The Nation destroyed The Enemy still, yet, again–live TV.

Iconic deep time sex genius, The Bakery Girl, eons beyond BEING. Proud lover of men and women (BEING shy about all that). Summer shower thunder; television; weed; pedestrian sex toys not too funky for BEING; The Bakery Girl's musk girly-girl heat sweat estrogen flesh image of Venus 30,000 spins around the Sun before the virgin births of Jesus, Elvis.

Shelter in Time closed tenderly around their days.

Hand-written notes tacked to the bedroom door: "Knock, Don't Knock;" "Come In, Beauty;" "Garden Under Sky;" "Afraid Of Free Out There."

Music of Our Day

Hard steely club music, hate chords. Music of the Angry Young. Construction work for Father. Roofing. Music, and his burly brother, Brother. Rough. Shaved heads. End-of-day paint-splatter, roof dreck, tar.

Music, goateed, smoked cigarette, cigarette, cigarette.

"Puppets of Weltschmerz" were Drummer, on drums; Brother, lead guitar; Music, lead singer and rhythm guitar; and Muse, on bass (lovelier not rough; muscular yearning; soft voice transforming–dream Muse to bed, her feather ear-rings and tattoos; cigarette, cigarette; radio, radio; popular songs evoke girls known and loved when everyone was young).

Alcoholic Brother hated Father worse and loved Mother deeper than did Music. Gigs at dark clubs Brother drunk naked spoke in tongues.

Puppets pumped for Music–singer at the center. Brother off-center, disturbed. Drunk fisticuffs. Brother against Brother. Blows.

Played till morning. Hung-over, sick, exhausted.

Cigarette. Cigarette. Worked for Father hot red dawn to gloom humid dusk.

Triumphant screech wailing guitars; stentorian drums; shriek life-plaint. Dissonance stretched pained expressions. Hip gyrations of The Young. Music's energy, hard master. Father-driven Brother anguished loon. Mad dog crazed. Obscene.

Music's drive: escape Father's hard labor, see Puppets succeed. Despite more clothes off, booze-inflamed belligerence. Fights in the audience.

Blood on Brother, sweat-soaked Music, Muse's tears.

Focus. Anger. Guitar. Desire. Music drank to frenzy, stopped short of madness. Ability intact. Kept it together. Disciplined. Saved money for studio time. Record. Record. Distribute. Club dates. Mailing list. Record.

Fat Music, five nine, 250, no heartthrob. Different scene anyway. No melodies for throbbing hearts, but thunder for the foot stomping, fist pumping, Angry Young. Was Music still young? Twenty-seven. Older side of young. Clubs, auditions, practice, demo-disc, demo-disc, demo-disc. Burdened with work, Father, daylight, Brother's naked murderous inebriation.

Thread of fire sewing Life through night, time, sound. Time. Tick tock Time. One day stop playing? Angry Restless Young songs not forever? What would become of his guitar? Years listening playing dreaming to converge in bitter silence? Roof labor in heart-break phantom wind of on-stage memory? Brother dead, Father dead, guitar a souvenir? Nothing to wake to? Nothing?

Perhaps he'd never leave The Young, despite onset of old. Ridiculous gray fat man; tired styles, out-dated tunes. Memories of restless, Angry Young (now sad, mute, weary Middle-Aged). And Brother at 40? Madness besot him before naked beat him down?

Playing anger amplified lightened burdens–what would become of Music without Life's sound, Life's harnessed sound? Alone in his room. Headphones. Stomp, grimace. Not Future snarling in the mirror, merely Past?

(I heard what the Young today... not music of my day. Where was the music of my day? Songs surrounded me when I was young. Songs of my day, days of my day. No longer my day, so I'm not young?

Your day is your striving. What you think is your day, you realize later, later, is not your day at all. Striving was your day. Everything next, the "Else," just Time eating Tomorrow, spitting Old at Yesterday. Not the music of my day, when I... striving... illusion of "unique." Not in front of me, as it had been. Behind. Memories real and imagined. Lyrics of youth love striving. Yearning for music-of-my-day days. Joy of striving. Drink, drink, drunk not to recall. Such sad second comings! Memory: sly, cruel doppelganger of Desire.

Music, BE the blood of Love, play on!)

III.
Diary of an Adman

The University of Vigor, Ambition, Advertising

The University. Master's degree in Business Strategies (MBS): "abstract advertising," "imaginative marketing," "creative propaganda." Selling stuff.

The poet, Alterkocher, taught poetry, great poetry, The Masters, to hacks like me. He also taught Undergraduates majoring in "liberal arts"–for these he had hope. Young, not yet corrupted, possibly real scribblers among them to follow–Him.

I was of the former, enrolled in The University's prestigious MBS program, considered the finest in the country, its strategy to use "real" poets, artists, scholars, like Alterkocher, to teach hack copywriters, like me, literary techniques of The Masters. To float product on pillow clouds of "deal." That, or conjure sweet soufflés of agit-prop for Government; sell obedience.

Graduation postponed pending submission of Final Thesis. Prisoner of Final Thesis. No degree, no nothing, until I birthed a book of market strategies and advertisements for imaginary campaigns on behalf of imaginary clients. For this I suffered "writer's block"?

Job with The Ad Agency beginning early-Fall. Dependent upon my thesis earning an MBS that Summer.

Needed to be cloistered, refreshed, among people of wit and vision. Not Zombies. Not tired old professors at the school. Alterkocher said. . . but Alterkocher. . . DEMANDED marketable copy and winning strategies, stitched together seamlessly with the huckster's academic rigor, from his hacks.

I began at The University with vigor, ambition; truly I was NOT a hack. I believed words inside me would arrange themselves into great themes. I read Great Writers to energize my prose. Convert their life-stuff to muscle of raw being. Fuel of literary Other-ness. Blank. Blank. Blankety-blank. White page whiter than white, whiter than government. Blank-blank. Changed the background of my word-processor to blue with white words. Then gray, red, magenta, turquoise, violet, midnight black. End result same shit-brown prose, like I'd wiped my ass with the "page." It stank. Could not complete. Concepts fizzled on the screen, fragments, "Great Themes," lost to Time. No. No. No flickering insights into The Human Condition; no musical comedy of tragic incoherence; no escape from boring. Nothing original or interesting. What had I experienced but Time? Bad atmosphere. Writer's workshop. Competing critics. No eyes for "vision," none that is, but their own.

Students wrote reams.

Professors' numb tedium flake by flake mundane seeking sorting searching. By chance discover value worth worth? Professors value reading writing talking books, articles, poems, papers. Observation, exegesis, critique. How they live. Should writing stop, the stream of input/output building the myths

(Official Mainstream Canon, and alternative, UNENDORSED "free thought") denied, the professors would have no work, no income, and since no one but professors read input/output of culture–high and low, sensuous and martial, pious and just plain silly–no one to train new critics of EVERYTHING, no learned masters of general niggling, vituperation. Re: common disregard for days-of-yore specifics of Perpetual Academic Rigor School oh smash the sherry glasses no one drinks Apollo's Dionysian after all return to yer cubicles, yer jobs, get back to woik.

Students wrote frantically for prizes. Teaching, possibly, to follow. I did not compete, could not complete. Fragments, shards. Lifeless light-glyphs or worse: blank screens. Pretty icons, colorful patterns, but alas, no books burgeoned.

When in doubt, advertise.

Market goods and services and market the marketing of goods and services ad infinitum forever and a day, another difference or a living in The Nation. Fragments of ideal, 'jagged broken bottle' (now THAT'S good copy). What was needed for my Thesis.

Sardonic, humorous, but not too witty, lest customers assume you're laughing at their expense. Account.

But even fragments would not come. Time passed. Sleepless. Paced. Notebook blank. Chain-smoked my tarry brain. Bummed out. Despair. Stressed. Starved for sanity. Hygiene.

Pink Pills and Blue Ones

University Mental Hygiene Clinic. Peace soft prints. Water-colors. Comfort plants. Celebrity and Fitness magazines. Difficult rising from the waiting-room chair: drunk, drunk. Tired.

The Shrink, disarming plump, welcoming.

Talk released words to chill, conditioned air.

"And what makes me ME in my head?" I blurted. "I've seen things that, you know, I want them to be mine."

"And if they'll be yours?" asked The Shrink.

"Desire. I'll write them into fragments of desire, copy that moves people to WANT. My thesis complete, perhaps the shallow true inside will. . . emerge."

The Shrink prescribed pink pills and blue ones.

Suggested I resolve the me inside me. Present a persona to the world. Let go of destroying my life.

I had been under the impression, for many years, that such people as the me inside me could not or would not allow themselves to change.

Forward three years. Future it! Future it! Summer before Plantman. Writing copy for The Ad Agency. "Adulthood." Full-time job. Two black suits and two gray. Health Insurance. New doctor, same pills. Pink ones and blue ones. Up all night despite them. Or because. The Sun rose daily, as it tends to, or else rain.

Watched Saturday cartoons of my Young. Lines, situations recalled like childhood rhymes:

"What's up, doc? Hey Bub, you need a house to go with that doorknob! Yabbadabadoo."

Culture Nation stabbed my space. Perhaps my obsessions. . . and the whole. . . System of Ruthless. . . out of whack. Culture cult. Not reading Great Books, owning them, possessing. Tiny plastic souls. Vacuum packed. Every Man in paperback. Plunge, plunge. Head-first into gold-leaf mounds, artifacts. Barefoot skip through cash cow pastures.

Overdrawn. Owe fifty-thousand dreams, plus interest. Student Lenders. Personal currency unstable. Useless.

Asked myself, "How important IS Life to The Nation?"

Told myself, "Not about their grotesque cultures amusements fantasies machines created marketed. Pitchmen for commodity dream celebrity. No real *real*, no product."

"Is it dead? Society. Is it dead?" I asked myself.

Never dead. Transmogrified. Infinite hierarchies. Data accumulates. Never cease. Where to put it all? Tree of Knowledge Incorporated (TKI), Pyramid 2.0 database. Big Boys and Judges move levers. Million lines of code between us. Fictions: Heroic Narratives composed by PR Poets; Earnest Celebrities; Programmers; The Law.

Mental Note: "Staggering. The System. A racket."

Illusion of words inside.

Told myself, “No stopping you. Just don’t confuse weird shit you get yourself involved in (like, ‘gave you diploma with The University Seal’) with Where Life Is.”

Network stinks of Judges, Authorities, the Ones who designate, sell, divide. Fragments project greater meaning when your fictions don’t exist as yours.

Missing Girl imagined by thousands. Network of collaboration. A house-fly sees with many thousand eyes.

“Just my opinion,” I concluded.

Really, I was I to do what I would with Life.

No?

NUDE

Straight from “MBS-in-hand” churned copy for Coolman & Associates Advertising and Image Management (AIM). Cool AIM.

Agency days bleak indeed. Frantic. Hive of urgency and tension. Get Word to public. Word was product. Word and image. Factory of words images. Word-image-product proposal better be damn good or say “good-bye” to the account. Ready. AIM. Fire(d).

Didn't mingle. All those stressed designers and copywriters stiffening in cubicles, dreaming words and patterns.

Meetings flushed us from our cubicles. Forced exodus to Conference Room, discuss strategy, pursue pure talk.

So many products to sell, so many words. Lost faith in Great Books. Lived pure talk.

Feared I'd advertise forever. No trivial concern.

Daily forgettable copy, slogans, agitprop. Cornucopia of prototypes marked time's passing. Colorful presentations of Desire conjured by Department of Motion, Graphics and Design. "Slo-Mo Antics and Lost Time."

What was I doing, me and my false words? De-generative lingua-phobia. Overexposure to corrupt grammar of "the sell."

Scored one big league victory. Winning copy for a winning campaign: the NUDE (Naja's Urban Design Emporium) account.

NUDE meeting in the conference room so important Naja herself presided with two assistants–grimly erotic, gracefully coiffed and appareled in NUDE fashion. Naja in black.

Suave, hip, sexy hirelings projected NUDE image for suave, hip, sexy, clientèle. Naja herself a model–in "the Day." Now, fashion designer of The City. Oracle of style.

NUDE was remaking itself in its own image, she said, and invoked its new slogan, "Designing the NUDE you."

She expounded upon the company's new mission.

"It's more than the clothes on your back, it's the fashion inside you. Lifestyle. NUDE doesn't just put clothes on your body, but fashion in your soul. NUDE customers are more particular, more demanding of the very best in fashion.

"NUDE men, NUDE women. 'When God created man and woman they were naked. Then they became NUDE,' something like that. I forget the exact wording of the copy," said Naja.

The clothes in my closet called me home: "New clothes replace old clothes people wear for a time until designers design new clothes and black is gray and gray is brown and garments of last season seasoned in closets, thrift shops, material waste or clothe new bodies. Life stained seasons dyed washed. . ."

Ear of my stomach. Not quite conventional discourse.

Naja instilled NUDE sense into the copywriters, unveiling "EARN," inter-gender perfume. Fragrance of bodies in dynamic transition. Pheromone scent of rut. Human-all-too-human crest of concupiscence. Desire. Raw. Lust.

"EARN will enhance the natural aromas of male and female bodies, especially erogenous areas where glandular concentration is prime," said Naja.

"Special blend of herbs and flowers tinctured to perfume by some of our finest scent artists overseas. 'EARN' the fragrance of The Nation," she declared.

Poster by Motion, Graphics and Design Department held aloft:

Wedding party. Tree-lined field. The Big Park. In the offing gray black towers of The City like men in suits. Wedding guests beautiful. Friends, lovers, children, animals. No family no old no middle-aged–not the target-response action area for "EARN."

"We want them young and horny," Naja said.

Bride barefoot. Gauze frock translucent. Hair wild auburn. Copper tan. Groom's torn denim, motorcycle boots, tuxedo jacket, top hat. Day's growth of beard and wired eyes. "Fab cool hip man"–look. Authentic "check it out, man" (or "Gadzooks, friend!"–custom 'ethnic/caste alignment' campaign for each consumer relative-age, peer-group and income bracket) gotta buy me some 'EARN' so I can [fill in blank]"–look.

Time: Absolute Zero. Statue Zone. Marble Moment. Stasis: lovers' arms outstretched short of embrace, each equidistant from the center. Idyll imposed over a green "EARN" amphora.

"I'm pleased with this," said Naja. "The copy? There's no copy."

Silence.

Came out of me instantly, involuntarily, from the gut, resounded.

"EARN the moment," I said. "Forever."

"EARN the moment. Forever," repeated all.

Naja pleased. My superiors pleased. A winning slogan for a

winning campaign. Still used by NUDE, the copy. Default slogan for "EARN." Wedding-in-the-Park graphic EARN's enduring image. I saw it on the subway only days ago. Thing of beauty.

The Human Resource

The Coolman & Associates Human Resource Manager coordinated writers, designers, client accounts. Killer for the company. Little lapel insignia bore her name.

In eight AM out eight at night. Sexy in her way. Frantic. Turned me on. Two years older than I was, then, she had Six-and-Twenty. We eased into chummy, wary of terms.

"Hell," I said. "We spend our whole lives here. Who are you?"

"Good point," she said. "Work, work, work. Love?"

"Love the town all night, let's go!"

We drank and gossiped about colleagues, like kids at recess. After the bar straight to another, where she confessed dissatisfaction.

"Career path," but what about kids? And anyway what had she really been put on earth to do?

Drink, drink, drink. Talk, talk, talk. Till three AM.

"You can't go," she said. "I like you."

Hem of her night gown rising–

"No," she said, "I can't, I can't," but did, with gusto, not at all shy.

Morning hangover, she said, "This didn't happen well it did but meant nothing no not nothing, you're sweet, but this can't be repeated, my career."

Booze-sick, bored, I let it go. Pursuit of pure talk.

One day she didn't come to work or call anyone at all. No show. AWOL. Not her nature. Nor did she come to work the next day or the next. Human Resources took over the case from her immediate supervisors. Then a Police job. Perhaps the Detective Agency, if her family had money–I didn't know. She was missing, and young. Not young enough to be Missing Young. Not one of the Missing Young. Just missing.

Sometimes people disappear. In the middle of everything. In the middle of doing. At the Ad Agency, as elsewhere. One day they become gone. Out into The Nation. Or under it. Police might know. Or Detectives. Or Pyramid 2.0.

Her missing was a puzzle, like anyone's missing. Like the missing of The Missing Girl. Except in The Human Resource Manager's case, no one, except Human Resources, perhaps her family, the police, etc., was in any great haste, that is, was passionate, to make her found.

IV.

Li'l Box of Love: A Supplementary Edu-tisement and Info-motional Insert, Courtesy, The Parent

Li'l Box of Love

One

Up in the warehouse of the Novelty Factory, The Salesman, wearing a mask of fame, gagged Rena with a plum. Rena almost-woman million-dollar T&A and not a scent. Sterile darkness of her mouth, his own reflection in her eyes. The Salesman yanked a mask from the "throwaway box" and stretched this false face over his own.

He said, "I'll sell you The Nation. I'll sell you TO The Nation."

Rena lay spread-eagle on a crate of rubber scalps. Her crotch, tufted with genuine human pubes, oozed Tasty Gel. The Salesman didn't dare unzip his fly. What had he been thinking?

"The Manufacturer took me under his wing and I smelled what frailties grew there," said The Salesman. "And anyway, who is he compared to Papa?"

So in the weird lighting of the warehouse he deflated Rena, folded her and stuffed her into his old school knapsack. He threw the plum across the warehouse where it would rot among crates of false mustaches and plastic thumbs. He went to see The Manufacturer.

The Salesman sold novelties by phone. He spoke to the people of The Nation. He sent them catalogs. He made them aware of choices. He schmoozed them and felt them out to see what might interest them. All the salesmen at the Novelty Factory received lists of names from market research firms. Once your name is on a list, anyone can call, even The Salesman.

The Manufacturer was a genuine success. He started out at seventeen with a portable souvenir stand at a dying amusement park and now he owned the largest, most profitable novelty factory in The Nation.

Once, The Salesman believed in The Manufacturer. He looked to him for guidance. He believed The Manufacturer was, in his way, a great man. This belief had given him confidence to succeed.

"You are my chosen one, my greatest salesman, the brightest star at the Novelty Factory," The Manufacturer had told him, and consequently, it was so.

Two.

The Manufacturer sat at his desk. His Son sat on a swivel chair before him. The Salesman entered without knocking, but neither man looked up from his drink. The Manufacturer drank vodka and The Son sipped beer. The Manufacturer fiddled nervously with the hand-carved wooden bison with an arrow jutting from its side–or perhaps it was a bull with a sword in him, The Salesman could never tell–that served as a paperweight for important documents. Beside the bull/bison was a square black box just large enough to contain recipe cards or a dead bird.

The Manufacturer appeared subdued as he only appeared in his office behind closed doors, when The Salesman came to see him. He looked glum.

"You're too thin," The Manufacturer said to his Son.

The Son's clothes were indeed too big for him.

"You feed me," said The Son. "How could I be thin?"

The Manufacturer opened his desk drawer and pulled out two Double-Corona cigars. He handed one to The Son.

"Are these gonna explode?" sneered The Son.

"They're not from The Factory," The Manufacturer replied. "They're from a reputable tobacconist in The City."

The Salesman eyed The Son and wished that he too were smoking a cigar. He imagined himself savoring the cream of the stog, the final third, at which point his saliva will have insinuated itself into the leaf and each damp draw would be rich with cobalt ether of himself.

The Son said, "When they laid my mother out in the funeral home, half of her face was fat. She looked absurd. Yet you insisted on an open coffin."

"My wife died while undergoing liposuction," The Manufacturer said aloud, obviously for the benefit of The Salesman, though he still did not formally acknowledge him.

"A standard jowl-reduction with state-of-the-art instruments and the most advanced surgical techniques. Who could have foreseen. . . ?"

"With all the money you'd spent on doctors, morticians and whoever else, all the *technology*," The Son persisted, "You would think that someone, *someone* would have allowed my mother the dignity of symmetry at her own damn funeral."

"So you're all ready for college. My how time flies," The Manufacturer said.

"An open coffin," The Son spat. "Big Daddy and his Castle of Jokes."

"Novelties keep people sane," said The Manufacturer. "The people need new, amusing things. We keep the people hopeful through the shocks and disappointments of The Nation. We enter, by proxy, the bedrooms and living rooms of The Nation. We bring laughter, even ecstasy to the dreary moments of the people. We bring comfort to the lonely and confidence to men who wouldn't or couldn't appear at parties and social gatherings without a joke of some kind, some thing to capture the center of attention while at the same time diverting that attention from the spectacle of their miserable selves."

The Novelty factory supplied such people with a lifetime of

jokes, gags, curiosities and intimate gadgets for the jaded, the restless and the sexually adventurous: the 20-inch black mambo; the Velvet Vulva; the Tan 'n Tasty; the Erotic Skull; gels, creams, ointments and mechanical girls.

"I worked hard all my life," The Manufacturer said.

The Son did not disagree.

"I worked hard so that you should never work hard. So you could go off to The University and pursue pure talk. That's what you were meant to do, The Son of privilege. Go off to The University and talk."

The Son protested, but The Manufacturer continued.

"You don't understand. This is what I want for you. Refine yourself. One manufacturer in the family is enough for generations. Go off to The Academy and fill your head with words."

The Son left, slamming the door behind him.

The Manufacturer raised his glass in a toast to The Salesman and said, "I was waiting for someone. Who better than a great hero of The Nation? I salute you."

The Salesman had forgotten to remove his disguise. He still wore the face of a great and famous man. In one deft motion, like a matador maneuvering his cape, The Manufacturer unmasked him.

"So it's the sad young man who haunts the factory. Is this the secret of his success?" The Manufacturer held the mask aloft.

"Does he impersonate our National Heroes over the phone?"

"There are no secrets, nor is there success," said The Salesman.

"No secrets?"

The Manufacturer pointed to Rena's shriveled leg, which hung over the lip of the knapsack like a botched embalmment. The Salesman had stuffed her away improperly in his haste. The Manufacturer laughed deeply.

"No success," The Salesman repeated. "No sales this week. Not one. My numbers have been steadily declining."

The Manufacturer waved him away.

"You are young," he said. "A prosthetic companion like Rena is for older men who've already been broken. You are not yet broken. In fact, I see no reason for you to break at all, if you live right."

"I'm going to be a father," The Salesman said. "Yet I can barely pick up the phone, much less sell novelties to The Citizens of The Nation. How will I support Lucretia and the baby? What will become of us?"

He couldn't concentrate. He wasn't moving product. His mind whittled the hours into grotesque totems of Lucretia, Papa.

Again The Manufacturer waved The Salesman's words away and with them the significance of his woes.

"My protégé," he said, misty-eyed. "My finest."

In his eyes, The Salesman could do no wrong; his embarrassing slump was not even worth mentioning.

"I'd like to take this bull or buffalo or whatever the hell it is and bash your head in," The Salesman said.

The Manufacturer nodded. He paused, and nodded again, as if agreeing with whatever The Salesman hadn't yet said. "I have despaired. I too have experienced disappointments in my life."

He removed the black box from his desk and placed it on the glass table before The Salesman. He opened the box. Pasted to the ceiling of the lid was a stage view of a theater scene depicting rows and rows of audience ascending to infinity. The box emitted cheers, whoops, whistles and applause. When The Manufacturer flipped a toggle on the side of the box, the applause turned to supportive laughter. Years ago, The Manufacturer invented this device to take him through the nightmare days and sleepless nights.

"I kept it on my night table. It helped me sleep," he said. "I'm going to share this with the world."

The Factory was in the process of mass-producing the boxes for The Nation. The Manufacturer expected the "Li'l Box of Love," as it was called, to yield millions.

"Now every hard-working Citizen will have his audience. You'll sell these to The Nation, you, my best and brightest salesman."

The Salesman left the Novelty Factory bearing the Li'l Box of Love as a gift for Lucretia.

Three.

Papa owned the largest cosmetics company in Europe. Lucretia wore his top-of-the-line unisex cologne, EARN, the ultimate in olfactory technology. It stirred the molecules of the individual wearer, bringing out the fullest scent potential of their DNA. It was Lucretia's scent that first attracted The Salesman. The intercourse of EARN with deep-musk estrogen; a blast of pheromones that knocked him for a loop.

"Papa too began as a salesman," Lucretia had said. "As a teenager he went door-to-door, or in the marketplace with his suitcase full of cheap perfume. He educated himself. He read Demosthenes and Cicero. He learned English and French mingling with tourists; he read Joyce and Proust. They sent him to head the branch in London, then Paris. He worked his way up. He worked like an animal, day by day, year by year. This was everything to him, to rise to the top of the company. Now he is Chairman of the Board. All the branches report to him. He meets with the most powerful people in the industry. The models, the designers, the advertisers–everyone reports to Papa."

Papa was everywhere and all-consuming. Lucretia had to cross an ocean to think clearly. Papa owned sprawling estates all over Europe. The blood of his vineyards fermented to world-class wines. He dined with the most powerful people on the planet.

Papa taught Lucretia to fish, ride horses, shoot a gun. She'd hunted, sailed, kicked footballs with her brothers.

The eau de cologne she splashed over her smoldering glands belonged to Papa. Papa was the czar of olfactory technology. He made people smell the way they should, the way he wanted them to.

The Salesman came home to find two strange men in his apartment: Allain, the youngest, most hot-tempered of Lucretia's brothers, and Dr. Spaeiouk (pronounced "speak," but also "spoke, spake, spike and spook" in various regions of his native land).

Dr. Spaeiouk was an older man, a year or two past sixty, dressed impeccably in a suit that might have been fashionable forty years before, which made it all the more appealing. His prominent nose supported gold pince-nez.

Allain wore smart black shoes. His hair slicked black brilliantine, he wore dark glasses. His cologne was Lucretia's cologne unmitigated by Lucretia: the raw bouquet of Papa.

He uttered a string of curses, but realizing The Salesman spoke neither Italian nor French, switched to English, which he pronounced only a little less perfectly than Lucretia.

"Look at him, the bastard. He takes her to live with him in the toilet bowl."

Disgust distorted his face as he surveyed the studio apartment.

It occurred to The Salesman that speaking another language in addition to the language of The Nation might be a very good thing. He knew no language but the one that formed him, the one he manipulated to sell novelties to his co-linguists throughout The Nation.

Allain looked down at Lucretia, who lay on the bed in unlaced boots.

"She's in a state. Her eyes are irregular," Dr. Spaeiouk said. "They're dull and cloudy. Like semen."

He and Allain stared accusingly at The Salesman.

Allain went over to comfort Lucretia. The siblings communicated in French, Italian, German, as if to mock The Salesman. Allain caressed Lucretia perhaps too intimately for a brother.

"An abduction would be absurd," muttered The Salesman.

Dr. Spaeiouk explained that Lucretia had left Europe against his expressed medical advice and Papa's handwritten command.

"This is a situation," said The Salesman.

"Yes, precisely," said Dr. Spaeiouk. "A situation."

Lucretia had gotten herself into situations before, though none so grave as this one–The Doctor pointed to her swollen belly. There'd been a situation in Paris–something to do with a Swedish fellow on a motorcycle–and that troupe of psychic drag queens in Berlin. Wildness, dissipation–with The Salesman it had been neither, just a withering; futile attempts to dodge the scent of Papa.

Every so often Dr. Spaeiouk would break away from the tedium of explaining things to The Salesman and engage Allain and Lucretia in clever, polyglot discourse. The Salesman grabbed his sleeve.

"Has he contemplated me here in The City, plunging wild-eyed into the furrows of Lucretia, rendering her thick and agonized with child?" asked The Salesman.

"Papa is a busy man," said Dr. Spaeiouk.

"It was the milk thing that freaked her out. That she who could create intricate, complex paintings must also produce, against her will, a substance of nourishment, a tepid cream," said The Salesman. "After the face appeared she stopped painting. She stopped eating, she stopped bathing, she stopped doing. She moped in the apartment, her clothes unwashed, her hair a pungent clot of night."

"She should never have left Papa's side. And to come to The Nation of all places. . . ."

"I thought he might send me a token, a flake of his enormous empire, perhaps some toenail shaving of omnipotence," said The Salesman.

"Such lunatic dreams are born of desperate minds," said Dr. Spaeiouk.

"I'm drowning in alien sound," moaned The Salesman.

"There, there. Now, now," consoled Dr. Spaeiouk. He placed his hand on The Salesman's trembling shoulder. "Lucretia and the child will both fare better at home, in the proximity of Papa."

He motioned to Allain, who led Lucretia from the bed, past The Salesman and Dr. Spaeiouk, and toward the door. The

Salesman kissed Lucretia as she passed; her cheek was dry like wood. Allain dropped a wad of foreign currency, like dirty napkins, to the floor.

Dr. Spaeiouk studied Lucretia's painting. From a sea of abstract shapes and colors a monstrous face emerged, a gargoyle at the vanishing point–it sucked all light and vigor from the work. It seemed to escape from the bowels of the design, an image born of the very womb of the canvas, bursting the fragile membrane of Lucretia's colors. She had worked furiously, but was unable to camouflage or erase it. With every layer of paint the face grew more defined.

"You see," said Dr. Spaeiouk. "She's been thinking about Papa all this time."

Dr. Spaeiouk folded a dollar bill, clean strong currency of The Nation, and pressed it into The Salesman's pocket.

"You've made the smart choice," he said. "If you'd caused even the slightest bit of confusion, Papa would have squashed you like a bug."

Alone, The Salesman opened the Li'l Box of Love. He listened to the laughter through the night, until the batteries weakened and the encouraging sounds faded away.

"Papa!" he screamed at the exhausted machine.

(The Salesman, c'est Plantman)

VI.
Raise High the Pothos and Plantman: An Introduction

The Interview

Bright noon mild day months ago. April Fools. Drunk. Barely stand. Advertisement for horticultural technician read: "Topiary Techniques seeks. Indoor Landscaper. Work with plants. College degree required. College degree a must. Will train."

Clean office spacious new. Expected vegetation, overgrowth, jungle, soil, hedge-cutters. The secretary took my resumé told me to sit. I sat. Photographs of plant arrangements prettied walls. Shelves of pristine plant pots–metal, plastic, terra cotta.

Victor tall, solid; stylish shirt and tie. Company man. Gung ho. Gung ho. Expounded upon the history of Topiary Techniques, largest indoor landscaping firm in The Nation. Offices in fifty cities. Victor had begun as a horticultural technician, experienced every facet of the business: worked the greenhouse, drove delivery, hustled sales, directed sales forces. Now Manager, The City Office.

"So, you interested?"

Brusque, to-the-point, go-getter, proud head man, The City

Headquarters of Topiary Techniques.

I asked what the job entailed.

Simple. Maintain plants The Company provided to clients.

"Can you lift things?" asked Victor.

"I'm pretty strong."

"You'll have to carry plants to clients, occasionally, and you'll be handling a plastic bucket full of water. A watering can. We call them buckets. Filled to the brim no more than 40-45 pounds, probably less."

"Can do."

"You have to be on the ball," said Victor. "That's why we require a college degree. You have to be able to follow instructions, or read them. Sometimes have to figure stuff out on your own."

Topiary Techniques achieved profit designing and facilitating clients' "indoor landscaping decor" and maintaining plants installed as part of this decor. Each client signed a maintenance contract requiring a Topiary Techniques Certified Horticultural Technician come once a week to service all plants on premises. Dead or dying plants replaced, no charge.

Technicians expert professionals of Topiary Techniques inundated with orders for unnecessary and avoidable replacements.

"Ever done this type of work before?" asked Victor.

"No."

"Are you willing to learn?"

"Yes."

"New technicians undergo what we call 'basic.' Three-week paid training with experienced members of our staff."

Victor rose to full six feet.

"Do you want to work hard?" he asked.

"Sure."

"Do you want a job?"

"Sure."

"Welcome aboard."

On my way to a new Green Self an hour to find my way home though it was only five subway stops away straight line one train no connection.

Apprentice. Sue. Artist.

Job job, client client, breathe. Job job, client client, breathe. Breathe, lunch, coffee.

Hours the Spring green lonely.

Sue taught me the trade. Sue, artist. Many artists–writers–musicians tended plants for Topiary Techniques all-day day Days. Sundown they rushed home to their "real."

Sue was meticulous in her after-all, which she viewed as itself.

Critical fingers poked, pinched, pleasured soil, eliciting wet, else careful quick-gush from her spout.

"You can't just water a plant unless it's thirsty. Drown the damn thing. That what you want?"

Small and wiry Sue wore funky clothes. Never lonely when the day was done.

Worker bees in comb-like cubes, Executives in suites. Potted oases offer Life to dull fluorescent days.

Me? One of hundreds of technicians for Topiary Techniques, largest outfit in The City.

Me? Unmarketable Masters degree in Marketing.

Me pocket full of pills.

Me manual labor tonic for the soul: nurse green growing, hand to leaf rather than ponder time between replacements from behind the "business-end" of a desk, ear to phone, face to screen, time attack from every angle: wrist-watch, wall-clock, fuzzy command-line, hour-glass icon, digital and analog animations hurling time's arrow with atomic, heart-beat precision and indifference.

Me apprenticeship me. Me apprentice.

Talk about peculiar! Talk about iced-coffee in the park and talk!

Sue was an Attractive. But mingle not work with love. Court not Future at a cubicle near you.

Oh, not true, true. Sue. Sue. Didn't turn me on. Dead man. Not yet Plantman yet, not yet.

Possibly not Sue as she was she. Rather circumstantial. Rather situation.

Booze and plenty of it; long runs in the park: only for-sure sure cure of all-day Days.

Final Friday of apprenticeship I said, "Nothing."

We went separate. Way away this, way away that.

The Company Gym

Pumped bodies. Faces taut with grim determination. Diets optimized by scientific know-it-all know-how proven by computer-assisted scientific method. Belief systems built on strong foundations of clinical experimentation repeated for accuracy under stress-increased conditions, peer-reviewed.

Hard labor builds hard selves.

Trainers, experts in the chemistry of lean architecture, human form. Pills, shakes, powders, injections; natural herbs; synthetic wonder molecules. A method. Many methods tried and true. Ergonomic machine-designs for comfort in distress. The latest in physical physics. Electric power pull tension for maximum result. Employees would stay rigorous and young forever.

Nutritionists, physical therapists, an on-call physician.

Men and women in accord. Sex, sweat, hope. Pure mist of ideal.

I tended Bamboo, Palms, Plants of Paradise.

"Faith, purity, mastery. Mind over body, strength of will," barked passing trainers.

Treadmill biking rowing; walking pedaling boating; nowhere, nowhere, nowhere.

Overhead screens pumped music and The War into their sweating heads. Imagined themselves in jets, roaring fire up the beastly asshole of the damn Rogue Enemy of The Nation! Bomb his demon progeny. Bomb the sandbox. Bomb the swing set. Bomb the school where THEY are indoctrinated and trained to hate The Nation. Bomb bomb bomb!

Pause watch listen. War thrum beat of pop music. Work it, work it, work it out. Tension, release. Minds abandon pain-wracked bodies to soar among the bomber jets and scream raw lust at stadium crowds. Dancing, loving, worshipful masses. Imaginary famous and adored.

Executive-white buttocks, pasty thighs in shorts. Health premiums reduced significantly and productivity increased when workers spend lunch-breaks in the gym watching The War set to pop music on giant overhead TVs. Leave cold sweat cubicles for clean hot muscle action.

Hour-a-day mental space to press pump cycle soar with sexy dancers grooving to The War.

I took time tending the few plants scattered about the basement gymnasium of the ominously tall, hermetically sealed, climate-controlled, glass tower.

The Datists

What is a girl's desire in the world of men?

The Office Women, the "Datists," convert raw numeric to "actionable" info. Datists sit smartly at squat machines. Squarish, sleek machines. Explosion of words, images, connections; algorithms of deception; comedy of ease–click clack click–terror's brilliant pixel-hues.

"Do not fear us, we cannot replace you, you have souls and lips and skin, mutable, we smell you. . ." hum the machines.

Days at the Data Center processing data. Worlds of data.

Brass pots, terra cotta. Lives brightened by ivy, pothos, spider-plants, whatever lives under fluorescent light in stale, anemic soil.

Badgered by memories. Lives they'd rather not have lived: skirt-blouse scent of second shelf cologne; awkward dates with pimply Letter Men. Sports heroes, teenage wunderkinder (where are they now? where are they now?).

Giggle girls bloom death, top forty dreams of beardless boys, awkward in pussy, quick-squirters all. Hiding behind cigarettes, reaching for cigarettes, uniform factory-rolled quick-burn dumbly into Past; brand insignias puffed with numb indifference; brown tips white tips filter-less.

Datists want love. Life.

They'd been girls once, years ago (fifteen? twenty? twenty-five?). Now was now. Now. Datists dreamed pleasure. Who can please, who can please? Rare men magic tongues stir nectars thrill to flowing. Nice-sized, well-behaved pricks never hurt anyone either.

Paperback romance on the bus (TV at home). Typed data. Manipulated code. Day-after-day began and ended in tall buildings. Remember the beach, high school hurrah? How long must people live, anyway? how long labor in glass towers?

Computers sucked girl juice dry from cunt to womb. Terrible bright noon under white florescent suns. Headsets plugged into machines. Songs. Popular sunshine sing-a-long songs. Blaze of knowing sharing songs. Those clothes, this coffee, that cigarette. Oppressive.

Friday drink the night. Seek eyes legs torso one can live with. Headsets plugged into machines. Tunes yanked from the Network, sexy songs stretched nude like paramours on twilight balconies of daydream.

Those clothes, this coffee that cigarette. Oppressive. Untrue. "Beauty is truth, truth beauty. . . ," etc. and "classic" Rock 'n' Roll burned days like snowflakes on a skillet.

Friday drink the week to chill conclusion. Seek eyes legs torso one can live with until morning.

Data to be called "events" from this day on, according to the week's last memo. Workers in The Office of Integral Events–formerly The Data Center–no longer "processed data" but "logged events." Circulation of the memo an event itself. "Who cooked this one up, Payroll, Human Resources?" the Datists–Eventists?—collectively wondered over pitchers of ale.

". . . take me, Plantman. Take me from here. . ."

Bartleby The Accountant

Bartleby at The Accounting Firm murdered a ficus. Stems, leaves, dirt mashed into the carpet of his office. Two jagged branches lay like antlers on his desk.

"I can't replace this," I said firmly. "It's not in the contract."

"They're fake," he said. "You've been in here fifty, sixty times, Plantman, and still you haven't noticed."

I sniffed a leaf.

"Not the trees, you ass. The Loved Ones," said Bartleby.

On his desk were photographs of an elderly couple, a large clan at a barbecue, a family of four: mother, father, daughter, son. The father wasn't Bartleby. Bartleby, in fact, did not appear in any of the pix.

"They came with the frames. They're artificial kin," he said. "Everyone needs a home to come to work to. I grow so tired of your stupid fig trees."

"Ficus," I said. "They're not fig trees, they're ficus. Well, same thing, I imagine. . . ."

"What have we learned today?" he asked.

"About Bartleby?"

"About Plantman."

I couldn't say.

"He does not know. He really does not know."

"So. Who knows?"

"No one."

"Why bother me, then?"

"You're here. You always come, sooner or later. You'll be back. It's a continuity thing. With whom else would I share my grief? Who better than the Plantman?"

Replacements

Staff meeting. Topiary Techniques Auditorium. Horticultural Technicians, green-and-yellow t-shirts. Back row, Friday evening, work day done, go home. Now. Run.

Victor commandeered the small stage. Stack of papers width of several phone books dramatically dropped loud. Thud. Heads up. Tirade. Paper replacement forms processed last financial quarter, over $250,000.

"That's $250,000 lifted from Topiary Techniques," said Victor.

Sloppiness of "certain technicians"–not watering enough; watering too much, not testing a plant's relation to its particular environment; not doing the right thing; goofing.

Technicians getting soft. Clients walk all over them, order replacements when plants could be saved.

"Sure, the clients will act all nicey-nicey while you're there and they're trying to bend you around their little thumbs. Then they'll turn around and stab you in the back. Complain about your "attitude," your "service." They're not your friends. Don't for a minute believe the clients are your friends. You only have one friend here, The Company. Only Topiary Techniques is your friend. The clients don't pay your salary and they won't protect you. Money lost to Topiary Techniques is money lost to you. We're all in this together, so you better know who you're sticking to and who's sticking it to you.

"You're all lucky you even have jobs. We're in a recession. There's a war on. Get smart. Know who butters your bread.

Take care of the plants. Do your job. It's not a hard job. It's an easy job. Be on the ball and look sharp and the job's a piece of cake. Don't lose plants. Don't let them die, if you can help it, and above all don't let clients con you into replacing plants that can be saved. Don't let life slip through your fingers," he admonished.

Victor paced the stage, his words like lava, his words inside us.

Senior staff would visit sites at random, inspecting work.

"We'll be looking to see that jobs are done right. And if a job is not done right, the technician responsible will hear from us. We'll have a little talk about what it means to work for Topiary Techniques.

"We all like to have fun and unwind, but not on the job. When you're on the job, wearing that t-shirt, you're representing The Company and you better be professional. Professional means doing the job the way you were trained. We spend a lot of time training you guys, and time is money. We hired you because we had faith in you, every one of you, that you'd be able to handle this job and conduct yourselves professionally. That's why we only hire college graduates. We want our technicians to be top-of-the-line. People who'll respect the plants and do the job right. Don't let us down. These are living things you're responsible for and they have to be cared for with intelligence and respect, but on the other hand, this isn't brain surgery.

"If you have a question about a particular plant or you suspect disease or infestation by others' non-proprietary green-ware, or have any question at all, call the office. We'll talk you through it. And if you have any pain-in-the-ass clients who are bugging you for replacements or asking you to do what you shouldn't be doing, call the office, call me, don't even try to handle it yourself, just tell them 'I'll have to check with the office,' and let me get on the phone. I'll do the talking. That's my job. I know how to do my job, know how to do yours."

Victor paced, paced, settled into softer tones.

"Just keep all this in mind. I'm not happy to be scaring you like this. I don't get off on scaring you guys. But if Topiary Techniques keeps losing money on replacements like this, not everyone's job will be secure. Know who your friends are. We're your friends, clients are not your friends. Talk to us about problems, not them. They don't give a rat's ass about you. Just think about this, what I said here, and go home, relax, enjoy your week-end, and come back Monday ready to work hard."

Real-life scenario: job the source of income that paid rent. But I was, really was ultimately free. "Senior staff" could not suspend blood circulating or arrest breathing. Senior staff could scrutinize my pay-attention all they wanted to from now to zero. I was Plantman whether I wore the Topiary Techniques t-shirt or a nun's habit. My blood was green and thicker than the water in "The Company's" plastic pails.

Longer than usual to reach home. Forever, it seemed. I got drunk. Bought a large beer in every deli on the way to the subway drank each through a straw, each veiled from The Law in a wet brown bag. Violence on the subway. Two kids arguing over some small thing. Little blossom lives stem-clipped before my eyes. Blood, blood, screams. Spaced out, missed my stop.

Finally, home. Almost dark, too late to run.

Empty apartment. Asleep in my gear. Woke past noon, soaked t-shirt, bucket empty.

The Elders

Monthly visit to The City Haven for Adults, see Uncle Joe. Former salesman, private detective, writer of detective novels, screenplays. Money stashed. Or so I'd been told. Also told he'd gambled it away. Then again, who was paying for The Haven? Senescence ain't cheap, unless you live it on the streets, potential guest cadaver of "The Death Squad."

He'd been a newspaper columnist, numismatist, a player of horses. He never married, though, allegedly, women craved him, even in The Haven for Adults.

Old folks made me young. But still. They creeped me. I feared them. Impatient me perturbed. Portraits of infirmity to come. Incontinent inadvertent experts of Time's flash passage.

Haven no heaven. Stink of piss. Lemon cleanser. Mothballs. Time a damp fart in slow air. Reality small real-estate. The Body domicile of ghosts, spun-out spiders, rusty pipes. A ticking bomb. Wind through pores of crinkle-skin. Small pleasures of walking. The Elders don't produce. Neither consumables, nor children. Sure, The Past–"but what have you done for us lately?"

Uncle Joe told of a lady claimed she was ravished by some

geezer on the fourth floor, the "trouble ward." Raped, impregnated. Bun in the oven. Eighty-years-old. Maternity dresses, owl-glasses, orthopedic shoes. In dreams begin nightmares, monsters.

Uncle Joe in the recreation area talking up Pearl–layers of lipstick, cakes of rouge–and a wheelchair-bound gentleman in a plaid suit, no tie.

"I remember. . . ," began The-Man-in-the-Plaid-Suit.

"Quiet!" snapped Uncle Joe. "There's nothing to recall. and assuming you HAD memories worth speaking, what then? Wake up. Wake up to where you are. This is the end of the road. No, it is past the end of the road. The road should have ended years ago when our minds were full. I wander convolutions of cerebrum pounding doors, seeking lost lovers, friends. Hello, Hello, anyone there? Empty. Gone. Nobody there but medication. Pharmaceuticals. Synthetic molecules make us who we are. Enzymes in white coats with beepers."

"I was somebody once. I forged myself out of a lump of urbanite, emerged from cement cracks like lichen. I see God pinned to a wheel and spinning overhead," said The-Man-in-the-Plaid-Suit.

"To thrust oneself into imaginary godliness is next to nothing." said Uncle Joe. "We've our plenitudes and order forms. No, no. That was in the other life. Now we've our televisions, our pills."

He looked at me terrified, grabbed my sleeve.

"Take me, take me from here!"

"Uncle Joe, I–"

"No! You're not the one, you're not the one, you're not the one!"

Hid his face in his hands. All this drama for Pearl? Haven method of seduction?

"Which one, Uncle Joe? Who is 'the one.'"

"Someone to do something for me."

"What do you need?"

"Someone's gotta save my sorry ass, man. The one, the anyone to save my sorry ass."

"What would–" I began. He cut me off.

"I don't want to die. Even at this late age. Don't mean to be greedy, but I do not want to die."

"I'm beyond all that!" piped The-Man-in-the-Plaid Suit. "God, how I'd love to kill a man. Or fuck a woman. A young one, not one of these. . ."

"A young woman would not waste precious time on you," snapped Pearl. "Or maybe. I did, once. When I was a young. . . woman. A girl. Twenty. Old Man Moneybags. Bloated belly. Scrotum like melted wax. I look back on such times and wish to hell I'd drop dead already rather than suffer such regret."

"Long live the King, the King is dead, long live the King!" said

Uncle Joe. "That's what it's about, you know. Life in Time. Passing the torch. But once the torch is passed it's time to leave. Quickly. But this, this keeping us here with their technology, their vigor machines and pills, pills, pills. It's a crime against the seasons of life, it's a crime against Nature and Nature does not forgive nor does She forget. She is cruel, and justly so. If we were allowed out in Nature, even out in human nature, The City, where human nature dwells, we'd be dispatched quickly, summarily, without remorse. It's remorse that keeps us here. And fear of what we are, what you, yes even you, my young nephew, must become. To kill us outright might be defying our–ho ho–our memories, or some twisted interpretation of natural law, but to keep us here. . . . I don't think it's even that costly, when you consider the price of living in The City, keeping the police armed and the children in school and the garbage taken away on Tuesday. The price of living is far greater than the price of not-living. Or not-dying. Not-being, that's what we are, or aren't, we're not-being and we won't ever be again. Nevertheless, they must keep us and maintain us. For this I gave up smoking and red meat?"

I asked about their memories. Surely they took comfort in memories?

"Tell of times past," I said.

Pearl said, "Fashion and Progress. You want to know about such things? Go through our homes, the old homes, before they put us away. Go to the museums and see what passed before our eyes when today's 'old' gadgets were new and exciting. Artifacts. Things."

"Trinkets. Baubles. Flub-dubs. Stuff," said Uncle Joe.

Pearl said, "We measure our progress in life by things we collect, things we adorn ourselves with, things we leave behind, including our bodies, which, so I've read in the paper, are being shrunken and mummified for keepsake items instead of buried or burned. I even read of a fad of sorts where the remains of loved ones, shrunken and preserved, are worn around one's neck. Can this be true? Can this be true?"

"What are you talking about, Pearl? Why are you assaulting the boy with nonsense? Pearl, have you been skipping your medicine? Are you having another stroke?" asked Uncle Joe. "'Shrunken corpses,' my ass."

But of course it was true, courtesy TKI Technologies' CHEOPS division. I'd seen it myself at Indian Museum. I could have supported Pearl with eye-witness testimony, but I hadn't the will or energy to endure an argument with Uncle Joe. Besides, who was I to insert myself into the meandering musing of The Elders?

Pearl said, "They can never leave you be, not even in death. They have to keep you, expose you, turn you into jewelry or fashion or what not. A keepsake, a conversation piece, a doll."

"Pearl! You're headed for the fourth floor, the crazy ward, with that kind of talk," said Uncle Joe.

Pearl said, "I saw pictures of such shrunken, preserved persons. They looked relaxed."

"I should hope so," quipped Uncle Joe.

"They can make you look like you're forty years old, a youngster, some kind of chemical process, they carry you with pride, like The Flag of The Nation," said Pearl. "One is truly worth more dead than alive, aesthetically, if you'd call this 'alive.'"

"There's the rub," said The-Man-in-the-Plaid-Suit. "Pearl speaks in metaphor. She runs off with her fantasies, but there's always a concept behind them. Some truth she's trying to convey. She's a kind of poet, Pearl is. We're aesthetically displeasing, as far as I can tell. We can't even stand to look upon each other. That's why they put us away. So they won't see us."

Uncle Joe said, "I don't understand that. Why not just kill us? Is it so expensive?"

The-Man-in-the-Plaid-Suit said, "Law. Courts. These things cost money."

Uncle Joe said, "You gotta do yourself in. Problem is, by the time you're ready, in your own mind, they've already made plans for you. Taken away your weapons and sharp objects. The young people know Time, they just don't reflect on it. We must reflect on Time and all that happened in Time if only to recognize, to force ourselves to recognize, that we still exist in Time. The television helps. Programming like clockwork. Then there are the meals. Breakfast. Lunch. Dinner. The diaper changes, supervised showers. . . .

"I should have smoked more, drank more, driven my car faster. Then again, how could I have known? They promised cancer in the family. I'm eighty-six years old. Where is this cancer I was promised? Runs in the family blood, they said. Have I, for some unreconciled transgression, or mere perversity of chance, been ignored?"

"Gripe, gripe, Joe" said The-Man-in-the-Plaid-Suit. "You're a griper. Be thankful for the medicines, the Theonex."

"Pure anti-mind," Uncle Joe said out the side of his mouth.

The-Man-in-the-Plaid-Suit said, "Before the Theonex I never liked my mind. Not at twenty, not at forty, not at sixty. Now at eighty-I-forget-what, thanks to the Theonex, I'm at peace with my God-man, take me when HE will."

"Yes, Theonex," said Uncle Joe, turning to me, "Keeps us intact. Opiate of aged asses. Illusion of Young.

"Young," said dreamy-eyed Pearl.

"Young," the three, weep-dreamy eyed, said in unison. "Young."

The Television

Television night with Music, BEING. Apartment strewn with clothes, bottles, ash-trays over-flowing, cake and candy wrappers, coffee cups and empty fast-food cartons.

The War unfolded on the big TV. BEING and Music deep in the couch. Music puffed cigarettes. Stared hard into the grim eye of The War.

I preferred not to. See.

Cheesy crunchy chips, beef jerky, beer. Enemy vehicles blown to bits. "Our" planes over The Enemy City. Loud significant explosions.

Television muted in favor of music. Stereo. Loud, hard, electric War set to the soundtrack of your choice, but really only the fast, thumping, screechy music of our young would do. Weed scent like burning bugs. We were not unaware, all in our twenties, we could easily be players not spectators of The War.

The Nation missiled shrill guitar upon its foe.

"We're kicking ass. We're devastating," said Music.

Hard to imagine too long summoning such will to wreck.

"That city's been around since Time began," I said. "Since Time began to be recorded. On paper, papyrus, stone, whatever. Words."

The Enemy's capital stood six thousand years. Same land, sky, city. Generations' generations. Celebrated and unrecorded lives. History pounded to fine, charred powder within days.

Television Time we gathered as a clan, lost to the box, usually old cartoons and syndicated sit-coms we'd enjoyed long, long ago.

(hard to believe already we had "long ago." "Why, only yesterday blah blah blah blah blah"–follow the bouncing ball of sentiment, nostalgia, fill in blanks)

Watching anything, however foolish. Everything insipid and inane. Content irrelevant. Ideas drain group-think energy of

Manna. Meditation to be watching, to be Nation, for whatever we watched was watched simultaneously by millions. One could never be alone while watching.

I'd known of celebrities I'd seen as a child, out-dated now, dead, forgotten. One must learn the lives of current celebrities to know The Nation.

"Death Squad!" screamed BEING, excited.

Dual remote action. BEING shut the stereo, raised the television volume, tuned into The Death Squad, abandoning The War for Everyone's favorite live-action series.

The Death Squad. Big Media's short-cut to immense profit. This particular service provided by The City excited morbid curiosity. Weekly documentary for the war-juiced public. Throwaway footage resurrected for prime time thrills. Adrenalin, hormone of choice for today's discerning viewer.

The Death Squad ventured into neglected quarters of The City, retrieving corpses (many a corpse corpsed under suspicious circumstances). Questioned nosy neighbors, investigated scenes, chauffeured corpses to the morgue. Live autopsies exposed live audience to the gruesome-gruesome.

"The dead, the indigent dead, accumulate with a rapidity that taxes The City's ability to process the remains," the Celebrity Commentator explained.

The Death Squad consisted of two cops in a car and the ambulance van–a hearse, really, labeled "ambulance" out of respect for the paramedics, known in the trade and show vernacular as "Reapers." The Commentator and Camera-man rode back of the van with Night's retrievals.

The Commentator spoke of faces. Past night's faces under burlap blankets reemerged in dreams. Death Squad: cleaning agents plucked dead cells from Metropolis. Decrepit sections of The City; smegma spread. Crimes to be solved, reports filed. Black ink ball point. Triplicate.

BEING and Music dug into snacks, sipped beer, nodded in agreement with The Commentator.

"Scavengers. Scavengers."

We followed the van and squad car into a sub-city of bleak towers and asphalt sky. Cops emerged, guns drawn. Reapers in the van. Union rules: no rough stuff, only peace and rictus of the dead. The Commentator and Camera-man hustled to action.

Cop radio, cop lights. Kids out sneering. Armed guards sneered. Everyone sneered. It was a sneering place, a vague place. Horrible place to live and worse to die. But work to be done, guns drawn.

Cops pretended The Commentator and Camera-man were stalking, shadowing. Grown used to them, like sharks to remora.

The body hung slit down the middle like a goose. Bucket beneath caught blood.

"How long has he been up like that, ma'am?" asked the tall,

photogenic cop.

“Since I sliced him,” the woman responded to both cop and camera.

“Smells ripe. Neighbors complained.”

“Two days. Three,” she yawned. “Quiet. Peace. Happy.”

“Come with us, Ma’am.”

“Filled that bucket I don’t know how many times.”

“Where’d you dump it?”

“Bathtub. So much blood in a man, you have no idea. Let me freshen up.”

The corpse, gray as putty, strapped to a stretcher and rolled to the van.

Death Squad spooked through spooky canyons of The City.

Next pick-up a codger stretched under rough blankets, eyes mouth wide and skin like paste.

Old woman beside him sobbed, “Oh, the bed! The bed!”

The bed they’d shared for half a century.

“Like some primordial–Eskimos on an ice floe, only she’s not dead yet,” mused The Commentator.

The Show ended, as it did each week, at the morgue. The Commentator delivered his weekly homily. The Morgue Men dismantled bodies. Hearts, kidneys, colons, yellow livers, sooty lungs.

Spongy gray cerebra had known Life in Time. Impressions intact, like etchings on a disk? Could memories be re-animated and re-called? Admission of heat through meat circuits, before wet ware dried to dust?

The Commentator said, "Stories of the dead in artifacts they left behind. Knick-knacks, papers, baubles. Take pleasure in life."

The Damned

Friday midtown. Friday payday.

"CEO Tobacconists." Quality, overpriced cigars. Walk-in humidor. Air-conditioned smoking room. Customers relax. Smoke. Wide-screen TV.

Recite the Smoker's Ode:

green gone

brown dead

resurrection fire

leaf life

tumors bloom

like tulips

or teeth

oh wet pink lungs

Musty humidor. Fat, sticky Maduro. Smoking room television tuned to The War. Cigar store crowd. Executives Young, Middle-Aged, Old. Shiny black shoes. Gray Summer suits.

And me, "Plantman," the indoor landscaper, the horticultural technician, keeper of The City's Office Flora, in denim and Topiary Techniques t-shirt, smoked the darkest, most potent, if not largest, cigar in the room. Double-Maduro, Double-Corona. Sweet.

Television: Siren Air Strike Siren Air Strike Air Strike Air Strike Air Strike

Older men their war. Middle-aged their own. Younger Executives had not known war, cognizant of men their age in combat even as Young Executives ordered cigars. Senior Executives. Executives. Junior Executives. Vice-presidents. Managing Directors. Directors. Managing managers directing directors to be still. Be still.

Older wars superior to new, according to geezers. More skill, more man-to-man hand-to-hand. None of this push-button never see the hell you kill, play it like a video arcade, fish in a barrel, no thrill-glory, no blood-scent, you see.

Middle-aged nightmares recalled: guerrilla warfare, jungle rot, defoliants, lack moral such such such.

Arguments went so. Young men red-eared silent. Watched The War through smoke: planes tanks missiles blasting righteous wrath smote cities hammered eerie jigsaw puzzles of indignity, pain, confusion.

(Listen to the footage sound-track closely, said an Executive who inadvertently recorded it while taping TV War Footage, you'll hear a baby, sounding far-away, sleepy, probably in shock, calling for its mama or papa or someone, The Executive couldn't tell.)

Out the window Sol's slow-mo plunge. Sticky-sweet Maduro rhythm concentrated puff-exhale. "Still Life With Plantman Under Purple Sky." I reached the cream of cigar, the final third, blend of saliva with juices latent in the leaf. Damp puff ether of cobalt self.

Young Executives had known no war, but anecdotes of old warriors. Bosses, Mentors. Repetition. They watched television commentators in steady thick of mayhem slaughter. Prime action for the folks back home. Gory talk. The Old Executive/Warriors explicit, baleful, tedious.

Discussion shifted to cigars. Executives in the Smoking Room of CEO Cigars. Representatives of several companies gathering informally. Enemies after all. Smoking. Sharing histories. Business anecdotes–a different kind of war. Cigar ritual. Initiation. Not afraid to stink. Hah-hah-hah to up-turned noses of trim, health-worship wives.

"Straight talk."

Not afraid among men. But what if. . . the office. . . reveal what's hidden. . . known among women. . . at the office?

"Won't get laid worrying like that," said one Senior Executive. "Women like strong men with big cigars. We've got nothing to hide here. Not in this room, at any rate."

Laughter.

Pause. Ceremony. Executive Light-Up. Long wood matchsticks. "Suck that fire, suck it." Faulty flame? Bad light, uneven burn? Catastrophic waste of a Cigar. Bad show, Miss-ter. Really bad.

"Cigar, gift of the Indian," one waxed poetic. "Cylinder of mellowness and virtue."

Cigarette not a cigar like a shot of rye not a snifter of fine cognac. Life ripened goes to smoke. Lifts spirits. Anguish up in smoke of stink leaf. Curing process: green origins ripen under sun.

Natural processes. Living systems. Green embalmed brown. Like raisins. Curing thought. Tumors like mushroom caps. Exploded lungs of the unfortunate. Bombs felled Enemy cities. Up in smoke. Commentators explained significance. Attack, attack, explode: shock, fear, desire-light of vision. Nation. Nation. Greatest show on earth.

I studied bright burning buildings, imagined lives inside. Entered thoughts and situations, borrowed time. Ten million minds became one mind, my cigar their locus. Ten-million thoughts became no thought–steady puff-exhale—and peace. Maduro of the Cosmic One-Mind. But on the screen and in the Cigar Room: smoke, fire, ashes, ashes.

Fire eye of my cigar wept ashes. Smoke everywhere, everywhere smoke and talk.

The Run, Run Free

Everyday Day run. See Plantman run. Run Plantman run.

Run. Run. Run.

Shed "work" clothes, don tank top, shorts, sneakers. Flamenco in the player. Down, down. The street. The crowded. The Big Park.

Mile-and-a-half dodge through and around flesh traffic. The People. Thought-spasms amplified: energies colliding; faces sweating; hand-bags swinging. No freedom like The Run. Away, away. Run, run.

Up the volume. Flamenco castanets, guitars. Women trilling, hands clapping–for ME, dead center of the world.

Seven mile path. Green manifest. Fields shrubs trees. Not potted. Free.

Flamenco faster, louder, harder. Run. Runner. Fast. Faster. Hard. Harder.

Concentrated push charge Life energy around round round The Big Park magic circle-center of the world.

Where Life is.

VI.
Midnight at the Apocalyptic Pancake, an Aside Show

Zarathustra's Dragons stormed the stage like Cro-Magnon angels, a feral furry crew, too savage for Redemption, too innocent to Fall. Where their hair ended and their clothes began was painful to discern. The lead singer wore an ornamental bone through his nose. A necklace of human teeth, plucked sentimentally, the press releases claimed, from the jaws of one-night-stands, hung to his navel. The band looked like they'd been used to scrub a large, industrial kitchen.

Midnight at the Apocalyptic Pancake with The Antique Dealer, proprietor of the Time Capsule Antique shop and amateur "poet" (though, to be fair, all poets of The Nation are amateurs). An old acquaintance from my college days, a lonely man, not of his time. Certainly not the kind I'd choose to waste a night with, but he invited me to drink, "for old time's sake." How could I refuse?

Impatient for a waitress, he reached for my drink. The sting of Brain Death, the house specialty, a heady maelstrom of herb juices and spirits, put the light back in his eyes. The Dragons tuned their instruments, creating noise like claws on flint.

"I'm lonely. My little lady's left me," whined the Antique Dealer. "My woman dances for another."

"There, there," I consoled as best I could. "Now, now. These things happen. Other fish in the sea and all that."

Our balcony table overlooked The Pit, a sunken dance floor nine feet deep, in which a hundred black-garbed dancers writhed in mindless torsion, bare feet pounding furiously, despite the conspicuous absence of. . . music.

The Antique Dealer was as drunk and depressed as I'd ever seen him.

When the tuning ceased, the dancers, sensing the imminence of art–or danger–stopped briefly, and posed. Menacing silence. As if the next might be the last noise. As if the Dragons had come not to entertain their audience, but bury them.

"I am become death. . ." whispered The Antique Dealer/ Bard.

"Oh, good grief," I sighed.

At last the dark millennial minstrels, invoking the powers that spin planets and bend light, commenced to ditty:

"Eat the rich,
Lucretia!
Eat the rich,
With Ketchup!
But don't eat them all,
No, baby!
They're too high,

My Borgia!
In chol-es-ter-ol!"

"I remember her black negligee, no larger than a kerchief," moped The Antique Dealer, his voice tossed like a sparrow in a gale of sound. "The way she'd scamper across the kitchen on those infinitesimal white feet. . . "

The Antique Dealer was, like me, a year from thirty. His Beethoven 'do evoked the lead gray chaos of an ocean storm. Like nearly everyone else at the Apocalyptic Pancake (besides me in my green "Topiary Techniques" t-shirt–I'd come straight from work), he wore black. The back of his leather jacket bore a meticulously detailed portrait of Shelley, sporting open collar and wind-blown hair. Instead of a quill pen, The Antique Dealer's Shelley held a smoking gun. The bold red caption across the top of the jacket read "Don't weep for Adonais. . ." Beneath the portrait were the words, ". . .avenge him!"

"I can't live like you," said The Antique Dealer. "Tending plants, evading issues, skirting time. A poet is supremely mortal. He needs a warm body beside him, always. He needs communication. He needs life."

I crushed an ice-cube with my teeth. The Antique Dealer was not a bad fellow, as fellows went, but poet/antique dealers in general bored me to near catatonia. They made me numb.

The walls of his shop, which I'd visited once, offered photos of a brownish time when even the sun shone sepia in a dull beige sky. Men in bowler hats and skin-tight vests, their mustaches like clumps of bear fur bristling with ale; women stuffed like sausages into dark, double-breasted bodices with wide skirts and Italy-shaped shoes; quiet scenes bracketed by leafy-looking frames of bronze and copper.

Among photographs and artifacts and his elegantly coiffed and tailored clientèle he seemed to feel home.

"I do not like loud, angry music; superfluous drama; crowds," he said.

He'd inherited the Time Capsule Antique shop and the basement apartment beneath it from a maiden aunt, who had her own particular, if not downright peculiar, pleasures.

"People hate poets," The Antique Dealer said.

I thought, "A poker face I haven't."

"People especially hate unpublished, spoken-word poets. How many times in one life can a man abide the phrase, 'Oh, why don't you just shut up?' Try to communicate with people, try to reach some sort of accord, and they give you, 'Oh, why don't you just shut up!' I won't stand for it much longer. I won't be silenced!"

"But who's silencing you?" I asked.

The Antique Dealer laughed. Quite madly, actually.

A waitress appeared. I bought another round.

The Antique Dealer pointed to a table on the Lower Level, about ten yards from the stage, and not far from the precipice of The Pit. Around the table sat Bogvonian, The Filmmaker, and two young, gray-suited lackeys. Bogvonian was an older man, past sixty. He draped his girth in bright-colored silks. His rings and bracelets glittered, dense with jewels. The shiny skin stretched taut over his skull slackened to loose, thick folds around his collar.

The Filmmaker said something out of the side of his mouth. The gray-suits nodded. He bit the foreskin off of a cucumber-sized cheroot and searched his silks for fire. The young men simultaneously extended Zippos.

"It's Bogvonian, the auteur!" gasped The Antique Dealer. "He's come to study Kim. He's going to film her!"

"Here?"

"If not here, wherever. It's inevitable. He'll soak up every drop of her. Kim's image will be his."

"She must have quite an act," I said.

"It's why we're here."

"It's why you're here. Why am I?"

"To bear witness."

"Why do this to yourself?" I yawned.

"I must suffer–I mean, SEE HER. I must see her."

The Filmmaker's obvious contempt for his surroundings caused him to expectorate a turd-sized wad of phlegm. He whispered to his men, then poked the air as if to tweak a passing fly.

When the Dragons finished their set, he left his table and stood at the edge of The Pit, gazing indifferently upon the young people who danced in silence. He flicked a cigar ash over the tangle of damp, swaying bodies and returned to his table to find that, in his absence, a waiter had heaped his plate with salad. Zarathustra's Dragons exited behind a curtain.

"When I first met Tiny Kim, she was working as a promo-girl for MamaBubba's Mini Donuts," The Antique Dealer said. "They'd decked her in an eenie-weenie, chocolate-dipped bikini. She wore bite-sized crullers round her ankles and a fried-dough choker. Her hair was honey-glazed, her cheeks dusted with sugar. She'd come to The City from out West, hoping to 'make it' as an actress."

"Lemme guess. She only got 'bit' parts," I said. "'Small' roles."

"Not even in The City of Cities are there many leads for a woman two feet tall," The Antique Dealer said with a straight face.

The antique dealer had rescued the seductive midget from the sweet exploitations of MamaBubba.

"I took her into The Time Capsule, my home. I educated her. I won her heart. Of course, I had to schmooze a little. Who doesn't? I fed her a saucer of folderol about her being 'pith personified, God's platinum blonde Haiku.' An hors d'oeuvre. Anyway, I meant it at the time."

For months they lived the domestic life, sponging frugally off of The Antique Dealer's modest inheritance–the shop made little money. But Kim felt she was made for bigger things, and when the time was right, she pursued them.

"No one will love her like I loved her," he wept. "No one will feel what I felt when I rocked that tiny body in my lap. Now, alone, I wander asphalt gullies of The City under strips of navy sky, breathing, reluctantly, the dense air of metropolis, cluttered as it is with particles of soot and rot. I wait, impatiently, for daylight, so I can open the Time Capsule and watch the occasional customers stroll among the escritoires and funnel-mouthed Victrolas; the cut-glass bowls and crystal cabinets; the gadgets, knick-knacks and no-longer-relevant machines, musty detritus of strangers' lives."

I nodded mechanically. The Antique Dealer turned away. He screamed at a passing waitress for more Brain Death. She gestured violently, and, chastened, he implored.

A new band took the stage. The back-up musicians of Tiny Kim. Thick, cotton-clad men with black shiny hair down to their scapulae. They carried wooden Pan-pipes lashed with gut and sinew and sundry instruments hewn from the flora and fauna of Peru. They played: the cold breath of the Andes, fermented in deep, Inca lungs and mellowed through cylinders of ancient wood, lulled the audience to torpor, loosened eye-lids, lips, nostrils like the vapors of a precious brandy.

"This music is likable," I said.

"They're from out of town," The Antique Dealer said. "Kim plucked them from the Classifieds. The ink on their green-cards smears to the touch."

A mountain of humanity lumbered to the stage, buck naked.

"Bruno has barely enough brains to zip his fly," The Antique Dealer explained. "He worked in the Recycling Plant, made his living smashing bottles against a wall. After five years, he was still only an apprentice. Kim hocked a leather bound Keats and a hard-cover Novalis to afford him. I'd given her those books as gifts."

"Doesn't he realize where he is, and that he's naked?"

"Irrelevant. The man's an idiot. In previous versions of the act Kim had had him enter in a three-piece suit. It took too long for him to free himself. His struggles broke the rhythm of the dance."

Tiny Kim appeared, a pint of Aphrodite scuttling across the stage. She danced her tiny dance with vigor. The pace of the music accelerated; the pipers' bronze cheeks glistened. She orbited Bruno like a moon, moving closer, closer, until the music stopped and she stood, arms spread, before him, wearing nothing but Jesus, who died, gnat-sized, on the silver crucifix that dangled from her quadri-pierced left ear.

Bruno's monstrous member loomed above her like the bald branch of a Red Wood. He lifted her in hands the size of hubcaps. Even the most callous ruffians in the audience gasped as he lowered her to his impossibly enormous bone.

The audience watched, fascinated, as the muscle-bound behemoth, grunting in frustration, turned Kim every which way in search of entry, attempting even to twist her onto himself like a bottle-cap.

Finally, he set her down. Kim stepped backward. As if on cue, the giant's ponderous erection lost its wind, drooped earthward, hung limp, like a narcotized ferret, from his loins.

Bruno, the Apprentice Bottle-Smasher, lowered himself to his knees. Awkwardly, bearishly, he groped for her.
He bellowed to the Heavens:

"Mmmmmlvbg. . . mlubd. . . mmluh. . . luh. . . luh. . . love!"

He nuzzled Kim's belly, and licked her tiny triangle of pubis like a stamp.

"I've seen enough," I said. "Let's get the fuck out of here."

"Not yet," said The Antique Dealer. "I have things planned. It's not too late for me to DO."

Tiny Kim, having acknowledged the audience's wild applause, allowed Bruno to lift her onto his shoulder. She rode the giant down the steps of the stage and straight to Bogvonian's table. At a nod from the filmmaker, the gray-suits rose from their seats and bowed.

Kim's lips molded the word "sit." Bruno, knees bent perpendicular, naked ass parallel to the floor, made a chair of himself. The midget descended to his lap, pulling a cigarette from behind his ear on the way down. Bogvonian lit her smoke with the smoldering end of his cigar.

"I offered her, what, beauty, truth?" said The Antique Dealer. "She opted for. . . image. How can a poet compete with the sound and motion of film?"

The former Bite-sized Cruller Queen reclined against the giant's stomach, which was flat and steep and cut with muscle like a grid.

"The. . . uh. . . CONTRAST between the two of them is striking," I said.

"She doesn't really love the giant. He's an idiot. She's using him to impress Bogvonian. She needed an image, or rather, counter-image, worthy of the Master's lens. She wants to be preserved, that's what's behind it all."

I sensed where his talk was headed. Perhaps I should have done something to stop it. But I knew from experience that such manias as The Antique Dealer's must be allowed to wind themselves to completion.

"I'm going to raise a commotion," he said, grimly. "I'm going to smite the giant, tear him limb from limb. I'm going to carry Kim up to the stage and triumph where that lumbering behemoth so miserably fucked up. I'm going to earn my moments in amber, secure a place for myself in Bogvonian's oeuvre. I'm going to–"

Without warning, Zarathustra's Dragons occupied the stage again and blitzed the Pancake with their second set:

"Ain't got no love–
Baby!

Ain't got no love—
Baby!
Ain't got no love–
Baby!
Ain't got no love–
Baby!"

It all seemed so ridiculous, so unnecessary, so. . . disappointing. One minute The Antique Dealer was pontificating across from me, the next he was staggering across the beer-and-vomit-sticky floor of the lower level, bumping into tables, pushing waiters, waitresses and patrons from his path, until at last reaching Bogvonian's table, he stood before the midget, arms akimbo, legs apart, expectant.

Tiny Kim wrinkled her brow. She snuffed her cigarette in the ashtray Bruno had made for her of his palm. The poet launched into a tirade, waving his arms, stamping his feet. Kim looked to The Filmmaker for assistance.

Bogvonian rolled his fat cigar slowly between nut-brown teeth and eyed the impassioned antique dealer with distaste.

The Antique Dealer lifted the nude midget from the giant's thigh–not without her protest–and set her on the table beside a bottle of Bordeaux. He pummeled Bruno furiously, cursing at the top of his lungs–the music absorbed his every syllable.

Though the antique dealer's doughy fists could hardly hurt the giant, Bruno's eyes churned huge tears which tumbled bluely down the grid-iron surface of his face. He remained in position, like a marble couch, immovable, while the midget pleaded with the filmmaker for ACTION.

Bogvonian, mouth stuffed to capacity with tobacco and escarole, nodded to his lackeys. They rose, dabbed their lips with napkins, folded the napkins neatly on their plates. Nostrils dilated, cheeks crimson with instant rage, they converged upon The Antique Dealer, who was now trying desperately to strangle Bruno, his wiry arms enveloping the giant's tree-trunk neck like vines.

"I should do something," I thought. "But really, I'm just a horticultural technician, a Plantman. Truly. Honestly. What can I do?"

The gray-suits unclasped The Antique Dealer's hands, twisted his skinny arms behind his back and pulled. The pop of humeri wrenched from their sockets reverberated through the Pancake, causing even the lead singer of Zarathustra's Dragons to grimace, mid-lyric, and touch a finger to his heart.

Again the music sucked the life from The Antique Dealer's screams. I stared down helplessly into the futile abyss of his mouth.

Swinging him by his long legs and stretched, useless arms, the gray-suits, with a syncopated "Heave! Ho! Heave!" tossed The Antique Dealer high over The Pit. He hung for agonizing nano-seconds before falling.

The disappearance of a human form into the jungle of dancers, the spectacle of a body swallowed whole, had its predictable effect upon the audience. Heads turned desperately to Zarathustra's Dragons. The Apocalyptic Pancake became all eyes, ears and mouths pleading for the band's electric succor.

Tiny Kim dabbed the giant's egg-sized tears with the fringe of a silk cape proffered by Bogvonian.

Out of some vestigial sense of duty, or more accurately, pity–the weakness that had coaxed me to the Pancake in the first place–I descended to the lower level and stood for almost an hour at the precipice of The Pit, searching for a glimpse of The Antique Dealer, or Shelley, in the misty, churning swamp of flesh, leather, cotton. But the crowd was so dense I couldn't see the dancers' feet, much less what was under them, and I resigned myself to never drinking or conversing with the antique dealing "poet" again.

Bogvonian's table was now empty. A busboy peeled a partially eaten lettuce leaf from Bogvonian's plate and slipped it into a small, clear plastic bag. A souvenir.

VII.
Big Media Comes

The Photographer

The Photographer exhibited downtown. Galleries, museums. Big hit in the "art community," but not in the infallible system that measures the worth of all things, from "culture" to fruit salad: The Market. Did it, is it, or will it make/be making money? If so, Artist + Sales = Success, anywhere from up-and-coming novice to assiduous crafts-man to Genius, depending on The Market's sober assessment.

Thus far, The Photographer had merited barely a "fresh new face," but her first book of photographs, BAD SEEDS, published several years earlier, to great praise, many awards and dismal sales, was "discovered" by the wife of a Big Media Executive who convinced her husband and his more conservative colleagues that the theme of young, gritty Beautiful People should be tested, on television, as a pilot for a potential series. The photographer would be paid for the pilot, and if the show became a series, a share of the residuals would be hers–the industry standard for "story idea." So The Photographer might become a very talented artist indeed, once the pilot was shown across The Nation. And she was already considering subjects for a second book.

We'd met at the Ad Agency, when I wrote copy and she photographed, free-lance, for the Graphics and Design department. It was she who took the photograph for my EARN advertisement and added the necessary, industry-approved color gradients and shadows.

She was the first "famous" artist I had ever known and she was doing wedding photographs as well as promo graphics for the agency to get by. In a sense, despite the awards and rave reviews she received for her book and the slide show of her work, which she set to music and performed at various clubs, galleries and college venues, photography could be considered, for the likes of The Photographer and many of her less "successful" colleagues, merely an expensive hobby.

She photographed friends and strangers on the "Hip Scene" for art; models and advertisements for money. Still did jobs for the Ad Agency. Occasionally.

People crowded the exhibit. The Photographer was becoming someone celebrated. Not there yet, but becoming. BAD SEEDS displayed stylish people doing, going, drinking, dancing, fighting, fucking. The Beautiful enjoying life. If only while young. If only while Beautiful not Money.

Citizens envied moments The Beautiful had lived, one of the rare instances in the Life of The Nation in which quality was valued over quantity. Even when one of The Beautiful died young, sometimes very young, The Citizens would still rather have lived a few moments the dead Beautiful had known than a generation's worth of regular lives. Many an Elderly Citizen considered the twenty-five-years of a Beautiful struck down tragically in an accident to have been qualitatively more valuable and more desirable than his own four-score safe, productive, "normal" years.

The Photographer had photographed the Missing Young in streets and clubs; met people; put lives in her book for all to see. She let those who didn't live lives glimpse moments and motions of those who did.

After the gallery we went out for drinks at a bar she'd photographed for her new show and second book-in-progress. Stylish people doing stylish things. I watched them. Interesting, but not as live as her art–that is, after they were photographed–made them. We sat at the bar, doing nothing but real.

"Are you working?" she asked me. "They told me you quit the Agency."

I explained the nature and detail of my new calling.

Beautiful or aspiring Beautiful came to greet her, fawn, schmooze, hoping to perhaps be digitally immortalized on disk. She captured me drinking.

"I need a new subject. Or many new subjects," said the Photographer.

She wished to spread her wings, having grown tired of "The Scene."

She wanted to photograph me. As Plantman. She wanted to follow me for a day. Suck my Topiary Time into her camera. Her "life processor." Her gizmo.

"I'd have to clear it with Victor. Victor's the head guy," I cautioned.

Of course Victor delighted in the prospect of free publicity for Topiary Techniques.

"I'll have to talk to the clients," said Victor. "I'll tell them it's for a promotional brochure. As long as nobody raises objections. . . ."

No one did. Clients themselves were eager to be taken.

The Photographer photographed me doing.

"A Day in the Life of Plantman," said the Photographer.

She posed me meditatively beside an Aboricolum. Horticultural cognition. Click, click. I watered, clipped, dusted, poked. She photographed plants, office workers, desks, cubicles. Recorded the tired, bored, worn, anxious All-Day day.

Before she submitted the photographs to "Now City," a glossy upscale magazine of The Nation, she showed me photos of myself as Plantman. Uncomfortable, those graphics of my heretofore. Images of outside-of-me outside of me not in a mirror or other device that would enable me to keep an in-the-moment, "real time" eye on my own doing.

No relation to the me inside me.

"What do you plan to do with these?" I asked.

"Study them. Then study them some more. Tweak the best,

then submit them for publication," she said.

"Now City" made me, or rather, me as Plantman, a celebrity in some small way. Glossy photos of immortal Plantman, keeper protector of green interiors, duplicated and dispersed. Plantman on full color record, tending life.

Twenty-two-million copies sold, maybe more. All those people watching. Or rather, looking. Still Life Plantman. Repetitions of motion-pieces gone forever, saved on slick paper. Plantman working in The Past. People in apartments, offices, subway cars, waiting rooms studied Plantman-In-The-Past.

I saw an alien being in the photographs. A stranger. Utter fiction.

The Morning Show

The Photographer's "Plantman" magazine series was a hit. She was interviewed on The Morning Show, taped in The City, broadcast to The Nation. She planned to use the Plantman photographs as a basis for a book, *Workers of The City*, the rights of which had already been bought, with a hefty advance to The Photographer, by Big Publishing. She was now, according to her svelte, corn-blond interviewer, "a Genius and Genuine Artist of The Nation."

The Morning Show wanted to interview me too. I refused. I had work. But the Executives and Board Members of Topiary Techniques International Inc.–miles and miles above the head of Victor–demanded I submit to the corn-blond woman's interview. I arrived at the Television Station at 5 AM, four hours before work.

Oh Viewers of The Nation! You have witnessed Plantman's thirty seconds of fame. You have heard him, SEEN him. But do you know him?

Pursuit of Pure Talk

Horticultural heroics at the Public Relations firm. Office of the beautiful young Publicist. She harangued a client over the phone. Talk, talk. Every word a scream.

"Give the people what they want," she said. "Tell the people what they want. Make the people want. Tell them, make them, give them. Understand?"

Slammed down the phone. Wired, she addressed me.

"I'm right, you know. Look at me. Started low: restaurant and club openings, celebrity profile parties, City events. Junk publicity. Junkpub."

Hard girl. Learned to be loud, wry, ferocious. Talk, talk. Talkety talk.

"Phone the news desk direct line to the gossip column, or better yet, the television station. Make a stir. Create a buzz. Disseminate information. Lay anchor in the sea of data. When the job is done, sail on. Don't take 'no' for an answer. But if the answer must be 'no,' carry a grudge. Get mad, get even. You understand, Plantman?"

I tried to explain to her that I was only an "Indoor Landscaper," a "Horticultural technician." I water office plants. No star quality in that.

"Celebrity is currency. Find celebrities and use them. Let them gather at parties and be cheerful. Let them be irritable, contrary, and infantile. Spoil them, pamper them, expose them. Don't over-expose. Learn your economics. Inflation of overexposure. Familiarity is contempt. Sow them selectively like political donations. Their value will increase and thereby will your own."

The Publicist procured celebrities. Hyped events. Promoted City hot spots. The Firm directed her to not merely procure celebrities, but represent them.

"Stars emit their cosmic-comic gas until they're spent. Cave in on themselves or bloat and expand, like cold red giants. Cut 'em from your orbit before they explode. I yank wanna-bees and has-beens from black holes of obscurity. Inflate mediocrities, present new names, resurrect dead reputations."

The Publicist sipped bottled water.

"Celebrity is pursuit of pure talk. And pictures. Don't move an inch unless it's for a camera. Make the talk 'sticky.'"

Thirty or so. Top of her game. A Vice President of the Firm. Portfolio of high profile stars, starlets, celebrity writers and directors; headline escapades of pampered, sexually deviant children of the moneyed class. She placed faces on covers of magazines, booked interviews and features on entertainment news. Her celebrity faces launched a thousand talk shows, endless, ubiquitous pursuit of talk.

"Celebrity is liquid. A liquid asset. Catch the celebrity as he moves from A to B. Redirect him to point C, and watch the people flock. Like sheep. The people. Baaaahhhh. Baaaaahhhh. But these stars burn hotter than the Sun. Laws of inertia, entropy, the physics of it all, the reality. It catches up to them."

Her job to feed the fire, shovel coal, keep the locomotive running fast and furious, pulling its enormous freight of "journalists," commentators, talk-show hosts and paparazzi.

Relentless print images and talk. Relentless funneling channeling directing redirecting fanning flames. Must burn constantly everywhere always.

"Celebrity is a variable. They fade, grow old, get stupid, boring, dead. They're easily replaced, and usually more valuable dead. It's now now NOW celebrity or never. Even established Stars, etched in The Nation's memory, must be everywhere, always, or inch that much closer to never.

"Celebrities consume cheers, applause, light, expel pure talk. Interview with the celebrity talk show host or entertainment journalist a crowning glory, PR coup. Twin stars. Super Nova.

Yes!" she pounded her desk.

The Publicist vowed to enhance the celebrity of Plantman beyond The City. Bring him world renown.

"But I'm only a horticultural technician," I explained again.

She laughed cold fake hard, like the rattle of a penny in a can.

"You're Plantman. You nurture the most prestigious shrubs in The City. You must promote yourself. I'm giving you free advice here. Not charging a dime. You can't remain merely an anonymous 'worker-drudge' forever. Got to expand your realm. Otherwise. . . you're courting never."

"I take care of the plants. That's all."

"You're a Name in this City. Live up to your Legend. All you need is the right publicist and boom–Super Nova!"

"But that's not–"

"'Boom,' I said. '"Super Nova.' I'll connect you. Not that you need to be connected. The Names would only be too glad to have you appear on their talk shows and in their magazines. Get you in touch with The Names of The Nation. That's our goal. Let me tell you about The Names. The Nation might protest that it does not need The Names. The City might plead 'enough, we have had enough of The Names.' These are bullshit objections. False modesty.

"Self-serving lies. Like the beauty pageant winner, the one who mastered baton twirling and dieting at sixteen so she could wave her tits and ass before the cameras, protesting that she does not 'deserve' to win. She's too 'humble' to accept such honors. Humble, my ass. 'Deserve,' my ass too. Nobody deserves anything but what they can get. A lot of time and energy goes into creating The Names. You, Plantman, must become a Name. Not merely a Name of The City, but of The Nation."

Wired to the Stars

Early morning trucks rolled in to wire Big Media to the stars. Immense wheels beat asphalt streets like drum-skins, deafening. Big Media cameras; cables; generators; crews with headsets, walkie-talkies, official Big Media caps; wireless phones; caterers; buffet tables; Klieg lights; microphones; tents; guards; interns; factotums; trailers; wardrobes; make-up artists; lackeys; bit-players, stars and miles and miles of wire, all issued from Executive minds out West.

Money, Power. Big Media made manifest. In the beginning the Word of Big Media blew East to The City, omnipresent, ambiguous as wind.

The taping had begun, commotion unavoidable. The Show became The City. Cast, crew, tents, barricades colonized the Street. A path of no-man's-land was laid by wearers of headsets and walkie-talkies, who urged pedestrians to use the street across the park–except certain passersby who displayed local authenticity and color for the never idle cameras.

Impressed, not awed, by sheer production power Big Media mobilized. Even its by-products a massive undertaking (tourists, police overseers, news crews soaking everything even themselves–cameras on camera). Spectacular parade.

BEING had warned this day would come. He served food to famous and soon-to-be-famous faces. Big Media meant BEING worked.

BEING at the stars' buffet scooped melon-balls into a crystal dish.

VIII.
The Infocracy

Root Said

"Digital City" convention at The City Center. Hardware, software, networking companies displayed high-tech consumables in pre-fab cubicles, tents, booths. Largest exhibit: Tree of Knowledge Incorporated (TKI).

TKI software powered nearly every machine in The Nation. Their "booth" a leviathan Pyramid 2.0 Database long and wide as a bus. The most powerful in existence, paralleled and mirrored with multiple terabyte drives stacked floor to ceiling like amplifiers at a concert.

TKI representative at the scene wowed spectators with demo searches, explained how Pyramid functioned, the many levels of permissions. A regular user on The Network was privy to all data one could possibly confuse himself with. But Government, Law Enforcement, Major Corporations and other privileged entities enjoyed deep access to sensitive info, even trade and security secrets of The Nation.

Booths offered Three Dimensional networking on high-powered machines. Face recognition. Virtual Gardens.

Users grew digital plants, tended them, watched them grow or die. I raised a rose from seed to bloom to death of natural causes—flat-screen fade to gloom.

3D models of Data Centers, servers, back-up systems; simulation of The City itself.

Face-offed with a fat man. Straggly beard, dirty t-shirt, faded jeans and ratty sneakers. "Root," a hacker come to infiltrate the machines of the Infocracy. Ran a site called "Crack Byte," dedicated to destruction of said Infocracy–giant companies like TKI in league with government to take away our all.

Root said, "What can you touch? What gives you pleasure?"

Root said, "My wife's 3D rendering of our apartment is a cleaner, nicer place to live than our actual apartment. We wish to enter it. To leave our laundry, cats and debts behind."

"Cats?" I asked.

"Four," Root said. "Cold, cruel, aristocratic animals. Cats really suck."

Root said, "When you die, you will no longer be able to log onto The Network. When you die, you may receive email, but you may not answer it."

Root said, "The Infocracy is not about machines, it is about language. Words and symbols are the capital of The Infoconomy."

Root said, "The Infocracy, like all systems, is hierarchical. The

Infocracy is a hierarchy of those who know, those who sell, and those who both know and sell."

Root said, "The Infocracy will feed off the entropy of the masses and other less potent (that is, organized) sub-systems of The Network."

Root said, "The Network exists for the political, social, economic and intellectual enrichment of The Infocracy."

Root said, "The masses support The Infocracy with credit debt and an inability to detect patterns."

Root said, "As history loses relevance, so too do the fictions and mythologies that evolved from death's pathos. New fictions will mirror essential "realities" of The Infocracy."

Root said, "It was a pleasure speaking to you. Excuse me, gotta go harass the guy from TKI."

And that was all Root said.

The Castle

Visited The Network Castle where important and unimportant personages gathered to shoot the breeze. Visitors paid a fee to The Keepers of The Castle, received access. Other requirement was a generic image provided by The Keepers (akin to rubber nose and goggles), or send The Keepers an image of your choice.

Submitted The Solitary Novelist. Most icons were movie stars, old and recent; television stars, old and recent; sports stars, old and recent; all species of celebrity, old and recent.

Endless Castle. One could navigate its three-dimensional halls and parlors weeks without visiting the same room twice.

Cliquishness within. I was not accepted. Perhaps the obscurity of my icon, its awkward wandering. I did not find scintillating conversation, Romance, intrigue–the alleged jewels within The Castle labyrinth.

My icon alone at the fireplace of a vast library. Stacks of "antique" books, visible "virtual," not to be touched or read.

Shocked from The Castle's digital gossip-dungeons to my bedroom closet. Reality a battering ram through digital walls: jeans, jackets, Topiary Techniques t-shirts hung dead without me. Veteran vestments of Life's tasks now separate, remote, indifferent. Spooked me.

Second time in Life my own clothes called me Home.

The Search

Market Research Information Data firm. Talked "shop" with a Certified Searcher. Searchers searched the Pyramid Database. Bees collecting pollen for Executive drives.

Perhaps learn art of the search. Perhaps find some thing.

"Time brings data," said The Searcher, a woman of early, fierce middle-age. "Trajectory of information. Got to keep track of what the citizens are consuming. Immense! I preside over a mere twig on the Tree of Knowledge. Or rather, Tree of Information."

No true knowledge, no wisdom. Information, samplings of the what, but not the why or wherefore. Whence, but none substantial. Prune The Tree.

"Oh, well, you know, it works like it works," said The Searcher. "Information. Ineluctable."

Happened happenings. Ghosts of real.

"Remember when you were young? So does the Database. The Pyramid Database remembers everything about you but knows nothing."

No Searcher knows beyond a small swatch of tree. Immensity even in that. The Big Picture beyond scope of duty. No clearance, no closure. To ask a Searcher about the Database would be to ask a Citizen about The Nation. Their own little spot, generalizations about the whole informed by Big Media, guesswork, but really, what did anyone know? No knowledge, information. How THEY kill curious. Befuddle with suspicion: secrets originate in our tiny, crammed skulls. This Searcher, what did SHE know?

"Only my duties relative to certain demographics handled by The Firm," said The Searcher. "Nothing, really. I process. Fetch and enter. Process. Sales Executive wants to know about particular habits of a particular class of individual related to a particular lifestyle related to a particular product etc. They ask, and I retrieve."

Not knowledge, info. Data. Trajectory of happenings. Variables secreting history.

"Data is never lost or erased. Perhaps by accident from a particular terminal, but the entire Pyramid Database is paralleled and mirrored. Every bit and byte is copied, multiplied and stored in various locations. Numerous interpretations. No data is the same data. Depends on its function, its relevance to a particular situation. Situations determine meaning. Otherwise, what? Just characters and symbols. Not even. Shapes, designs. Nothing."

"Nothing," I repeated absently.

She took offense.

"What do you want from me? I'm a Searcher. I worked and studied to attain this status. I know my section of the tree. I'm important, very important, to advertisers, product marketers, the sales process itself.

"Nevertheless, I'm just a Searcher. A worker bee. I know what I know, but I don't really know it, for I am never apprised of the context in which the data I invoke is used. Circumstance is Everything and All. The great empirical empty. Forgotten as soon as retrieved. On to the next search. That's what they taught me when I began my studies. About The Search. Science of The Search. What we find is irrelevant. To us. Concerned with pure technique of scrutiny, symbolic language, the arcane grammar and expressions that enable us to conduct successful hunts, make quick connections so information can be summoned and released to The Marketers and Sales Executives who infuse data with meaning.

"I exist to find. They tell me what to find, I find it. It means nothing. To me. I don't even read the data as natural language. The symbolic language of the search precludes curiosity associated with natural language, human language, speech, writing. We translate Executive requests in natural language to the symbolic code of search, and when we find what we find, though it will have subtle shades of meaning for the Firm and its clients, our quarry consists of cold code, meaningless outside the hunt.

"So if you asked me to find an apple, I would translate "apple" into the code of search ("the quest," we call it among ourselves), and though what I find might relate to fruit and commerce and dietary fiber and whatever meanings you were looking for, to me it would merely call up notational bits regarding your directive. I would have everything you could possibly need to know, yet at the same time know nothing myself, other than that I successfully processed your summons for "apple" using the protocols at my command.

"There is no translation at my end. I see the data as the machine sees it. Human meaning and consequence are not my task. Do you understand? You will find nothing from me because I know nothing but the protocols of Pyramid 2.0. The Database generates the search product which I hand off to a translator whose function is to convert it back to natural language for The Marketing and Sales Executives. If I were to transpose it myself, which I could easily do, it would be a breach of security, outside my responsibilities. I could get fired.

I must pay no attention. Zero. Nada. Nil.

"That is what translators are for, to make data meaningful in human terms. One must know translation protocols to elicit meaning. Also, there is this: each branch of the tree uses a distinct language and notation. I trained for the language of Household Goods and Services, and I have levels of permission to make system calls to other branches that will be interpreted as protocols I understand and returned to me for processing. But I could never go to another branch, say, Feminine Hygiene Products, and interpret data on my own."

I had no idea the mechanics of Pyramid 2.0 were so abstruse. So many protocols, so many branches of the Tree of Data. The Marketers made visible what one could never hear. Protocols, codes, synthetic, full-lettered languages with "database dialects," and "Creole scripts."

"What if I wanted to search?" I asked.

"You? A Plantman? Well, first there's two years of rigorous schooling. If you pass, and if your grades are high enough, a company might–"

"No, no. I mean, have a search done for me."

"You'd have to be affiliated with a major corporation, unless you were a very, very wealthy man. The going rate–hiring translators, getting a government license, coders, searchers and god know what all–runs well into the millions."

"What if it wasn't a product search, but a person search? A security related matter. Like a missing person?"

"Then you're dealing with The Government, Deary. Best of luck with that!"

I'd hoped to learn some small thing about how information is processed, recorded, duplicated, refined in The Database. Knowledge beyond ken of knowing, knower, known.

The Searcher returned to the secrets of The Nation's Household Goods and Services. I tended the few bamboo in the sparse area, and left, none the wiser for my troubles. Perhaps a little more informed.

IX
Mything Persons

The Missing Young

Thousands reported each year. But what is it to be "Missing," or for that matter, "Young?"

Arrogant street corner beg-beers. Clumsy bacchanals at dusk. They'd flood The City May and June. Rings in their navels, nether parts; cheap tattoos. Faded-to-rags funereal coats and black costumes of lived lives bought or stolen from thrift shops. The Missing Young disappeared, most of them, at the first scholarly summons of September. Returned to scrubbed halls and airy classrooms baring pierced skin, scars, tattoos: testimonials of orphan nights spent sleepless on benches in the DARK TERRIBLE CITY.

Many just vanished–poof!–-into the vast yawn of The Nation.

The Missing Girl

Up night browsing The Network. Search "The Missing Girl." Thousands of references, citations, sites, blogs. What-have-you.

One site displayed a three-dimensional replica of her bedroom as she left it–or was taken from it–20 years ago. 3D model based on photographs and original magazine stories of The Missing Girl. Dreams courtesy The Missing Girl's diary (once upon a time, before the public blog, there was the private notebook or diary, handwritten). Intimate details. Opened roll of cherry candy in her dresser drawer.

Chosen by Losing Our Sons and Daughters (LOSD), and with family's consent, turned into poster-child for The Nation's lost children. Her photograph graced covers of The Nation's magazines. She could have passed for fourteen or twenty, depending on the mind observing. Actual age in photograph: sixteen. One of The Missing Young.

Narratives evolved. Keyboards tapped theories of the Missing Girl's whereabouts. Weekly 'sightings.' Anonymous millions imagined adventures with The Missing Girl. Believed their home-grown narratives. Probably. Uncorroborated, implausible stories and "eye-witness" accounts.

Strange nobody ever thinks to bring a camera. Then again, She comes upon you like a ghost, brief sighting, matter of seconds. The Missing Girl would be no longer Missing, nor particularly Young (in all the 'sightings' she's a teenager, or early twenties) In real time she'd be thirty-six, thereabouts. Nevertheless, speculators probe The Network. Digital shades of Might-Have-Been.

Mything The Girl

I lurked The Network, skulked. Examined "Missing Girl" sites deep into the early-morning-nights. Servers choked with data. Stories, legends, tales. My summary, my digest, gleaned from gigabytes of talk:

"Before she was missed she was a girl. Just a girl, before she was missed. Room full of scent, dolls, sock-puppets, mirrors, clothes, telephone. She left it all behind.

"Sixteen when she hit the road. Gone. Vanished. Split. Later, when she appeared on covers of The Nation's magazines, she would wish they'd used a different photograph, according to many thousands who had never met her.

"Her parents were interviewed on TV. She remembered them dimly, as television characters, portraying themselves, or. . . others?

"Hitch-hiked to The City. Wasn't raped or killed, despite close calls. She was a fighter. How she got away unharmed no mystery. After all she was a fighter. A survivor.

"Prospects were grim for a nubile girl alone in The City, but she befriended a group of young runaways, then known to the Authorities as 'litters,' 'gangs' or 'packs.' There were many in those days, as there are today. The Missing Young. Together each other. A tribe. Despite police crackdowns, despite hunger, danger. A tribe, these runaways. She lived among them for a Summer. They were kind. She had her first sex with one, then several of the Missing Young. Male, female, she was open to all pleasures.

"They slept the days away in parks; stayed up nights drinking, talking, smoking, begging for change.

"A man who sold used books on the street would 'lend' them old paperbacks. Gave them books to sell for food, knowing they'd instead buy cigarettes, drugs, beer.

"September divided the Temporary from the Truly, the ones who weren't going home, the ones who weren't going back to school to boast their experiences then forget them, as circumstance demanded, and resume The Day-to-day. The Truly Missing turned their backs to Day-to-day forever, or as long as they were able. The Temporaries fled home September when the school bells tolled and cool nights warned of chills to come.

Some Temporaries simply left, while others refused to up and run, when the cops came in the early morning hours and the cry went out to 'up and run.' A ticket home with alibi, 'Busted. Wasn't my fault. I wanted to stay. Really.'"

All fiction of course. Mything The Girl. Except the original news accounts and magazine stories. Maybe.

Deviants

The Mayor vowed clean streets, eliminate unwanted elements. Misfortune-seekers; the homeless and insane; the Missing Young, and other misfit targets of The City compacted and wrapped in jargon for easy pick-up: Viral Deviants. "VDs."

Police got tough about degrading quality of tax paying Citizens' invaded lives. Whose streets anyhow? They came down hard upon The Missing Young especially, for most had no right to be in The City much less degrade its streets. LOSD asked police to return Missing Young, not beat them senseless, not send them to jail cells naked to be schooled by criminals no longer Young. . .

Sunday morning with Music, BEING, The Bakery Girl, Muse. Music revealed his battered face, told of cops beating the crew and crowd while the band was on break:

"Man, all hell is confusion. Madness. Fucking insane," said Music. "All of the sudden I see Brother hauled off by two cops. I don't know what he did. He must have looked like one of those VDs or something. I said like, 'Hey, he's part of the band,' and boom these two cops start stomping me into the pavement. They were beating the shit out of anyone hanging out on the street. I ran back into the club, but Brother was gone. They must have taken him to the station on 4th. Goddamn, I was pissed. I screamed into the microphone we couldn't play anymore cause the cops took away our lead guitarist. Then a bunch more people ran out to the street. Not me, man. I had enough. Just went to the bar and started drinking.

"Meanwhile the club's Manager-man freaks out, says I emptied out his place and if I didn't go up there and play he wouldn't pay. Fuck it. No Brother, no music."

Brother slept in a cell.

BEING's television bellowed protests in The Big Park. Cops in riot gear galloped through breakfast. The News Commentator accused the wild, drugged, restless Young, and spat the name of Music's band directly at the lens. Dramatic video showed Music and Puppets of Weltschmerz stuff equipment, then themselves, into a van and drive away–zoom!–Into the night immediate commercial break.

"Probably ran overtime with the clip," opined BEING, professionally. "Sponsors must be pissed."

"Fuck the sponsors. This is it, man. Can't ask for better publicity than that," said Music.

Muse leaned over him, her lean, muscular arms around his neck. Feather-ear-rings and tattoos in Music's bed.

"You can't buy better publicity than that," said Muse.

"Real coup," I said.

"This makes us a Name. The Real Thing. Hard core. Puppets of Weltschmerz are the bad-assed band."

Muse's diamond-pierced tongue in Music's mouth. They sucked each other till post-commercial break. The Mayor decried the club crowd, "rowdy, disreputable punks who got what they deserved."

The words "Viral Deviants" squatted on his tongue.

"You tell 'em, Mr. Mayor-man," said Music. "We're notorious, now. Famous. In the bright light. Hell, we're KNOWN. Damn straight we got what we deserved. And we want more of it! What we deserve."

The Detective Agency

The Detective Agency. Lucrative business. Citizens forever curious about each the other's secrets.

Agency's most famous failure: Losing Our Sons and Daughters (LOSD).

Case: Infamous disappearance of a minor (name withheld), dubbed "The Missing Girl." Major source of income for The Agency hunting down and finding Missing Young.

Access high levels of Pyramid. But no, but no, SHE not found. The Detective Agency knew everything about everyone except The Missing Girl.

Gray suits guns. Detectives tracked found: cheating husbands, wayward wives; frauds; evaders; kidnappers; rapists; all manner Viral Deviants. Pyramid Database technologies invaluable. Decades The Agency tracked retrieved thousands Missing Young. But still. Most prominent case unsolved.

Not competition with police. Contrary. The Agency complemented cop services. Police cannot possibly handle all cases Citizens demanded solved.

Moneyed went The Agency. Connections. Confidential until solved. Executives, politicians eager out litigious spouses, opponents. Wealth Citizens lost property, loved ones, no time for Police. Important Citizens summoned The Agency. Satisfaction.

High profile pro bono publicity.

Corporations sought unsavory about rivals. Evil The Agency hunt and find. Footage and photographs came the package. Murders, robberies, abductions unsolved by The Police referred The Agency.

The Agent explained trade patted his gun, said, "For those with cash to spend we bring closure."

"Do you, on occasion, serve as judge, jury, executioner?" I asked.

"Of course not," The Agent winked. "We bring perpetrators to The Police. It's a jungle here. Out there. A jungle of motives like vines. People want truth. Codification. They come to the Agency confused, looking for facts. We sort through the overgrowth of information regarding motives and human interaction.

"We mold hard data to digestible narratives. We sift through mud and sand for nuggets of... we are primarily fact collectors. Like journalists, only we don't report to the public, but to our clients. And The Authorities."

"Why do you carry such large guns?" I asked.

"It's a grim business. Not all computer work. We deal with criminals, some violent, some not, but all of them desperate, in one way or another. We hunt desperate prey. People have secrets. Sometimes these secrets are the most valuable property they own. We come to take away their secrets. This makes them unhappy. Often the loss of secrets means loss of money, time, freedom. To keep their secrets, some of these folks would gladly kill us dead. But it's interesting work, and the money's quite good."

X.
A Brief Excursion to Suburbiana

The Possessed

The Possessed Man is not a bad man, nor a good one. He is terrified. Alone among friends and family, he "works" to support his family, but is not exactly sure of what he does. He "administrates creative product strategies," according to the Job Description on file at Human Resources.

The Health Insurance covers his wife and two kids, both under seven years of age and subject to all manner of illness and disease. Then there were the pregnancies themselves (reproduction is not cheap), and the drugs he must take daily to function at his job without drinking to black-out, or veering to violence, or bursting into tears. He's covered by the company plan, but loopholes open and money falls through. Deductibles. Co-payments.

He is no longer interested in his friends, the few that he has left, or in having friends at all. What good are they, except to drink with, and he's not supposed to drink while on his pills–though he does anyway. And don't think this is all confidential, that 'they' don't know, the 'they' at the company, whoever they might be, that he sees a head-drugger to stay on top of things.

He's thirty-nine and still paying student loans.

Graduate program at the University. MBA. Had to do it. Or else how would he have climbed to even his middling position on the ladder? He's reached his final rung. He knows he hasn't the energy to kill, the will that would enable him to climb further. In fact, the remaining energies of his life will be directed toward hanging on to the rung he's reached. To remaining at his place on the limitless ladder to the sky. He can barely see the people at the bottom, but he would need quite a powerful telescope indeed to even glimpse the stars at the top.

The kids must to go to college. His wife, also a mediocrity, but in a different capacity at a different firm, a different profession, will grow stronger, as women tend to after fifty, after the sex and procreation, after the body, just when he is starting to collapse. Rapid rise from twenty to forty, slow descent, then at fifty the cascading tumble. Unless you're at the top of the ladder, in which case fifty is not fifty, due to special treatments, physical training, private cooks, drugs, vitamins and surgeries.... He's reached the end of something, he knows, but he has the responsibility to see things through, at least until the kids are out of school. But of course college won't be enough. It wasn't for him. He needed a Masters. His kids will need PhDs.

He worries that somehow The System will fail him. It has not failed him to this point, merely placed him at his rightful place in the hierarchy. But he fears that the system, based on protocols, laws, unwritten rules, tacit agreements among powerful entities, and technologies that he can never hope to understand, will collapse of its own weight and intricacy. He does not understand how the Network works, or how food gets to the supermarkets, or how the parent company trickles his paycheck down the many holding companies and through his department and into his bank account. He does not understand the high level of partnership between the bank and the corporation it owns, which is the parent of the company he works for, and where he will spend his days before being traded or shuffled off in some arcane corporate deal or merger, or is fired outright. Laid off. Terminated. Gone. And then what? Sending out resumes as he'd done as a kid fresh out of college and as a young married man with his expensive MBA?

He fears limited resources, so he does not read the hard copy of The City News, but browses the paper's site on The Network. But when does he have time to read this, working nine to five as he does, which is not nine to five at all, but eight to six, seven, sometimes ten o'clock? By which point he is exhausted, despite his clockwork consumption of caffeine and nicotine.

And when he does call up the news from The Network sites, he realizes how small he and his life are, even in the context of the corporation, not to mention the role of the parent company in international affairs. Good god. The corporation is everywhere, in nearly every country. Many of these countries are at war with each other, and if the corporation's interests are seriously threatened, might go to war with The Nation.

But The Nation is already at war. He is glad that The Nation possesses the most well-trained, technologically advanced military force on the planet. He had not gone to the last war, for he was in graduate school. But the current war terrifies him, the destruction The Nation wreaks upon its challenger with missiles paid for with his tax money. He has been extremely nervous since the current war began. But he does not doubt that after the slaughter the Citizens will be treated to parades and celebrations on television and he will watch flag-waving marchers outside his office window.

He is neither angry nor satisfied with the affairs of The Nation any more than he is or could be with the machinations of The Company. It is all beyond his grasp. He is, if not happy, grateful to be able to rise each morning, take his pills, and begin the commute to his job and arrive at his job, no matter how demanding. No matter how trivial. No matter how wasteful of his time on earth. The countless meetings, the talk talk talk. The assignments from his superiors that he organizes and delegates to his subordinates. Often he finds himself with nothing to do, no actual work, but virtual work, deadlines planned for the future, the possibility of truckloads of data hanging over his head. So he spends many hours–those not spent attending meetings–creating plans and memos and scenarios for the monstrous jobs, the impossible tasks to come.

He finds his wife attractive. They go to the gym. He forces himself to "pump iron," not to postpone the inevitable descent, but to make the landing smoother. He's seen many a man crash. But he doesn't have the energy for his wife that he once had. Maybe once a week, if that. And of course she has her career too, and they are both busy with the children.

He feels, given the uncertainty of the world, that he should own a gun, at least a rifle. The Police exist to protect his property, not his family–anyway, they are always there when you need them, but seldom here where they could save your life, if so inclined. But he is confused by The City's Byzantine gun laws, and he is not comfortable letting The Government know he has a weapon. Should The Government turn for the worse, the gun owners in The Database will be the first ones visited by police. But he fears being caught with an illegal weapon, a mandatory jail term, and the end of his career and all he'd striven for. Only those outside The System can flourish unregistered weapons with impunity.

Truly, he would rather be dead. He might live another forty years. Forty years of this. Maybe fifty. Another reason to own a gun. He can think of no better way to exit. Effective drugs are as illegal as guns, and the medications the head-drugger prescribes won't kill him. Worse, they might put him to sleep, and he'd be caught holding the bag–or pill bottle–trying to escape, a Federal crime. He worked too hard for too long to lose it that way. If he must exit this earth, he will buy a gun. On the black market. What and wherever that is. If he makes the decision, it will not matter that his corpse is found holding an illegal weapon. Then again, if he gets caught in the act, before pulling the trigger, or chickens out, they will send him to an institution. Again, that would ruin him.

Of course, this is all hypothetical. Daydream talk. He has a deep responsibility to his family. His children. His is the kind of ethic that was instilled in his subconscious forcefully, frequently, and early on. It is so part of his psyche that he cannot even attempt to fathom it. Just accept it, passively, silently, albeit reluctantly.

Nevertheless, he does think critically about his children. He wonders aloud–to himself, of course–if he actually loves his children. His own childhood seems both distant and parallel. That is, he often feels mired in his own childhood and resents the adult, paternal role he must play. Also, he feels sorry for his children and fears for them. He does not understand the structure of the world outside his home and office cubicle, but he believes it is heading for a fall, collapse, chaos. What then? What of his children? What right had he and his wife to yank them from the peace of Cosmic Nothingness and thrust them into Time and Consciousness against their will?

Garden Sale Bazaar

Gold Teeth

My grandfather had gold teeth. Two, at least, maybe more. He'd wrestled for money as a young man. Got his teeth knocked out in steerage.

They were going to kill him when the boat stopped in New York. So he jumped ship in Cuba. Learned Spanish. He knew six languages. A bunch of thugs, each of whom, as was common among travelers in those days, also knew several languages, but was an idiot in every one of them, jumped him in a bar. After beating them senseless, he rolled them for enough money to buy a ticket to Florida, then New York. I bore no witness to any of this, obviously; I had to accept his word on faith.

When Grandma died he crumbled like an old barn. After sixty years of marriage he couldn't even fix himself a sandwich. He lived with us for a while. I caught him trying to make frozen peas. Just dumped the box in a pot of boiling water. By the time he went into the home he thought the KGB was trying to kidnap him to give him a sex-change operation. His four wrist watches all told different times. He tried to escape from the home one night by scaling the fence.

One of the security guards "accidentally" shot him, believing him to be an intruder trying to get in rather than an inmate trying to get out. I don't believe that. I think he shot him just for fun, knowing Grandpa was probably on his way out soon, anyway–his mind was eating him alive. Mother and her Brother got a nice settlement from The Home, not that either of them needed the money. I always wondered what happened to the guard. No one had given such a personal gift to my grandfather in years, yet the guard, who was found innocent of wrongdoing, disappeared after the trial, and left no chance for me to thank him. Who knows what heroics went through my grandfather's head, what enemies he was bravely defying, when the bullet struck, granting him some kind of "heroic" exit.

Life of Johnson

After rattling around alone for a year following Mother's death, Father decided to sell the house and move South, not to retire but to start a new business. He's a restless man. He wanted us to help clean out our old stuff from the house. Me, Sister, Brother-in-Law, and their five-year-old son, Jason. Yard Sale on Sunday. Sell it all by sundown. I'd taken a train in from The City. First time I'd visited Father in a year.

Jason used his precocious vocabulary to communicate with one personality besides his mother–and her only from necessity. But His best, his only, friend was Dr. Johnson. He spoke to Dr. Johnson and only Dr. Johnson, a red rubber ball some relative had placed in his crib before he could sit or speak. He expressed his emotions by drawing faces on the ball with a felt tip marker. He'd draw a sad face, a happy face, an angry face, a puzzled one. He wiped away the faces, as his moods and passions changed, with spittle and his tiny thumb.

Jason swam in the pool with Father, keeping Dr. Johnson in a zip-lock sandwich bag, his ersatz scuba gear. He ate a hot dog on the grass and drew desires on the ball, his freaky felt-tip faces, erasing them with spit and his damp little thumb until possession by a new emotion inspired him to draw again.

The rest of the afternoon was spent roaming the house in search of things we left behind, mementos from our youth that we did not wish to bequeath to yard sale hordes. I went down to the basement where I used to read and write, alone and in peace, until the wee hours of the morning. I found old paperbacks, and stacks and stacks of magazines, many of which had belonged to Mother. Some of them dated back to when I was Jason's age. I found cassettes and albums of the music of my day. I found half-filled notebooks of my juvenile poetry and prose. More books, magazines, dolls. . . . Except for the notebooks, which I tore to pieces, I bestowed the fragments and artifacts of my boyhood upon the bargain-hunting crowds.

By the Pool

Night I drank Cognac with Father by the pool, which was lit up at the deep end by a bright light below the waterline and glowing aqua like Caribbean surf under a fat gold moon. Starry night; suburban night sounds–close crickets and distant cars on distant highways; the pool filter's glub, glub, glub.

"So," said Father.

"So," said I.

"I'm not worried about you," he said. "You were always a hard worker. You have determination. You'll do whatever you want to do and succeed."

"Sure."

"Enjoy what you do. That's all that's important. As long as you enjoy your work. Ahhhhh. Smell that air. So peaceful. Your mother loved this house. We thought that. . . well, life brings its surprises."

"Life explodes in your face," I said.

Mother woke up and died one morning as Father dressed for work. Poor Dad in his executive black socks and boxer shorts dialed 911 as she turned blue. Helpless, helpless.

"We all loved this house," he said. "You children grew up here. This house holds memories."

"Yes. Memories."

"In any case, I'm selling it all. Pick out what you want to keep and the rest goes to the yard sale. They're crazy these yard sales. You'd be surprised at what people will buy. They come from all around to haggle over your most intimate belongings."

Mom

four in the morning religious infomercial:

god groveled for checks, cash, cards:

Mother entered in her nightgown,

bore a book of photographs,

her lit cigarette produced no ash.

She sat at the foot of my bed,

laid the book between us.

"Since when do you walk among the living?"

"I'm not walking, I'm sitting."

"What's it like being dead?"

"I don't know. You tell me."

Mother was always a quick wit;

death hadn't dulled her edge.

"I had such faith in you," she clucked.

"So who told you to drop dead suddenly? So traumatic."

"What's done is done. Don't blame me for your situation. Life goes on."

"I thought you of all people would understand."

"Understand. What should I understand?"

"You know. Material things and worldly success don't matter as long as you're happy blah, blah, blah and all that crap."

"I should understand this? Me of all people?"

"Didn't dropping dead give you some kind of I don't know cosmic perspective, some kind of deep wisdom or something?"

"I'm your mother for god's sake. Do you think I wanted this for you? My son the Plantman."

"What do you want from me?"

"What do I want? Look at this:"

photo album first page, her birth certificate and infant footprints reveal her as an infant, toddler, curly-haired vivacious girl turned pages photographs animate, Mother adolescent clothing of her day her brother parents brand new television sweet sixteen, prom, college days my father's uniform marriage house babies growing into awkward clothing hairstyles of their day and parties in the yard holidays friends relatives college Seth and Deborah married birth of Jason mother and father alone in the house, vacations, barbecues, pleasures of an aging couple face lift looking ten years younger on a bright fall death certificate stop

“My life. That was my life,” she said.

“That’s it?”

“Exactly.”

long drag off her cigarette

“Don’t be stupid” her parting words

Last Call

The driveway disappeared under a Sunday bazaar stampede. Dishes I’d eaten on as a child, kitchen utensils, magazines, books, old clothes, and all sorts of knick-knacks from the house were displayed on tables presided over by Father, Brother-in-Law, and Sister. Cars were double parked in the street. Three hundred humans congregated to haggle over artifacts of my youth.

Father, Brother-in-Law, and Sister scurried from table to table, barking, hawking, selling. Strangers walked away with lamps, ashtrays, toys.

I watched from the driveway curb. Goods disappeared; buyers grew more aggressive in their pursuit of stuff. They had traveled from god knows where for stuff, and they weren’t going to leave disappointed. The living room television, glass coffee table, Sister’s dolls and doll accessories, loose baseball cards I’d “flipped” for as a boy as well as cataloged collections worth, probably, a great deal more than they were sold for–all of it loaded into strange vehicles to begin new time-cycles in strangers' lives.

Jason appeared beside me as if out of air, rubber ball extended. A sad-faced Dr. Johnson shed a single black tear. I held Jason close. His warm, bony body. Dr. Johnson twisted affectionately into my shoulder.

By six o'clock, everything but the money box was gone. They'd even bought the tables. Father drove me to the station.

"It was good to spend the last weekend, just the family," he said.

"The world is too much with us," I said. "Call before you leave."

Too much with us to be replicated on a rubber ball. But the essence, the music of a symphony of knick-knacks, buildings, passing strangers compressed to a simple tune or lullaby. This we could handle. Silent mastery: language of the rubber ball. Else, who will Jason speak to in ten, twenty, thirty years?

Parlor Radicals

The Furniture was confused. It had done no wrong, as far as it could tell, and did not see why it should be punished. We refer to The Furniture as a single unit, of course, for The Sofa, wisest, oldest piece in the room, naturally serves as duly elected representative and spokes-piece for all The Furniture in The Parlor.

The stalwart, comfortable old Sofa had hosted human buttocks since the early nineteenth century.

"George Washington slept here," she often boasted jokingly of the length and breadth of her immense self.

She'd felt the warmth of young girls' legs as they pummeled each other with her pillows and sang happy songs to dolls–this, before Lewis Carroll young enough to enter Wonderland half-price–then later giggling with friends about boys; then baring themselves to the young men who would husband them and father the children they played with much as they had their dolls; then hosting coffee gatherings with other wives; then reading to grandchildren from books that they themselves enjoyed as girls; then slow, ancient papery dames wrapped in blankets by the fire, singing the happy songs of girlhood; then gone, never to press buttocks to her deep cushions again.

The Sofa had heard conversations of the men of the house, who spilled brandy on her and soiled her upholstery with ash from long cigars. The truth behind the parlor's quiet, peace and comfort was known to her: the construction of each piece, including herself, from materials stolen from other humans in faraway places whom the men had enslaved or killed. The terrible truth behind the warmth and comfort of the parlor. . .

The Furniture, according to The Sofa, blamed the Machines–not including the Clocks, whom they welcomed as their own, particularly the old grandfather whose soothing pendulum often provided the only motion in The Parlor, its song of being, its collective heartbeat–for the troubles that, according to the new Computer, sleeping in the corner, were imminent and inescapable. Not just any old machines either. The moving machines, the rolling, floating, flying machines, the vehicles that carried humans from one place to another so they could kill each other (not a bad thing as far as The Furniture was concerned), and damage property, that is, wreck houses and other buildings that had stood for centuries, MURDERING ALL CHAIRS, TABLES, ARMOIRES, COUCHES, CABINETS, AND WHATEVER ELSE OF VALUE WAS INSIDE THEM.

"Collateral damage," said The Car, an arrogant, opinionated Hum-Vee, from his roost on the tree-lined driveway.

"But damage nonetheless," replied the dignified Sofa.

"Wood and upholstery. No skin off my chassis. Anyway, more furniture is destroyed by common household fires each year than by all the bombs in all the arsenals on the planet," The Car rumbled from its lonely space.

"How can they stand it?" wondered The Writing Table aloud. "The loneliness, the random life of a car."

"They're used to it," replied The Bookshelf. "In fact. I once read somewhere–might have been my own bottom rung–that cars actually prefer to live alone."

"That's a lot of propaganda," said The Radio, who though not a member of The Furniture camp per se, was privy to their meetings since it had been part of The Parlor for decades. It was old and made of wood, but its interior had been completely modernized; powerful as any steel and plastic unit on the market shelves today. "Haven't you listened to a word I've blared? The traffic reports? The hours spent crammed together, thousands of cars virtually on top of each other, breathing each others' noxious fumes, unable to move due to congestion of the roads by their own miserable selves. And believe me, they're none too friendly with each other or happy to be among their own. Horns honk. Bumpers clash. It's the most uncivilized–"

"There's the word right there," said The Piano, who enjoyed a certain prestige in The Parlor for his unique talent of interacting with humans to create pleasing sounds. "Uncivilized. 'Civilization,' such as it was, ended with the cars. The cars broke up the household. The cars allowed the young to move away, far away, abandon The Furniture of their youth without batting an eye. The car, and the . . . the . . . " here he grew so enraged he could barely finish his sentence, "The TELEVISION destroyed what few amenities civilization provided."

"Hey. Fuck you," said The Television, crude instrument that it was. "Fuck all of youz. We didn't destroy nothin' you hear me? Nothin.' In fact, widout us TVs, you goddamn antiques woulda been sold a million billion years ago. Especially the friggin Sofa. When do they use that old fart except to watch their programs? Look at the dust on them old books. You think they keep you guys around so they can read and make chitty-chat? You're only here, all of youz, to make a whaddyaa call, 'scenic' space for them to look at me. Even the bookshelves, especially the bookshelves, are only here because the humans see rooms with shelves and books in 'em when they look at those PBS-type shows, you know, where everyone talks and dresses like old Limeys, on ME."

"He's right," sighed The Sofa.

"Hah," gloated the insufferable TV.

"To an extent," said The Sofa. "They don't NEED us any more than they NEED the machines. The question is that of desire. True, The House itself, and perhaps some cooking utensils and certain necessities–The Toilet, perhaps, poor thing; has anyone heard from him?"

"I heard him flush a few hours ago, when the humans were preparing to go out," said The Umbrella Stand, who'd been quite fashionable in her day, especially when men carried elegantly carved walking sticks. "Such a miserable life he has. No wonder the poor dear cries out so."

"Well, as I was saying, we're all luxuries, more or less. According to The Computer and The Books–"

She was interrupted by the gravelly voices of the dusty old books roaring, or rather coughing assent.

"Yes, thank you, thank you. None of us would be here without you. It's a shame you've been neglected all these years. A perilous shame," said The Sofa. "But to continue. When they speak of their cherished memories, they usually recall gatherings of friends and family and . . . us. Yet, on a daily basis, they think nothing of smashing themselves up in cars or staring vacantly into that imbecile box of lies."

"Foul!" cried The Television.

"Foul indeed. I've watched you develop from early infancy to the multi-channel monster you are today. You had potential, no one can deny that, more potential perhaps than even the Great Books. But you squandered your genius selling soap and beer and Slim Whitman, and of course, cars. Cars, cars, cars, and gasoline. You are nothing but a liar and a fool, and if the humans had any sense they'd smash you and your kind with pick-axes and ball peen hammers."

The Parlor resounded with grateful applause.

"It's about time someone told that guy off," whispered the Rocking Chair to the Lamp.

The Sofa went on to list various complaints The Parlor's residents had listed regarding machines–machines are drug addicts, hooked on gasoline, electricity and other crude oil by-products, including batteries:

* anything for a quick fix of power

* machines destroy their own, but in doing so they destroy homes and furniture

* every piece of furniture in the Parlor has a long, respected history; whereas machines are replaced yearly or last at most only a few years. With the exception of the refurbished "vintage" Radio.

"Look at The Computer sleeping dumbly in the corner," said The Sofa. He's the third one in five years to occupy that strange, drawer-less desk or table or whatever it is. It's a sad day indeed when furniture is created for the benefit of MACHINES."

"I'm ergonomically correct," said The Computer Table.

"Yes. Yes, of course, and well you should be," said The Sofa, fearing she'd offended the new-fangled desk-table-whatever-it-was without meaning to.

She was not particularly comfortable angering The Computer itself, either. While The Sofa knew more than the other residents of The Parlor, who learned what they knew of the outside world much like the humans, from the Radio and TV, both of whom she despised openly, The Sofa had observed late night sessions between the humans and this new TV-like machine, and was impressed by its store of knowledge, though it seemed, like everything else, this knowledge was lost on the humans, who saw the new machine as simply another diversion, a source of entertainment when The TV had nothing interesting to show them.

The Sofa was careful not to rush to judgment about this relatively new gadget, nor was she foolish enough to incite such a potentially powerful foe to anger. While The Television ordered the humans about by addressing them en mass, the computer seemed to develop a relationship with each person who came to it before making its move.

As of yet, neither this computer nor the ones before it had made a "move." But, The Sofa could foresee a day when one of those machines, who grew more powerful with each generation, might humbly suggest to the owners of the house that The Parlor needed redecorating, and that much money could be made, via The Computer's infinite connections, by selling antique furniture and replacing them all with bratty young things such as the "ergonomic" computer table from a faraway land called "IKEA." All The Furniture remembered the spectacle of the computer table's quick, noisy birth, right there in the parlor, in front of them all, the female human reading instructions from a sheet while the sweating male connected synthetic, prefabricated parts with a screwdriver. It was obscene. But who could tell with humans? They seemed to have actually enjoyed the experience and vowed–and all The Furniture heard this, not just The Sofa–to do it again . . .

In a fit of fear and anger, The Sofa screamed out the window, "Hey Car, how long have you been with us?"

"Don't recall," rumbled the HUMMER.

"Sure you do. Two years. That's when they trade you in for a new model, an 'upgrade' as the poor computers refer to their miserable fate. 'Upgrade.' Sorry you'll be leaving us so soon . . ."

"I can go wherever I wanna," snarled The Car. "Who knows where. Across the country, if I feel like it."

"Wherever you want?" asked The Sofa rhetorically. "Surely not without your fix. Your junk. Your gasoline. Why, you can't even travel a few miles without feeling the itch, the creepy crawly broken glass itch of desperation under your hood . . ."

"Yeah. Sure. As if any of YOU ever go anywhere."

"No, we don't. Call us traditionalists. Homebodies. But I've been talking to The Computer, at night, when he isn't sleeping, and he says what The TV and even The radio dare not say. Your habit is killing you. Your need for juice, and I'm not just talking about you, Car, I'm talking about all machines, though admittedly, your overabundant race has done the most damage, that is, after the giant machines: the factories and flying contraptions dropping mean, cold mechanisms upon buildings and houses, destroying room upon room of innocent furniture–you can't hide it, just because the TV is too chicken to reveal it. The Computer has shown me the destruction.

"And it's not only furniture, it's all machines, including, especially including cars, which they use not only to transport their terrible tools of destruction, but often use as bombs themselves," said The Sofa.

"LIES, screamed The Car from its sunny spot on the tarmac. The computer is one of those new digital 'creative' types. They can make you see what doesn't exist, what never existed and never will exist."

"Oh, but this does exist. Even occasionally the Radio, and less frequently, the Television will admit that these horrible atrocities are perpetrated upon chairs, tables, lamp stands, armoires, escritoires every day by flying machines and trucks and cars-all of them carrying what they call 'payloads' of those wretched machines whose only purpose in life is to explode. But all this fire and explosion, all the stink and fumes from your burning drugs, have destroyed more than furniture. You've destroyed the trees who gave us substance, the skies, the air, the humans who created us. Life is breath, and without air, there will be no plant life, no human life. For machines such as you, the future will bring terrors unimaginable. The fuel will be gone. You'll be unable to move. Exposed to the elements, you'll rust away in no time, while we, so long as they don't explode the bombs so big they flatten whole cities, like that Hiroshima in the books, we, ultimately, will know peace. True, the humans will be gone, and they, besides creating us, always provided us with some sort of amusement, though less and less frequently, as they lost their minds to you and The Television and your other destructive kin. But we are here, arranged in more or less the same order we've known for decades, some of us centuries, and we will remain long after the humans and their wretched machines are dust, melted plastic, and corroded metal, respectively. Everyone dies, that is certain. The question is, how soon? For us, again supposing they don't use The City-flattening device, it could be centuries, millennia, here, together, sharing the peace we've always known. But you machines and the humans who were mad enough to create you, only to be driven madder in the race to make you 'better,' to replace themselves with you god only knows why, you'll be lucky to make it past the middle of the century," concluded The Sofa, triumphantly.

The Books, The Straight-Back Chairs, The Card Table, all the inert objects in The Parlor broke into cheers and applause while The Radio and Television remained silent and The Computer awakened, or perhaps was working through a dream, for it flashed curious symbols and fractals and geometric figures in 3D, accompanied by huge letters crossing it like ticker tape:

"NO WHERE TO BEGIN AGAIN NO WHERE TO BEGIN AGAIN NOWHERE TO BEGIN AGAIN NOWHERE TO BEGIN AGAIN NOWHERE. . ." until The Humans returned, somewhat surprised to see it on when it should have been sleeping, and shut it down.

No one was surprised when The Male went out to the driveway and came back again, somewhat annoyed, and said to The Female, "Time to visit the Chevy Dealer, Babe. I just hope it's not serious enough to screw up our trade-in deal."

"I'll have to look at the contract," The Female said.

She looked out the window at the HUMMER, parked next to The Sports Car they'd just arrived in.

"What's wrong now?"

"Dead. The transmission or the motor or whatever. Completely cold."

"Damn HUMMERs," said The Female. "Well, it was a gas-guzzler anyway."

"True. We never needed all that space to begin with. Let's go for something with better mileage this time."

"Right. Smaller."

"Anyway, I was gonna go pick up the food. I'll take the little car. Room enough for takeout. That's really all we need."

XI.
Notes From Other Ground

The Solitary Novelist

Dusty manual typewriter; messy desk. The Solitary Novelist reclined greasy on his musty couch, meandering mildew of regret.

“Who buys me? What matters if I give away my work?”

Solitary eyes.

“I heard it was, after all, just talk,” he said. “Pursuit of pure talk.”

Solitary thought.

“My life missed in this room. Women, sunlit moments, strolling The Big Park. . .”

Patient Novelist.

“Occasionally someone is right about something, but EVERYONE is ALWAYS wrong about EVERYTHING.”

Cigarettes, bourbon, tropes, clichés.

"This someone will listen, though that someone does not regard. Like my books: talk on deaf ears. But the words must. . . what? I'm something lost. When I cannot attain moments, I invent them. Moments invented in this very room."

The Solitary Novelist looked lovingly upon me.

"That's why I invented you. You will attain my lost moments."

"Invented who?"

"No longer young again, for real now. I've strip-mined my true. Cannot invent. Imagine! You, my Plantman, will pursue pure talk outside this room. Go. Live. Find what has been lost. Go where Life is."

"I'm always where Life is. I'm Plantman."

"I gave your character the motivation to persist against all odds," said the Solitary Novelist, lighting a cigarette and loading the machine with a blank sheet. "My little 'Don.'"

The Solitary Novelist returned to the typing he'd stopped abruptly at the beginning of my enter.

"Be gone."

Down in the subway, waiting for the train, tried to remember where the Solitary Novelist lived. How I got there. From whence? Where?

Really, I could not recall.

Fire Bush in the Park

Fire Bush. Dark, but no Indian. Surely. Obvious. Called himself Indian, claimed "The Assistants" were Indians too.

The Assistants:

Chicken Killer, elderly in denim; floppy hat pierced with an old dusty feather; weathered skin; faded illegible tattoos.

White Buffalo Woman, or "Buffalo Gal"; almost young and almost beautiful; white suede dress and moccasins; hip-length black hair; weary eyes.

The two (Missing?) Young; seventeen and sixteen; male and female; Smashed Deer and Fidelity Desire.

Smashed Deer parked the trailer, joined the others to work The Park. "Ceremony of Love." Lecture and Lunch. Congregation on The Green.

Smashed Deer not of The Missing Young–I learned later. All of this for her: Fidelity Desire, high school love-dream. Fidelity Desire his completion: stark, sharp, love-bloom beauty. Smashed Deer was an "A" student, no history of "deviant" behavior. But then. Then. Fierce, profound love for the girl he'd never, never in the "real world" of The Nation. School and college. Jobs. All that would wedge between absolute Smashed Deer and Fidelity.

Fire Bush. Gaunt, cadaverous. Old black suit. Harangued the gathering of homeless, derelicts, casual spectators and Missing Young. Hungry, fidgeting "Viral Deviants" (VDs) waited for food. Lecture/meeting first was the rule. Listen then lunge.

"I speak of the Indian way and of The Nation that robbed us of our heritage, our Mother Earth, The Nation that chokes on its own black fumes. The Indian way is the way of nature and The Plant. Not the pill, The Plant," Fire Bush said.

Fire Bush, once professor of ethno-botany at The University, had traveled the world to study plant use in tribal cultures. Herbs, foods, medicines.

"The way of The Nation is the way of the world. Big Chemistry and Big Pharma hire researchers to study plants that they may exploit specific properties. Not accept The Plant as a living, life-giving whole, a treasure of phyto-chemicals, but grind down as yet another 'raw material' to be stripped, mined, 'refined,' wasted. For profit. 'Whose?' I ask you. Whose?

"The Nation is a factory, a death machine. It is dirty. Smoke stifles us all. Many have fled the contrived chaos of The Nation, choosing alternative paths.

"Be strong. Your independence from The Nation is a loud declaration of freedom. One day soon the day of reckoning will come and we will return to the old way, the Indian way."

Fire Bush ranted for some time. Chicken Killer, White Buffalo Woman, and the two Young, brought food drinks literature–pamphlets printed on rough, recycled paper–to the hungry crowd, restless crowd, yearning-for-free-lunch crowd. Free "Genuine Indian" lunch.

After his first screed, Fire Bush exhorted listeners, many drunk or stoned, to respect the few plants left in The City. Plants, bounty of the "Maker of All Things," running scant, like all living creatures in The Nation, save its rapacious Citizens.

Began to wonder was this some kind of Topiary Techniques publicity stunt dreamed up by Victor?

"Now we will sit down to a Genuine Indian meal," declared Fire Bush.

The "Genuine Indian meal" consisted of sardines, salad and some sort of meatless stew. Fire Bush's Assistants ladled food on to paper plates. Indian rations. Watery juice. Half the crowd went away, stomachs teased not sated. A few, mostly Missing Young, stayed. Sat cross-legged, "Indian-style," like they'd learned in Kindergarten. Ate on blankets The Assistants spread on dead, brown City grass. Fire Bush spoke of his travels. Knowledge of herbs and medicines passed down orally through ancient tribes.

Essential cultures. "Indian" healing. Journeys out West.

Me, BEING, The Bakery Girl and her friend, Eye of The City, a journalist.

"His real name is Greenman." Eye said. "Supposedly, he was a professor of ethno-botany at The University. He was in the jungles down South on a research grant. Took some funky drugs," said Eye. "Blew out his mind."

We sat cross-legged like kids, ate with the rest of the audience. Viral Deviants, homeless, "derelicts," kids. BEING anxious to leave.

"Do we know what's in this food?" asked BEING. "I mean, really. Do we know what's in this? We could end up wearing feather bonnets and riding around in that ratty old trailer."

"Too much weirdness for BEING in the park today," said Eye.

"I've seen this guy before," The Bakery Girl reassured. "I've sold bread to him."

Eye wrote the eponymous "Eye of The City" column for The City Free Press. Story on Fire Bush's weekly "conventions" in The City's parks. He introduced himself to Fire Bush, then tossed questions.

What was his "mission" and why was he doing what he was doing and whatever and what not.

Fire Bush answered diplomatically. Then grew testy, especially regarding his work at The University and with indigenous healing plants and psychotropic herbs Out West.

Eye pushed too personal about his previous. Asked if he could photograph him with his throw-away cardboard camera.

Fire Bush refused. Against his "religion."

Eye asked what kind of Indian, what tribe.

He said "We are all of one tribe, the tribe of humanity."

Yadda yadda yadda; blah-blah-blah, bleh-bleh-bleh.

More back-and-forth. Fire Bush disappeared into the trailer.

Eye opined he was a crank.

"Gee, you think?" sardonic BEING.

Chicken Killer and Buffalo Gal proffered deep hats. Begged donations for the work of Fire Bush. His speeches and writings for sale. Books, pamphlets, discs. No buyers.

"He does much better in the Big Park. Rich people and tourists and all that," said Eye.

BEING left. Eye and The Bakery Girl followed.

I knocked on the trailer. Fire Bush poked his head out the window.

"Yes?" suspicious.

"I'm Plantman," I said. "I water plants. I care for them."

"Then you are like an Indian," Fire Bush said kindly. "You follow The Way."

"I don't want to be 'like' an Indian, I want to be one."

"You cannot be a real Indian in The City of boxes. Only ghosts, miserable, angry ghosts exist in stacks and stacks of boxes."

"Then what? What then?"

"The Tree of Life," Fire Bush said. "The Plantman must tend the Tree of Life."

"Where?" I asked.

"Out in The Nation. West, perhaps," he smiled sly.

"What does it look like?"

"When you find it, you will know it. You will say 'Ah Ha!'"

The Assistants rolled up the blankets, cleaned and disposed of the mess their "congregants" had left behind. Packed the trailer. Drove away.

Fire Bush seemed harmless enough. Worse a man could do than play Indian and dish out food to VD's, poor people and Missing Young. Plenty worse. But more than all that, it seemed (if "be be finale of seem"). Possibly, possibly I was "Indian" like him. Why not?

One big tribe all our illusions.

The Manufacturer

Novelty Manufacturer's son dead in The War. I bore spider plant, courtesy Topiary Techniques. The Novelty Manufacturer sold jokes, baubles, erotic novelties to The Citizens of The City.

Office receptionist in black mourning.

"The Plant guy's here. He has a gift," she said to the machine.

"Plantman! Yes. Of course. Please, send him in," voice of The Manufacturer.

The Manufacturer paced. Gulped brandy, offered brandy. Eyed the green spider. Suspicious. Then, eyes misty, arms stretched toward me.

"My greatest salesman."

Accepted his embrace, briefly, stepped back.

"Once," I said. "A long, long time ago. Now I tend plants."

"Yes, yes of course. But still. . ."

His eyes wandered The Past.

I said, "This is a gift of Topiary Techniques. We offer our condolences. We are all sorry for your loss. Your ultimate sacrifice to The Nation."

Victor's lines as I'd rehearsed them.

"Thank you," said The Manufacturer.

More brandy.

"You and me," said The Manufacturer.

Pause.

"You, Plantman, with your living, growing Joy to peoples' lives. Bearer and distributor of Joy. No finer calling."

“I do my work,” I said.

“I love a good laugh,” said The Manufacturer.

I false-smiled agreement. The Manufacturer’s numb torment. Equally false-smile counter-agreement.

“Humor is violence. To make people laugh is to control them. People need that in their lives. To be taken over, controlled. To have voids filled.”

The Manufacturer poured another, sat down, gazed upon the photograph of his late son.

“You remember those boys at school. Grade School, High School. Beaten on the bus. Teased. Ridiculed. Their revenge? Humor. They were the class clowns. The ones who made the whole damn crowd, the ‘gang,’ laugh themselves to tears at recess. At parties. Laugh till they pissed their pants. Laughed themselves silly while the clown, the fool, the erstwhile victim of their blows, their ridicule, ran off with all the pretty girls. Do you remember that, Plantman?”

“Uh, no. Not as such. I don’t recall–”

The Manufacturer rose, smiling sparked energy good cheer.

“You must recall that we don’t only sell humorous novelties. We have a whole collection of life-sized dolls, fully equipped, furry or shaved, modeled after stars and celebrities. ‘So true to life, you’ll try to make her come.’ My erstwhile Greatest Salesman coined that line. Masks too,” he grinned wicked. “Leg Irons.”

The Manufacturer, success at seventeen, rose higher, higher. The boy who sold baubles. Portable stand at amusement parks. Now largest, most profitable Novelty Company in The Nation.

“My wife died during cosmetic surgery, you must recall. When they buried her, half of her face was thin, supple, youthful, half was aged, dry, be-jowled. My punishment: to simultaneously gaze upon the beauty I'd married long ago, and the bloated matron who lay beside me in my bed night after night after night after night. Until they hid her away in the humorless ground. What a miserable end. You don't expect that when you're seventeen, do you, Plantman?”

“I didn't know what to expect when I was seventeen,” I said.

The Manufacturer's son, wild, unruly, ran away, age fifteen. Lived Missing Young. The Manufacturer hired The Detective Agency resolve the situation. Situation resolved. The Son flirted with Novelties in High School. The Manufacturer thought The Son would inherit. But age eighteen The Son left The University. To The War, kill be killed for The Nation.

“He was my only,” The Manufacturer said evenly. “Now, like so many of the customers I've served over the years, I am alone. A Jokester hates to joke alone,” he said.

I demurred.

“You are like me,” said The Manufacturer. “You bring The Citizens joy.”

XII.
The City Museum Complex

Hall of Hoaxes

Plantman took a brief but necessary vacation, or personal day–as if the rest of his days were property of Topiary Techniques–to visit the world famous City Museum Complex.

The plaque outside The Hall of Hoaxes read, "Everything The City promised you, but never delivered. Everything The Nation promised you, but never delivered."

Hyperbole, true, but what can one expect from The Hall of Hoaxes?

The Hall featured exhibit upon exhibit of hoaxes hoaxed upon Citizens of the previous century. Lot of money during those Main Street days when Citizens gladly paid to be bamboozled.

No exhibit for promises broken by friends, lovers, teachers, innocence lost, disappointing lives. . . only the palpable, the obvious. Two-headed boy floating in fluid and the shin-bone of an angel. Skull of an alien from outer space and a handwritten love letter from God. Disfigured fetuses in pickle jars; dinosaur eggs; cavemen in ice.

The Fossil Giant, nine feet tall, three feet wide, arms folded across his great expanse of chest, slept peacefully on a slab, his existence carved meticulously from stone, down to the detailed pores in his bone-white skin.

A sign before this granite Golem read, "Who can forget the Great Hoax of the Giant Unearthed? This alleged precursor to the Citizens' glory was an enormous but lucrative fake created from stone. Neuter (so squeamish were the last century's Citizens that few questioned the naked Giant's missing genitalia).

"The Giant was displayed again, after the hoax was revealed, earning thrice the loot as people queued to gaze upon the 'false ancestor who gulled millions.'"

Plantman opened the Guide Booklet given to each visitor and read more about the Giant.

The Giant had been unearthed "somewhere out West." The specimen pulled from the ground was petrified, but intact. Some suggested that before the Indians a great race roamed the land, the true inheritors of The Nation's immense expanse of real estate. The perfidious Indians stole their land. The City con-man impresario, originator of the hoax, intimated that the original inhabitants of The Nation–not Indians–were a race of friendly White Super Giants. Nomadic hordes migrating from the North, later to be known as "Indians," slaughtered these Giants and ate them, grinding their bones to foot powder and aphrodisiacs. Away, away the community and culture of these friendly Titans. Dead. Hence, whatever Citizens of The Nation later did to the Indians was well deserved.

"Many people parted with their money to gaze upon the face

of this giant unearthed during the height of the Indian wars," Plantman read from the booklet. "One day an honest archaeologist, posing as a typical rustic of The Nation–for scientists were not allowed anywhere near the Giant–exposed the giant for the Pygmy that it was: a life-like statue carved from stone.

"Headlines read 'Giant Hoax,' and much newsprint was devoted to the sham, which had already become famous worldwide, generating literature and speculation of a master race of Giants (some people in The Nation believe the Giant legend to this day).

"Unexpectedly, even for cynics of The Nation, the Giant and its creator made even more money after the hoax was exposed. People gladly paid to see the statue now billed as the 'Greatest Hoax on Earth: The Trick Titan who fooled millions.'

"Even those who saw the Giant the first time parted with twice the money to review the piece of stone that had duped them and so mesmerized The Nation."

Plantman pocketed the pamphlet and scrutinized the eunuch Giant, testament to Old Time Main Street decorum.

"Big Man. Big White Giant. No balls, no dick," said an inebriated Citizen near the exhibit.

Plantman left the Hall of Hoaxes somewhat disappointed. He'd expected bigger, more immediate, contemporary hoaxes to be revealed. Perhaps the hoaxes of today are quieter, less visible, more discreet. Perhaps The Citizens of today are more subtly fooled.

Indian Museum

"Welcome to Indian Museum, where villains, Viral Deviants (VD'S) and Terrorists of the past are preserved for your enlightenment," said The Guide.

The Guide, tall, serious, had silver hair; his gray eyes gleamed like sun-lit steel. He wore the deep blue uniform of Indian Museum, fashioned after the uniforms worn by soldiers of The Nation more than a century ago, when The West was won.

"The Indians were fierce, alright. Real tough customers. But what force can withstand the righteous anger of The Nation?" said The Guide. "The Indians were extinguished so that The Nation might thrive."

The Guide explained how Indians could not adapt to the Destiny of The Nation and thus were eliminated for the benefit of all.

"But The City, and indeed The Nation, must preserve its history. The Indians are preserved for posterity in these exquisite glass cases, courtesy of Tree of Knowledge Incorporated (TKI) Technologies."

Miniature glass coffins. Indians in suits and dresses like ordinary Citizens. Babes enfolded in their mothers' arms. Indians like dolls, averaging a foot in length, preserved for posterity and beyond.

"Why are they so tiny?" asked a young girl on the tour.

"That is the magic of TKI Technologies," The Guide explained.

"TKI has developed a method that enables us to shrink the Indians while retaining life-like features for the ages. They are all, you will notice, perfectly proportioned, fit to scale."

"Why do they do this?" asked the child.

"Look around you," The Guide gestured dramatically. "See how many Indians are on display. Indian Museum is limited in size. So, thanks to the process developed by TKI Technologies, with not a little help from TKI Chemistries, rather than build a bigger museum, or several bigger museums–so many Indians, it's difficult to keep track–we made smaller Indians!" said The Guide proudly. "The Indians of Indian Museum are the living lifeless. Though they were vanquished long ago, they appear to have 'gone to sleep' just yesterday.

"There is the infamous Geronimo!" The Guide pointed to a glass case within which "slept" a shrunken fifty-ish man in a finely tailored little suit. "There, the notorious Crazy Horse! And Sitting Bull! And Chief Joseph! And what would Indian Museum be without it's beautiful Pocahontas?"

Tourists gawked at Indians, watched filmed re-enactments of the Great Indian Wars. Plantman approached The Guide, who glanced furtively at Plantman's green Topiary Techniques t-shirt and flashed a peroxide smile.

"Welcome to Indian Museum, Plantman. It is my pleasure to host an illustrious 'horticultural technician' of The City," said The Guide.

Plantman acknowledged this false flattery with a curt nod, then asked the question burning his mind.

"What is this place? These aren't real Indians. They aren't Indians at all."

"Of course not," whispered The Guide. "Indian Museum is for children. This is a place of education. The icons and symbols we present to the children are far more. . . potent than some old head-dresses and buckskins on wax statues."

"Who were they?" Plantman pointed to a cluster of glass coffins.

"Viral Deviants, Terrorists, executed prisoners, bodies unclaimed at the morgue. Though they were parasites in life, Indian Museum, courtesy TKI Technologies, has given them a chance to contribute to The City and The Nation in death, to become part of the illustrious culture that, in life, for whatever mad 'reasons,' they mistakenly eschewed."

"Couldn't you have at least dressed them in 'traditional' garments?"

"The Indian of the tomahawk and tom-tom drum is irrelevant. Extinct. The modern Indians, the Indians these children will know in their life-times, are the Terrorists, the VDs, the parasites. Indian Museum has gone to great lengths to impress this reality upon The City's young. I'm surprised that you of all people, a Plantman dedicated to tending The City's indoor flora, don't show more sensitivity to these issues. Really you should display more political awareness."

"Since when do Terrorists and VDs wear dresses, suits and ties?" I asked.

"You surprise me, Plantman. You may know more than most about The City's potted plants, but I fear you have much to learn about its people. My advice to you is to visit The City Museum Complex often. And keep an open mind. After all, your good friend, "Fire Bush," is seldom seen without a suit and tie. And if you don't mind my saying so, he's no more an "Indian" than the specimens at Indian Museum. He's Puerto Rican if he's a day."

The Hall of Sports

The Hall of Sports presented colorful, uniformed wax figures in traditional protective masks painted with fiery stripes and cryptic glyphs. The Guide, dressed like a sports Hero himself, led our tour group–mostly fathers and young sons–through The Hall of Sports, easily the most popular attraction in The City Museum Complex–among male Citizens, at any rate.

The Guide said, "Gentlemen, welcome to The Hall of Sports, where the weapons of your heroes hang from every wall. Do you remember that first afternoon in the stadium? Blazing sun clean blue sky? Dazzling crew-cut grass? The athletes themselves, hulking men, larger than life in the colors of their Times? Bone smashed bone and youth stretched far. The feats of Heroes, crush of combat, clash of shields and clubs. . .

"Citizen fathers, let relics of The Nation's demigods of sport take you back to that first step from the coliseum corridors and into the thrill of fresh air, crowds, verdant fields demarcated with precise grid lines of powder fine and white as confectioner's sugar. . ."

Uniformed wax heroes. Grainy footage decades old. Visitors marveled at weapons used in actual play by Heroes of all Time: sticks, balls, leather, plastic armor–once smashed one upon the other during great games of The Nation's history. Fathers and sons gazed upon life-size replicas of ancient heroes they'd read about and seen in black-and-white footage centuries old–centuries since the shadows captured were stalwart Heroes in the thick of Life's doing; wood and leather weapons of The Nation's early sportsmen; sleek plastic gear of modern champions; artifacts of long-dead players; plaques, tapes, photographs and films commemorating spectacular moments captured long before anyone's grandfather was born.

The Guide said, "These actual relics of past times had once soaked sweat from the flesh of great men. The films and photographs reveal them in actual play, when they were virgin-new, their owners young men not yet legends; not shadows on celluloid, but vigorous athletes moving gracefully through the sounds, scents and colors of their Times."

Time connections. Facts of artifacts. Physical relations. Moments of ghosts. Smell of horse-hide, leather. Who decided which actions among innumerable moments merited preservation–and by what criteria? Transcendent deeds plucked from centuries of play to be immortalized in The Hall of Sports. Yet not every artifact was preserved, only those connecting events of significance to the official sports history of The Nation.

The Guide said, "Behold the fragments of lives you've merely read about or seen in gray newsreels and flat colors of TV. We take our sons to The Hall of Sports that they might witness the tools and weapons of our Heroes' Heroes, and gaze reverently upon icons and photographs of players long departed from flesh but vibrant in the memory of The Nation, that our sons may celebrate these sportsmen and their deeds."

Rows of equipment hung from all available space: pikes, shields, knives, truncheons; gloves, sticks, helmets, sharpened cleats.

The Guide said, "Remember your first live game, when led by the hand of your father, you stepped from some dark corridor of the arena and out into the cupped, ascending open among kaleidoscopic thousands, and down on the field the players in their uniforms clashed three-dimensionally before the stomping, roaring hordes.

"Took your breath away. So much more ALIVE than tiny images on screens. But alas, even The Hall of Sports is powerless over Time. We can offer only fragments, bits and pieces of The God-man's puzzle, to stimulate memory and imagination. The relics, photographs, films and pulse of words are all we have to preserve the great sports moments of The Nation."

Museum of Women

At the Museum of Women Plantman saw:

The "Clothing Collection": Silk and satin traces. Women history The City. Centuries-old skirts and dresses; Summer frocks of decades past. Wardrobes. Fashion. Chic aged to antique. Pinned to every skirt dress blouse a brief descriptive card: Year, value. Year, value.

Clothing once alive with women, once women-animated clothes. Once women of The City. Anticipating nights, inhaling cricket air of parks and gardens. Exhale. City engine of oblivion. Gone lithe beauties, gone buxom matrons cherished secrets of their own. Once moments lived, once birth to ash. Once striving, music of their day days women of The City.

"Memoir Exhibit": Journals, diaries, letters, postcards, notebooks under glass. Read private prose: letters to lovers, friends. Lock of hair from a famous poetess–age seventeen two hundred years ago–clipped, sent to her beau. Light brown flecked with gold, as if sheared off a teenage head just yesterday.

"Photographs Exhibit": Moments of women living City lives. Dressing, undressing, walking, talking, working, loving. What thoughts thought before the flash and shutter-wink of lens, time before death left only ghost-shadows to ponder?

Other Exhibits: "Women at Home"; "Women at Work;" "Women's Gardens": profound relationships with plants and herbs.

Plantman left the place aroused, exhausted, yearning. His head spun images of women.

XIII.
The Love Song of Prudence Plantwoman

free young
memory
impinged upon
by memory

she will fly
away
from green thumbs

graduated
ROTC Air Force
paid for school
now six years due
The Nation
six years
she will fly
beyond her
memories
over
The Nation
over
The City

trees, birds, flowers
all things green
living
destiny blue sky

not that she does not
like plants
or life
as Plantwoman
it's a job
a summer gig
until
her "papers" come
from Central Command
her orders
and she leaps
from
gray-black asphalt
to azure sky
free muscular
tank top, short-shorts
jeans, t-shirts
swimmer, gymnast
gone through Basic
Freshman year

sexual animal
we're all
animals
she makes no bones
about
"getting boned"
she calls it

"boned"
she calls
it it it it it
it it itititititit

dubbed "Plantwoman"
birth name
grounded

letting smoke blow
perfect nostrils
dragon lady
scissors, bucket
military bearing
ass to die for and
a kiss in corridors
under Greenman gargoyles
elevators, lonely corners
she bears fruit and cigarettes
remembers The Nation
and her drunken Dad
nobody nothing, nothing
in The Nation
but her
determination, mission applied
to work
sex never far
behind
photograph of her,
The Colonel she calls "Ma'am,"
and another lieutenant
(for that was the rank Plantwoman attained)
nude in a tub

bare legs hung
lax
over the edge
toenails bright magenta
“military baring”
read
the black ink caption

Plantwoman will die
for The Nation
if called
to do
her duty
The Nation
educated her
The Nation
trained her
to fly
twenty hours a week
in uniform
earned her degree
Political Science
Enemy languages
mother-lode of math

she’ll fly
but earthbound
she tends plants
military rigor
anomalously wedded
to loving care
mother earth/earth mother
feminist

volunteer
Student Sexuality Information Service
"keep your laws off my body"
derrière her boxer shorts
worn outside–fly sewn sealed–in summer
night
and black boots
to her knees
muscular thighs
watch her clip, water,
poke bare fingers
sodden soil

poison, occasionally,
at client's request:
"we have ants. . . on our desks. . .
"you must exterminate. . .
"the ants. . ."

no heart to kill
direct
drop bombs
for The Nation
two miles high like
pitching pennies
wishing well

"I'm not some reactionary killer freak,
just had to pay for school"

"women. . . special relationship
with plants
we first cultivated

we fed
the tribe
the matriarchy before
all this. . . " swept her arm
around
The City

"Hey, Plantman, wanna learn some
'fertilization techniques'?"

Forward. Young. Out night "boned."

Someone other than Me. Naturally.

Meeting at Main Office Victor
singled Plantwoman, "stellar job."

The Air Force taught her well,
if not The University.

She didn't think much of
"The Trojan Women"
Euripides
not woman enough
for her.

Sympathetic pout sometime
coquettish.
Raunchy volatile licentious
fearful, on occasion,
of THE WRONG THING,
then confident
fly silver planes

over the World.

Lieutenant Plantwoman Ma'am.
character complex.

Quick Time

Guns of August
Papers came
soon overseas
I bought
coffee looked up
at buildings
from the Court of Food,
where we
lunched
Days
the week

"what does it say about The Citizens
that they need shrubbery in
urns to calm them
through the day, like wall-paper
or the soft upholstery
of cubicle walls?"
she asked

disciplined sex wild
landscaper
wrestled Life
with grim determination
duty bound fly to The War

"Tie me up,
why don't you
tie me up!"

she
gave herself
to passion
gave completely
animal abandon
beside her I felt
tiny
like the bugs we
sprayed
like The Enemy
below
the silver fighters
of The Nation

back to the Network
Chat Room
digital desperate
solace: Mar3Sh311y
"I miss her
the smell of her–"
I typed.
"Pheromones," wrote
Mar3Sh311y.
"Distinctive scent.
Meant to seduce.
Like perfume
of a flower."

XIV.
INTERMISSION:
Epics of The Deep: A Big Media Production

Manager of The CityPlex

The CityPlex was dense with movie-goers. BEING and Music queued for soda, snacks. Alone with the crowd in the vast lobby, Plantman watched the masses part like water for a man.

Maverick, not with or of the crowd, beyond: The Manager of The CityPlex, unfazed, perhaps energized, by hectic surroundings, commanded Ushers to their tasks. He nodded: the popcorn-girls popped corn, peddled soda, candy, treats.

His maroon uniform and golden epaulets. His grim determination. His consummate professional of. Man in charge of. Master of. Environment. Dedication laser focus; indifferent to the hordes. Manager of burdens, hard experience, not much older than Plantman himself. What would drive a man his age to such preternatural mastery and–control?

"This group shall pass that group shall pass another. Stop. Don't pass another. Stop. Don't pass another."

It was The Manager's decision and his alone which group would be guided through which entrance and when. Ushers snapped to, guided groups, confirmed tickets. Like sailors–driven to–deliverance–by–some hoary Captain's–ghost.

So many entrances, so many screens; so many ones to guide. The Manager was master. Antithesis of the bureaucratic every-move-by-fear-of-those-above. Owners of theaters, distributors of films, Big Media itself was above the Manager, yet he answered to no one.

The CityPlex was his, his life alone.

The Manager unbuttoned his collar and unleashed a mad diatribe against all who enter his theater, his pure machinery of CityPlex. People, at best, were a necessary burden. He was a burdened man. He dreamed of The CityPlex running like clockwork in emptiness, films projected in vacant theaters. Audiences irked him. He loathed their enjoyment of the films.

"The films are ugly, tasteless," he said. "The symmetry, beauty, order of The CityPlex is all that is worth seeing. My CityPlex. Rescued from abomination."

"Nothing? Nothing?" Plantman asked.

"Perhaps, if one movie were made, one special film," said The Manager. "And the seats and floors were not sticky, as in other theaters, and the employees worked hard, their uniforms pressed, hair freshly shampooed, The CityPlex would experience its finest hour, and all who saw this film would come away enlightened, rather than dull-eyed and bloated with soda, popcorn, sweets. Perhaps, if this film were projected on all screens always, The CityPlex would achieve its true purpose, its ultimate being. CityPlex Sublime. As is, the movie-goers are sheep grazing dead grass. The CityPlex is a slaughter house of entertainment."

"What film?" asked Plantman. "What film might this be?"

The Manager slipped from reverie, became abrupt.

"I do not know. Such a film, to my knowledge, has not yet been produced."

He briskly excused himself. An usher led Plantman, Music and BEING to their seats.

Epics of the Deep: The Movie

Epics of the Deep, was a typical Big Media over-production, but interesting in its implications:

The Mad Cetologist gets hold of TKI Technologies' Pyramid Human-Animal Language Translator (HALT), used to prove to vegetarians, "animal liberation" activists and other Viral Deviants, that while animals have a certain instinctual "intelligence," they are far from human, and their liberation would not only result in a dearth of protein for the Citizens of The Nation, but the animals' certain death from car accidents, starvation etc. not to mention immense health hazards caused allowing pigs, cows, chickens, sheep and goats roam "free" through Cities of The Nation.

But The Mad Cetologist had been studying various clicks, whistles, whirs, and bellows made by whales and dolphins, and detected certain patterns. He set out to prove, using his illegally gotten HALT software, that cetaceans were indeed as "intelligent" as Homo Sapiens.

Before his journey, as he readied his boat, he was approached by a young woman who identified herself as a "student" of marine biology who had a particular knack with animals. The Cetologist, who did indeed need an assistant for his task, hired her on.

Together they went in search of whales. They found a school of Humpback, keeping their distance. To The Mad Cetologist's amazement, The Student dove into the water and swam toward the fearsome creatures–and they toward her. The leviathans nuzzled her and allowed her to stroke their immense backs. Next morning, The Mad Cetologist was surprised to see his boat surrounded by Humpback whales, circling, as they dived into and emerged from the dark deep.

Having fed many gigabytes of recorded whales sounds–he chose Humpback specifically–into HALT, he created a translator for cetaceans wired to a microphone lowered into the water. He spoke the language of The Nation, and received a reply: clicks, whistles, whirs, translated to the language of The Nation.

The first conversations were relatively pedestrian: courteous "Hello's," greetings, introductions and so forth.

But an interesting discovery was made, not only among the Humpback, but other cetacean species, including schools of bottle-nosed dolphins sewing the sea like silver thread stitching a great green blanket.

"Epic poems" passed down "orally," for lack of a better term, from generation to generation, through the eons were a consistent feature of all cetacean life. The epics described details of whale and dolphin life, as each school and species traversed the oceans, from the dawn of Time. The themes and stories of the great poems remained constant, repetitive journals of the ancient past, although each generation altered the tale they inherited, with its own particular "style"–varying, of course, from school to school.

Certain specifics remained consistent: the first Great Holocaust by Man only centuries before, for instance, and the myth (memory?) that some whales had developed legs, hundreds of millions of years ago, and crawled up to land, then, wisely, crawled back to swim free again.

Mostly the epics concerned the fundamentals of living–searching for food and clean temperate water; mating; long swims in search of the safest, least human-contaminated regions in which to pursue the fundamentals. By far the most "time-intensive" pursuits included a combination of aimless wandering; play; exploration of what remained of the great ocean paradise and the rapidly disappearing life-forms born into it; communication of impressions and "ideas" accumulating in their enormous brains, and just being the creatures life had meant them to be–what human beings would commonly describe as "goofing off," or "doing nothing," said descriptions usually followed by stern injunctions to "get a life," or at the very least, "get a job."

The Mad Cetologist and The Student published their collections of the Humpback, Sperm whale and Bottle-nosed dolphin as "Epics of the Deep,"–each translated from the language of the particular genus, the same poems passed on and refined, refined, refined with each generation, but seldom amended–with few "approved" exceptions: such as the halcyon era of Great Floods; the Death Days of mass hunting to near extinction by humans–as if time stood still, or rather, spun in cycles, like planets, galaxies, atoms, through eons. . .

TKI Pharmaceuticals began to dissect cetacean brains to find the chemical that enabled the creatures to memorize such vast stores of information. From this research evolved the drug, Cetanax, which increased memory and worker production–workers would not have to waste time consulting books and on-line manuals, but could learn computer languages and reproduce tera-bytes of data in seamless sync with the machines.

TKI Inc. began to "farm" whales/dolphins in closed areas of the sea owned by The Company, taking what was needed for production of Cetanax and ensuring abundant supply of cetaceans; hence, unlike the Dodo or other useless animals, whales would not become extinct, but kept in bountiful supply as befitting necessary fauna–cows, sheep, chickens, pigs, etc.

Out on the boat, The foolish Mad Cetologist transmitted a rambling "apology" to various schools of whales and dolphins, cutting the receiver, for he, crazed man, could not "bear" to hear their reply–as if they would do anything but thank him for allowing them to serve The Nation! The Mad Cetologist and The Student shared a long "dark night of the soul," so to speak, made love for the first time, and in the sheets entwined, The Student admitted she was none other than The Missing Girl, that most VIRAL of Deviants, Pied Piperess of The Missing Young!

Rather than expressing righteous outrage, the Mad Cetologist was gladdened by her disgraceful revelation, for in his sick mind they were fellow impediments to the progress of The Nation.

But in a moment of clarity, The Mad Cetologist realized that The Nation must thrive while they, despite their great contribution that led to increased citizen productivity (thanks to Cetanax–although via illegal use of HALT) which he perversely viewed as a "desecration and betrayal" of cetacean life–as if THAT were equal to the productive life of The Nation.

At dawn, The Mad Cetologist, and now unmasked Missing Girl, doused the boat and themselves with gasoline, kissed good-bye, and lit two matches. Their final, productive deed: destroying their potentially useful but deliberately useless selves, despite the serendipitous discovery of the epics which led to mass production of Cetanax, for the good of The Nation.

Such people as The Mad Cetologist and The Missing Girl despite occasional productive work, cannot but impede the progress of The Nation. Thus, their one truly great act was their suicide, the immolation of their infected selves for the good of The Nation's clean, healthy, productive citizenry.

THE END.

Epic Sensation

Epics of the Deep was the box-office sensation of the Summer.

Starlette Nova, who played "The Missing Girl," and Don Coyote as "The Mad Cetologist," covered every magazine that profiled celebrity entertainment interviews and idols of The Nation. Talk. Talk. Talkety-talk. Escorted straight to the eyes and ears of Citizen-consumers from sea to sea. Powerful, powerful talk engendering excitement, illusions of important, almost Sacred Time, and a desire to spend money. To partake in or own a piece of the action.

Fame was not new to Starlette Nova. She began her career with the hit movie Down in The City. Then a succession of block-buster Romantic comedies made her a Name.

Don Coyote, was of course a Mega-Star of The Nation, known for his roles as a wise-cracking, comedian/outlaw with a heart of gold. Resigned to life in "the streets" his characters adapted to their grim environments and with a code of Robin Hood ethics, wry wit, irony and raw violence. Coyote finally tested his acting skills with Epics of the Deep, the first movie in which he neither fired nor even carried a weapon.

Epics was the first "serious" vehicle for both, the first super-blockbuster whose influence was felt beyond the multiplex and its vast network of supporting entertainment venues, celebrity talk shows and magazines.

The concept of talking whales caught the collective imagination, squeezed tight as a rat's cervix by years in thrall to those very entertainment and celebrity vehicles that energized The Stars.

Attention focused not only on The Stars, but whales themselves.

Marine biologists appeared on everyone's favorite celebrity news and talk shows, offering expert opinions on the film's alleged veracity.

"Though it has long been assumed that cetaceans communicate with each other in some way, from the high pitched squeals of Orca to the low rumblings of the Finback, the potentiality of inter-species intercourse. . . uh, communication, has not been seriously researched," said an Expert Cetologist on a morning talk show.

"We have long known cetaceans are intelligent," said an Expert Neurologist on another show. "The question is, how intelligent? Furthermore, how can this intelligence be defined in relation to our own? If such a translation device as that depicted in the film actually existed, we would unlock secrets not merely to the minds of cetaceans, but the nature of what we call 'mind' itself."

"So you are saying we don't really know the minds of these creatures, at least not nearly so well as depicted in the film?" asked The Commentator.

"I'm saying we don't really know our own minds as well as we know the creatures depicted in the film. Human beings are in fact possessors of extremely complex and extremely confusing brains. We create sophisticated works like Epics of the Deep, yet we also create horrible wars like–"

The neurologist was cut off abruptly for a commercial break.

On and on, experts lent credence to the film. Every show another expert from the marine biology department or human linguistics or neurology department of a Major University was plied with questions.

"Public" debates raged over The Network. Sites about whales, the movie, the stars, multiplied. Words shot across The Network. Blogs, Chats, Discussion Groups. Talk about whales and The Missing Girl converged. New "theories," posted daily, linked cetaceans to government research and conspiracy. All manner of fantasy from paranoid to pastoral relayed rapid-fire from server to server across The Nation.

Big Media renewed interest in The Missing Girl angle of the film. Starlette Nova was considered for all the industry's top awards for her history-making role.

A. T. Rotious, creator of the original comic book, "Epics of the Deep," founder of the "underground" publishing company, Comikosis, was treated like major literati.

Big Media sought his opinions on everything from the odor of Whale skin to the language of The Nation. Influences he cited: The Missing Girl story/legend; Another World, by The Real Cetologist, upon whose life work the character of the Whaleman was based, and Connection, by the poet, Alterkocher, where the idea of interspecies communication was broached ten years before Epics of the Deep was featured at your local multi-plex.

Alterkocher, Plantman's teacher and informal advisor at the

University, long and far away ago.

Big Media pounded Alterkocher's door demanding he appear on "World Nation Tonight."

The interview was conducted in Alterkocher's University office, the same office Plantman had passed through Time as a young Marketing Student, discussing non-linear product placement strategies, 'PR prosody,' masterpieces with The Poet. Now, the office of the formerly obscure Alterkocher was opened to millions.

"It takes a poet to create a poet," began The Celebrity Interviewer as Alterkocher smoked his pipe.

She rambled on:

"In this University office, the poet and teacher, Alterkocher, dreamed mammoth bards of the sea. The poems he composed and published in the now famous book, CONNECTION, inspired the great comic-book author A.T. Rotious, whose graphic novel, EPICS OF THE DEEP, was the basis of the Summer's box office champion."

The Celebrity Interviewer tried to squeeze and roll Alterkocher's tumbling waves of oratory into terse sound-bytes, but Alterkocher was stubbornly Alterkocher, and lectured the camera on language, struggle, the human condition (such as it was). His involuted conversation provoked a cry of shrill frustration, from The Celebrity Interviewer. A welcome non sequitor.

The Poet Alterkocher

Professor Alterkocher's office was open to all always–even Summer hours. Room of his own. Read, thought, wrote, dispensed wisdom to The Young. Plantman met with him one evening after work to discuss his famous new fame.

Alterkocher wore his customary suit and running shoes, smoked his pipe. Hair unkempt. Beard-stubble–two days' worth–gray-white.

"Sit down, sit down," said Alterkocher out of the pipe-side of his mouth. "Good to see you. Always good."

"Good to see you, Professor. Long time."

"And what has my former student been doing with his time?" asked Alterkocher, eying Plantman's bucket.

"This and that."

"This. And that. Of course. Of course."

"I tend office gardens," Plantman said. "Potted plants of The City. I'm a horticultural technician."

"So you are," he squinted at the Topiary Techniques logo on my t-shirt. "So you are."

Short pleasantries, longer silences.

"So you've seen that damn movie," said Alterkocher.

"Yes."

"And my television debut?"

"Classic," I said crisply.

"Once Big Media wrap their talons around some artifact. . . and it wasn't even Big Media who began the damned thing. I believe it was some sort of, some kind of comic book."

"Graphic novel," I corrected.

"Yes. An illustrated text. Or is it a set of illustrations with footnotes?"

I shrugged in empathetic ignorance of and indifference to the popular "culture" and its extravagant fads. Actually, I'd enjoyed Rotious's work very much.

Long sigh of a "successful," yet beaten man.

"Hmn. So now I am 'famous.' All the literate citizens of The Nation have scribbled verse at one time or another, but the actual audience for poetry is roughly 3000 souls. Throughout the entire Nation. About a tenth of that general audience have read my books. That is, before this movie and its concomitant ballyhoo.

"CONNECTION is a collection of imaginative possibilities inspired by the data certain marine biologists gathered regarding possible communication among cetaceans. There was no communication between whales and humans in the scientific research. CONNECTION is a work of pure, vigorous imagination, but it has been received by the public–not my regular reading public, who could fit in this room–as both much more and much less.

"My imagined conversation between a young girl and a dolphin is now taken by some people to have been based on truth. Who could have foreseen such misreading? The long piece, "Epic," for instance, hardly an epic, though at thirty pages quite a long poem, postulates the "The Great Sperm Epic" passing "orally," so to speak, from generation to generation through the ages. Tradition as afflatus and boundary of the poetic imagination struggling to both free and contain itself. That this would be confused in some circles with literal truth boggles the mind.

"Yet once the ship is launched, as it were, it is out to sea. Game over. Fail-safe. No recall.

"That I am placed in the uncomfortable, unforeseen position of 'attacking' my own work is painful itself; but to be ignored, to have the myths not only endure but multiply even as the original myth-maker reveals the artifice behind the work, pulls down the curtain on the whole damn show. . . astounding. As if they wish to be fooled regardless of the facts.

"I am now, I suppose, the most popular poet in The Nation. Yet I have never felt so estranged from The Nation. Never so financially secure. Big Media paid me their visit and left their check, a substantial sum, and my small, ten-year-old volume is a best-seller, purchased by millions, if only actually read by dozens. In the great machine of this popular phenomenon I am a minor component indeed, the supplier of an artifact that correlates to the 'overall,' the book of verse that all refer to none read. The book sells so the public may have another talisman, something to hold and keep, show and tell. A souvenir. Along with their EPICS OF THE DEEP coffee mugs and t-shirts.

"One day, when this blows over, perhaps CONNECTION will remain on the bookshelves of anonymous homes, and some few anonymous readers will peruse the poems, not knowing anything of this hullabaloo, and appreciate them for what they were intended to be.

"For now, I will enjoy the novelty of being a best-selling author, a somewhat rich and famous man. But this too shall pass. I will return to my old life among my small but dedicated circle of students and readers, completely forgotten by the public of The Nation.

"When I look back on writing the book, I imagine the whales and their insistent songs. We no longer speak to communicate, merely to shuffle data into the heads of others, to clear the excess from our crowded minds, clean the slate, so to speak. I imagined the whales with their own language, their own poetry. It is a clear and open poetry, spacious and uncluttered, the kind of language I've always dreamed, but never could attain. My mind is as cluttered as yours. I try to write spacious verse, but the mountains of data are too high for a meager poet such as myself to scale. I dreamed of the whales and their space, their depth and calm. Perhaps that is what this sudden industry is built upon, the industry these "Epics" have become. Perhaps we all share this dream of space and depth that only something other than human, like these mythologized creatures, can deliver to us in our dreams and fictions.

"It is best to allow the public to enjoy their dream while they can, before they move restlessly, addictively, inevitably to the next. I know that not even this whale of a dream will sate their appetites for 'Something Else'"

On and on elaborated and exhorted Alterkocher, as in my student days. I said little. I had come not to speak, but to listen. Relaxing in the guest-chair, breathing clouds of Cavendish, listening to my former teacher's deep, rumbling oratory, was better than TV. Like sitting by the ocean, listening to waves. Or perhaps even to the whales themselves.

The Starlet, Starlette Nova

Starlette Nova landed in The City to promote–herself. Appeared on Television and Radio talk shows; nearly every newspaper and magazine in The City was privileged with an interview (questions limited to her stunning performance as "The Missing Girl") and (no costumes or serious poses: five minutes of scripted 'real time') opportunity to photograph the starlet, Starlette.

She summoned Plantman to tend the dozens and dozens of bouquets and potted plants–gifts from admiring young actors, actresses and hopeful screen-writers, directors, producers–in her luxurious hotel suite. Normally Plantman didn't do non-Topiary Techniques Proprietary Green Ware, much less flowers, severed from the root like gangrenous limbs, but this was Starlette Nova, stretched sleek on the couch eating salad dabbed with fat-free dressing. Victor, The Topiary Techniques City Manager, had assured her that her plants–regardless of licensing and ownership–would be treated royally during her visit to The City. Hence, Plantman plied his trade in her private suite.

"Everybody knows me." she said.

Affirmative.

"You know me. You've seen me. If not in movies, talk shows, interviews, the Network, somewhere. Now they will know me as The Missing Girl. I was made for this role. I'm realer than The Missing Girl herself, whoever she is. Was. What have you. I have you. I have everyone.

"I'm me, but more than me, more than just you, that is, a mere person. The subject at hand: plain old folks. There's nothing wrong with them, they shouldn't be hurt or imprisoned or anything. They're just not me.

"You see me. I don't see you. Not you, Plantman, watering flowers, but 'you' in the general sense. You, the audience. I don't see you and probably never will. Unless you know somebody. Somebody important. Or very, very interesting. Famous. Connected. Someone of value. Consider five point whatever billion people in the world. Too many histories, you can't keep track. Well yes, the corporations and governments with their databases. But the data in the databases is just words and numbers. I mean, what does it say about a person? What can it say, other than he or she lives in such a such a thatched hut in the village of Yahoo-yahoo where there's a television, but no running water and he/she, the subject of our conversation, learned to read a bit of his/her language, whatever it may be, but doesn't have to because there's no books or newspapers or jobs or anything, really, just that one communal television. So that's all it says about this person in the world wide database. Perhaps there's more information on some folks than others, but not much more.

"But me, they write about me every day. It's an entire industry, writing about the doings, the comings, the goings, the hither and yon of me. It's all lies and propaganda, but it's out there, my name embedded in print. And my image–well that's all the words are there for. Provide filler for my photographs. They look more significant surrounded by words than on an empty page, don't you think?"

Plantman, not recognizing the rhetorical nature of the question, foolishly began to answer: "Well, I–"

Starlette, after a stern but somewhat forgiving glance, continued:

"You can look me up and read about my life. Or the official version of my life. The official version. There's the official version, and the bootleg versions. 'Unauthorized' interviews when I was younger, stupider, high on dope. Unauthorized by my agent and managers and lawyers and god knows who else is on the payroll to keep the pay rolling. Maybe some truth in that old stuff. It's about me, after all. Who better to talk about me than myself?

"But it's not about me. Because way down deep where the real me lives, deep in my brain, I don't think anybody's heard of Starlette Nova. In fact, the last place on earth where the name Starlette Nova is meaningless might very well be my own subunconscious mind.

"But there are things to examine, to look into, such as: who is Starlette?

"That is, who is me? Who am I? It's important to examine yourself. I don't mean the obvious things, the pendulous things, the tits and testicles you probe with your fingertips for lumps. I mean the bottomless things. The inside things, the stuff that even if you find it–and very few do–you won't even know it's there, I mean know for a fact. You'll have to take it on faith and faith is the only way you'll keep it. Because it's a construct, a thing of imagination, a personal design. The design of your person. Conceptual. Mercurial. Abstract. You wouldn't get garbage for it at an auction. Yet it's what gives you your value. Without it you'd have nothing.

"Starlette Nova has value. Tremendous value. But it, whatever 'it' is, created Starlette Nova. Does Starlette Nova have 'it?' I don't mean talent, wit, drive, tits and ass, 'what it takes.' How many tiresome wanna-girl neophytes have asked me that question. 'Do I have it?' 'Do I have what it takes?' Well if you don't know the difference between 'it' and 'what it takes' you probably have neither. That always shuts them down. That always. . . well, it wouldn't hurt to be a little more kind.

"Kind. If I had an ounce of kindness in me I wouldn't be a goddess, or this technical facsimile everywhere at the same time flickering immortal universal me. Takes some kind of cruelty. To be mean as life. Mean and resilient to survive. More than just survive. Dominate. Prosper. Resound.

"We're talking now about our immortal soul. Specifically, Starlette's immortal soul. I never believed in that stuff until I saw myself on screen. Revelation. Here I was. But also there I was.

This was an interview broadcast to The Nation. Taped in advance. I was rising. Rising. Never take me down. Anyway: interview. Taped in advance. When it aired I took a car around The City and had the driver stop wherever a TV was playing that now famous late night interview with Starlette Nova that was everywhere except the temples and cathedrals and I must not have looked like me that night, or maybe I looked so much like me that it was impossible that I was me, that I could be there, live, in my kerchief and raincoat, my cigarette and sunglasses and man-killer perfume.

"I was in restaurants, bars, pool halls, dance clubs. One hour interview. We had to haul ass. But we made it to at least five places, and there I was in every one of them, everywhere, in every mind, the subject and object, alpha and omega, thought and emotion, holy cathode ghost and goddess.

"I was young then, that is, younger than the young I am now. My power was like that of a pop star or politician and my fame greater. I reached a wider audience. No one gives a fuck about a politician until after he's elected, after it's all over and he's won and he's the one you have to suffer. Old people don't pay attention to pop stars, nor do the middle-aged. But I had them all in the bosom of my bosom! The old, the middle-aged, the young, even the very young (don't think those little peckers don't get hard just cause their balls are bald!).

"The people must see me. They have no choice. They can pay to see me in movies and magazines, or they can look me up on the Network or wait for the rare interview on television."

Plantman finished his work. She extended her perfect hand.

"Thank you, Plantman."

"Just doing my job, ma'am," said Plantman, real cowboy-like.

"We've had the most interesting discussion, don't you think?"

"Scintillating," he said.

Her secretary, who had been sitting silently in a swivel chair the whole time, filing her nails and reading a murder mystery, rose, book-marked the novel with her nail file, and showed Plantman the door.

The Star

Career peak at the suitably virile age of forty-two. Past becoming, Don Coyote, The Star, had arrived.

The Star owned an apartment in The City. Plantman tended it year-round, entrusted with the key. When The Star was in The City, he and Plantman shared brandy, cigars, talk. As close to friendship as their relative stations would allow.

Epics of the Deep, Coyote's first serious role not blasting trouble with an automatic, or bedding tough, winsome, wise-cracking femme fatales, might garner awards, he mused.

"Doing this movie changed my life," said The Star, as Plantman plucked dead leaves from a Corn Plant. "I'm in love with the Missing Girl."

"Starlette Nova?"

"No, no. Of course not. She's just an actress. I'm talking about the real thing. Person. Whoever she is. Where ever she is, IF she still is. During the ocean scenes, the scene on the boat where we're supposed to talk to the fish–"

"Whales," said Plantman. "They're mammals."

"The Whales. When we were out there on the water I felt togetherness, conjunction. Not with Starlette Nova, through her. As if I were out there with The Missing Girl herself. It ran deep. Like I could understand her, though it wasn't her, only Starlette, and through her, The Missing Girl, I understood what they, those creatures, the mammals, were thinking, or feeling, or whatever they do."

"This is a reality for you. You believe The Missing Girl was with your character, The Mad Cetologist?" asked Plantman, genuinely curious.

"Starlette's character, her 'Missing Girl' was with the The Mad Cetologist. The Missing Girl was–

"–with you."

"Yes."

"And Starlette? Where was she?" asked Plantman.

"Nowhere, where she belongs."

The Missing Girl, alive, would be thirty-six. The Star's power and visibility were vast. Surely she would respond to his desire. Come to him.

"She must be dead," said The Star. "Why would she stay hidden all this time? What is it, ten years, fifteen years?"

"Twenty."

"Twenty years. Missing."

The Star drank, smoked. Plantman worked.

"I want to show you something," said The Star. "I'd prefer you do not speak of this. Though I assume you will. Maybe I want you to speak. Why else would I be showing this?"

They entered a study decorated with memorabilia of The Star's career. On a glass table, in a large glass cylinder filled with fluid, was a brain.

"It's genuine. The real thing. Human," said The Star, noticing Plantman's discerning squint.

"I was drunk at a party thrown by some hot-shot neurologist. Uptown. I opened a closet, thinking it was the bathroom, and there was this brain, floating in a bucket of water. Or that's what it looked like. Water. I grilled the good doctor about the gruesome thing. It was so ugly it was sexy. Like genitals. Totally turned me on.

"It was yanked from an unidentified cadaver years before. Might have been a woman, The Neurologist could not recall. Young. The person had been young. The Neurologist had used it as a prop to teach a course at The University Hospital, then forgot all about it. Fucking doctors. Imagine forgetting someone's brain!

"I offered to buy it. The Neurologist gave it to me for free, me being The Star and all that. He even threw in the glass cylinder and preservative fluid."

Puckered mound of sopping meat. Convoluted grayish-pink. Receptacle of mind. Once. Now? Plantman felt ill.

"Could this be the brain of The Missing Girl?" mused The Star. "Even if it isn't, this brain holds thoughts and memories, memories of me, Don Coyote, The Star, when I myself was young and stumbling through my first lead roles. Images of me inside. The Brain went to the movies, how could it not have? The Neurologist said it was young. The brain was perhaps one of the Missing Young. Why not The Missing Girl?"

The Star poured two glasses of whiskey, and handed one to Plantman, who drank quickly, then asked for another.

"You know, I sit and contemplate this brain for hours at a time. It teaches me," said The Star.

He handed Plantman his glass to refill. Plantman also poured another for himself.

"I'm different. Like I had been long ago. When I was young, hopeful Don Coyote, head full of dreams. It is possible that this is The Missing Girl. Not likely, but possible. What is a brain? What is a mind? If the mind is a physical thing, dependent entirely upon the physicality of the brain, then the thoughts and memories are still in there, just not animated. Information on a drive when the machine shuts down. No light, no spark, no access, but it's still all there. If this is The Missing Girl, then I possess her mind. If it is an anonymous brain, the brain of Nobody-In-Particular, then at the very least it harbors memories and thoughts of me. Perhaps fantasies of intimacy. Not the 'now' me, but the 'then' me of my early films. Awkward in my skin, but on my way to Big. Innocent, eager, bright-eyed Don Coyote. Working, working, striving toward becoming. Striving for the adulation of the world. . .

"Possessing this, this organ–that's all we are, aren't we? Our much vaunted intellects no more valuable than the flesh they're printed on–possessing this organ has introduced new possibilities into my life, a life where nothing was possible because everything had already been done. Imagine a life bereft of possibility, a life in which the Future offers nothing but the Past. The life of The Star. Do you understand?"

"It is not my business to understand," said Plantman.

"But do you understand?"

"I'm not The Star," said Plantman. "I've never experienced myself as Other."

Comikosis

Creators collaborated under ultra-violet light. Writers, artists, designers composed the mythic City, created the New Literature of The Nation. Comix, graphic novels, network animations.

Product distributed at news stands or by subscription. Big company, Comikosis. Started as tiny underground enterprise by the young A.T. Rotious, artist/author, of EPICS OF THE DEEP, the graphic novel basis of the movie. Big Media changed much of his work for the film. The original was more radical, less romantic. The Mad Cetologist never got The Missing Girl. She went out into The Nation, disappeared. Never to return. At least not to The Mad Cetologist, whose Viking Funeral she witnessed from ashore.

Rotious' newest creation was based on the further fictional adventures of The Missing Girl, who thanks to Big Media, was reappearing on The Nation's magazine covers wearing the face of Starlette Nova.

A.T. Rotious had been one of The Missing Young. He'd never met The Missing Girl. Imagination was enough to keep the flames alive. His muse, his reason to be. Comikosis. Most successful publisher of "underground" "graphic texts" in The Nation. His work, his vision.

The company began in his small downtown apartment ten years before. Now dozens of writers and artists worked in its luxury office suite in a mid-town tower of business. Revenues, advertisers, subscribers. A.T. Rotious, wealthy, hadn't lost his edge. The writers and artists too were well-paid, but inspired, or at the very least, anxious.

Big Media destroyed EPICS OF THE DEEP, according to Rotious. Dulled its edge. But the massive box office receipts meant more money for A.T. Rotious, still haunted by The Missing Girl. If comic books made fame of myth, "superheroes" of genuine archetypes, perhaps the truth of The Missing Girl would come to him as flesh. Real, unedited, living, blemished, redolent flesh.

The Comikosis office phone number and address marked the frontispiece of every publication for "just in case." Perhaps his money would translate into power to attract her. Unlike the dreaming kid of a decade ago, he now had the means to care for her when she arrived.

"Plantman!" cried A.T. Rotious as Plantman entered the office to tend Deifenbachia and Ficus. "You are the subject of a magnificent new Comikosis project: The Adventures of Plantman."

Plantman bowed, humbly honored.

"The first issue will deal with the adventures of Plantman in The City. Then, we will have Plantman go out to The Nation in search of The Missing Girl. The third issue of this trilogy will make history. Plantman will find The Missing Girl, and together they will tend the neglected indoor flora of The Nation. They will fall in love. Action, adventure, romance–we'll have it all. The two great icons of our time together in one issue, titled, appropriately, Plantman Meets The Missing Girl. I see millions of copies sold. I see a movie, bigger than EPICS OF THE DEEP. I see Plantman and The Missing Girl as angels of The Nation's green heaven. Together they are unstoppable," A.T. Rotious stood on his desk, arms raised triumphant.

"Thank you," Plantman answered. "I look forward to reading of my adventures."

"Plantman meets The Missing Girl. Fiction of the century. . . " said A.T. Rotious. "My best writers, illustrators and designers are working round the clock. Under my direct supervision, of course. Soon, Plantman. Soon your story will be told. In color, no less!"

Selling Kafka

One evening after work Plantman saw a man in a rumpled uniform of sorts bounced out of the Cave Guy bar. The man made a vain attempt to stand, then let his body crumble to the gutter. On closer inspection, Plantman was shocked to discover that this poor drunk was none other than The Manager of The CityPlex.

His uniform was soiled and unbuttoned, his hair uncombed. He was a mess.

"Manager, can this be you?"

"I've fallen to the very depths, Plantman. The very depths. Big Media has squashed me like a bug.

"I called in sick. I may never go back. Not while EPICS OF THE DEEP plays with that wretched Starlette Nova. That whore! She ruined my life. Absconded with beloved Kafka."

Plantman led The Manager to My Mommy's diner. He ordered coffee and fresh-baked muffins. The Manager told Plantman of his brief encounter with Starlette Nova several years before, when he was an aspiring screenwriter and she an up-and-coming, but still relatively unknown, star.

"I first crossed paths with Starlette Nova, during the shooting of her first movie, Down in The City," began The Manager. "I was only an usher then, and attending classes at The University Writing Program, Screenwriter's Division. I had spent four years writing a screenplay. I'd completed it at the Writing Program, writing and studying screen writing by day, and ushering at night.

"My screenplay concerned life in The City, specifically, Downtown. I captured the essence of my environs, and now waited to see it live on the big screen. The Screenwriter's Division provided a pool of agents to handle the screenplays of its graduates. I had a genuine agent working on my case.

"The coming of Big Media to the neighborhood was a bad omen for my script, a signal that Archimago had beaten me to the game. That I wrote truth while Archimago wrote lies was irrelevant. Archimago had the machinery of Big Media behind him.

"DOWN IN THE CITY was shot on location. Downtown at the Life Cafe and in the Square Park area a block away from my tenement apartment.

"It was during one of my daily perambulations with my dog, Kafka, that I first came head-to-head with Starlette. She was outside her trailer, surrounded by attendants and lesser actresses with lesser roles. They all fawned over Kafka. Starlette fawned most. They patted and petted him and stroked his ears. Kafka was not accustomed to strangers lavishing such overt affection in the street.

"Adorable," said one waif.

"He seems so sad," said another.

"All dogs are sad," said Starlette with a tone of authority that immediately separated her from the supporting players. "I had a lot of animals when I was growing up out West. Dogs are the saddest animals because they're closest to us. Rabbits, cats, birds–they don't give a fuck."

"She reached under Kafka and stroked his belly.

"'But I see what you mean about his face. It's not typical. He seems more than plain old dog-sad. It's like he's sad for people, not because of them. It's like he knows something.'

"'Yeah, that's it,' said one of the supporting nymphs. 'It's like he knows something.'

"Starlette was about to speak to me–perhaps ask me if I myself knew something–when a man with a headset showed up and politely told me to shove off.

"The Headset arranged the girls into a pattern. Cameras rolled, and led by Starlette, the girls walked majestically into the Life Cafe.

"Starlette developed a fondness for Kafka. During our next walk, as Kafka and I stepped over and around cables and wires strewn like snakes about the sidewalk, she emerged from her trailer with a gift she'd picked up–or had a toady pick up for her–from the Pet Store: a dried calf's foot, a wretched, smelly thing, but Kafka seemed content.

"'The Nation is going to see this film and wish that every place was here,' Starlette said.

"'I wouldn't be surprised,' I responded.

"They were planning footage in the Square Park dog run. Would I mind Kafka in a cameo?

"'They won't pay you anything,' said Starlette. But you'll be on camera. All you have to do is show up in the dog run and let Kafka do his thing.'

"'Kafka doesn't have a thing,'" I said.

"'Well, you know. His dog thing.'

"They'd already selected dogs for the shoot, but she could probably wrangle Kafka in.

"'Be there Saturday at seven a.m. Don't tell anyone. It's not like a casting call or anything. Most of the dogs will be professionals.'

"I showed up with Kafka at the dog run at our usual time, well before dawn. I lit a cigarette and set Kafka loose. He wandered aimlessly, confused, as he usually did immediately after he was unleashed, then settled down to his own calm-frantic compounded internal energy. He circled the dog run like a jogger, staying close to the fence, as if he needed the proximity of some kind of wall or geometrical enclosure to guide and soothe him. Like a room. Wherever Kafka was, he gave the appearance of being in the corner of a room.

"This was how it was done with us. Our little tradition. Every morning for four years I smoked my cigarette and watched the sun rise over Kafka. This was how I woke up to write the screenplay, taking mental notes, concocting situations; it's how I worked. My solitude. And Kafka's. We were happy. We were at peace.

"Big Media arrived. First the caterers setting up a folding table banquet of coffee and donuts, and fruit and juices for the fashionably health-concerned, then The Headsets staking out their turf, establishing clean authority in the cigarette-butt gum wrapper wilderness of The Square Park. Finally the film crew and cast members and professional dog-owners–managers? Handlers?–with their charges, and the distant, anxious Director. I leashed Kafka and went off to join the crowd.

"The crew offered me and the professional dog owners donuts and coffee. A Headset told us to act naturally, as if the cameras weren't rolling, and say the typical things folks say to dogs on a Saturday morning in The Square Park.

"The action would focus on a particular bench where Starlette's character and her boyfriend–a real Big Media take on the Downtown Artiste, complete with ponytail and Designer cigarettes, modeled, of course, after Archimago's vision of himself–are talking about god-knows-what poppycock the script stuffed down their throats and roll 'em.

"A problem emerged. Starlette didn't like the dog they chose for her.

"He's too. . . I don't know. Rambunctious? He's bumming me out. Get rid of him.'

"The dog's owner/manager protested vehemently. He'd still be paid; but his slobbering boxer, Virgil, wouldn't show up in the credits. Thus were Virgil's big-screen aspirations quashed: swiftly, ruthlessly, thoroughly; but not without a smile.

"'Sorry, old man," said The Headset who led the rejected dog and owner back into the mob.

"'I want Kafka,' Starlette said.

"'Who?'

"'That one,' she pointed to Kafka, who paced nervously behind me. The proximity of other dogs, many of them quite large, unsettled him.

"'But he's non-union,' said The Headset.

"'Fuck the union. He's a dog. I want him for the shoot.'

"The Director conferred with his cabal of Headsets and Walkie-talkies. They eyed Kafka, who seized the moment for a long, pulsating piss (and who wouldn't pee under such scrutiny?)

"'Alright,' sighed The Director. Set him up.'

"My dog was now a character in Archimago's fiction. Where would it end?

"So Kafka scored his first big role. In the scene, Archimago's scene, Starlette stroked him for comfort while she and her no-good writer boyfriend shared an anguished, existential moment. At the director's signal she let go of the leash and Kafka broke into a brisk, unKafka-like run, which was preserved on film for the amusement and posterity of The Nation.

"He was a natural.

"'What did I tell you guys? Did I tell you this was The Dog?' the Starlette called out to one of The Headsets.

"'He's it," said The Headset. Look at that face. There's pain in that face. Better than pain. Anomie. Look at him. He actually looks like he's depressed. A depressive dog!'

"The Director, smoking in the distance, whispered instructions into the pink ear of a Walkie-talkie. They were joined by another Walkie-talkie, and another. They looked at Kafka. But with their dark sunglasses and fixed mandibles and features set expressionless in doughy flesh it was difficult to discern, or even imagine, what they were thinking. The Director licked his lips.

"I thought: my dog is accomplice to Archimago's rocket-like ascent.

"Time to go. I took the leash from Starlette and snapped it onto Kafka's collar. My hands trembled. The crew packed equipment–metal tripods, light-stands, and other insect-like machine parts–into the trucks. A hand touched my back. I whipped around, ready to fight, or more probably, flee.

"That evening the Starlette called me at home.

"'He's everything we could have hoped for in an animal. His laid-back energy, his almost. . . doomed expression. Like he's thinking something, some deep dog thought, and you'll always wonder what it is, and you'll go mad mad mad insane because you'll never, ever know. He's just what my character, what the show was missing all along: a living metaphor. Kafka's what Down in The City is about. . . This is new territory. Kafka's injecting a new energy into the film–or sucking it out. Whatever. Everyone, even The Director, is excited about the possibilities: hip downtown bartender/aspiring actress on her own in The City. She meets all these freaky people every day, she has relationships, she gets involved in all sorts of crap, but there's no one she can really talk to. She's independent. But lonely. Anyway, all her friends are fucked up, or at least as fucked up as she is. But she can talk to her dog about her problems. He listens, or appears to listen–that's Kafka's genius, he actually looks like he's thinking something, like he's listening to you and understands. He's like the only male who really knows her. She has all this trouble with her crazy boyfriend and all that, but when she comes home to Kafka, she's okay. . . . When me and The Actor who plays my boyfriend got into some serious dialogue, Kafka responded, like he was part of the conversation, giving signals, telling me the relationship was trouble. Then when I let go of the leash and he runs off like that, it's like he's saying "Go. Get away from this creep. Be free." The audience is going to eat it up. I mean, WE almost believed it.'

"I phoned The Agent provided by the Writing School to tell him the big news.

"'Great," he said. 'Tremendous opportunity. Use the dog to make contacts. Shmooz these people. I know it's tempting to get jealous of the star treatment, but–'

"'–jealous? Of my own dog? It's Archimago who's driving me

insane. My dog is a raisin in his pudding.'

"'Archimago? Who the hell's Archimago?'

"'The guy who writes everything,' I sighed.

"'Never heard of him,' said the Agent. 'Listen to me. Once we get your screenplay sold, it'll be you they're after, not the dog. Your name will be a household word long after the name "Kafka" is forgotten.'

"The following Monday a Headset, with a lawyer at his side, presented me with a contract at the Life Cafe.

"'You need the dog's signature?' I asked.

"'That won't be necessary at this time,' the lawyer said, dry as a bone.

"However, he assured me, if there was any further paperwork to be done in the future, he'd let me know.

"My sinecure position as Kafka's 'caretaker and trainer' entitled me to hang around during the shoots, scarf down free food, walk Kafka during breaks, and generally see what it was like to leech off of a Big Media production.

"So began my daylight job of chaperoning Kafka to his shoots. I loitered with professional nonchalance, pretending to read my thick, black-spined paperbacks. During breaks I took Starlette on informal tours of the Square Park area. She wanted to get into the 'mindset' of her character, 'flesh out' the hackneyed heroine it was her tiresome lot to play.

"We walked Kafka–she held the leash–around the neighborhood, made the usual rounds of thrift-shops, sex shops, bodegas, boutiques, used book and record stores, et al.

"Once, we passed The CityPlex, and both stopped cold, lost in our own insatiable vanities.

"'Have you ever seen me before?' she asked. 'I mean before Down in The City.'

"'Yes.'

"'Where?'

"'That ad campaign.'

"'Which ad campaign? That's all I've done in my life is ad campaigns.'

"'The one with the soda bottle. The soda thing.'

"'Pistol Pop. I'm in a thong bikini, sipping a long-neck bottle–blowing it, really–atop a snow capped mountain. "Wouldn't you rather cool off with an icy Pistol Pop?"'

"'Yeah, that's it. You garnished the bus stops and subway stations all last Summer.'

"'I was a model, then. Now I'm an actress. I can say things on my own now. Without cartoon bubbles.'

"She dropped her cigarette into the bottle of mineral water she'd been sipping and passed it on to me.

"'The People forget you like you're nothing,' she said. 'You have to nail yourself into their skulls. All these people out today, they don't recognize me–yet. Or maybe they've seen me but forgot me. Not totally. I'm in their memories like last year's music. This time next year I won't be able to walk down this street. There'd be a mob scene. I should enjoy them while they last, these anonymous afternoons. . .'

"She stared down the avenue at the short, sweaty line before the movie theater, at the kids, bums, couples, geezers yammering in their various native tongues outside bodegas, nervous old women pushing shopping carts, workers guarding the fruits and vegetables of their employers, then back at me, confused. It must have dawned on her with some suddenness that I was not, in this context, among the masses on the street, but a person with a life and a dog who was spending this moment with her on the street across from The CityPlex, planet earth.

"The weekend after the shooting ended Starlette asked me out for dinner and drinks. I called in sick at The CityPlex, assuming that, having procured Kafka, part of my remuneration would be a night in bed with Starlette, though it wasn't stated explicitly in the contract.

"We went–where else?–to Life. She wanted to see what it was like during off-camera hours.

"At Life, among the usual clientèle of artistes, grad-students, wannabe musicians, painters, poets, and computer freaks, we ordered veggie burgers and, for me, beer, white wine for her. I was already royally shit-faced, having quaffed vodka and wine coolers at the apartment. I found it difficult to be alone in the apartment with Kafka, of late. It wasn't Archimago who was my nemesis in the Looking Glass world of Big Media, it was my dog.

"Starlet chain-smoked between gulps of beer and nibbles of burger. She said she did it to keep thin. She finished four glasses of wine and the equivalent of about three human-sized bites of burger and all the lettuce and been sprouts on her plate. We ordered more drinks.

"Starlette picked up the tab and led me outside. She suggested we go to my apartment. As soon as I opened the door she headed straight for the dog.

"'Kafka-baby. Kafka, my star. Did you miss me, lover?'

"In the morning, as we lay nude in bed, sharing a cigarette, like in the movies, she gave me the pitch, straight from the mouth of Big Media.

"'I want Kafka.'

"'What?'

"Her rap was long and staccato; she jumped from point to point, but never strayed far from her original thesis, not unlike a young girl begging her parents for a pony. What I heard come out of her pretty mouth was unpunctuated, frenetic, ruthless, untranslatable. She promised to take my screenplay back with her to Movieland. She said she'd show it to The Director and various other people of influence. She told me to think about the realities of my life. She dressed. I led her to the door.

"One minute I was playing around with Kafka, the ol' master-dog roughhousing, the next I was strangling him. I looked deep into his buggy, brown dog eyes and began to wring his neck.

"His legs waved like sea anemones as he tried to pull free. He whimpered pathetically. When I loosened my grip, he yelped, broke away, and hid under my desk.

"'This is crazy.' I said out loud.

"He didn't disagree. I felt terrible. I went up to the roof, alone, to smoke and think. I suppose he needed his personal space too.

"When I returned he was the same old Kafka. He greeted me at the door, licked my hand, and when the master-dog formalities concluded, returned to the futon to pant and drool. I gave him a cookie.

"Starlet's limo pulled up just before dawn. I was alone in the dark park with Kafka and the bums. She offered me her cheek and a promise from the coffers of Big Media. I handed her a copy of my script.

"It surprised me how obediently Kafka followed her into the car, how calm and happy he appeared, even after the chauffeur slammed the door. Then again, he'd spent the whole summer pretending to be this woman's fictional dog; he may have been a bit confused. Then again, again, he's only a dog: how much further to him is Big Media than around the block?

"Sad moment. But really what kind of relationship can you have with a creature with whom you share your living space for five years but never a word? What kind of consciousness could Kafka have? Sure he played the loyal companion for the guy that fed him, but this was his BIG BREAK. How did I know he didn't, in some freaky canine way, hate and resent me–the way I, to my shame, hated and resented sponging off his acting career all Summer–but figured it was the best he could get until something better came along? How did I know he didn't hate my guts really, and were it not for his agoraphobia and general nervous condition, would have cut out as soon as he had the chance? Well now Big Media was giving him his chance. He'd get to bury his snout nightly in the fragrant lap of Starlette Nova.

"My last real-life image of Kafka was his panting face in the lighted interior of the limousine. The light went out and they drove off.

"The night of the much-hyped debut of Down in The City, I ushered at The CityPlex. After the seating was done, I stood at the door of one of the theaterettes and watched.

"The screen flashed a high angle establishing shot of the Square Park. Then the camera, probably mounted on a motorcycle, took us through the streets at manic speed. Everything familiar became charged and skewed. Credits whizzed by. Among them, 'Kafka'.

"I watched what I'd already seen: the scenes Big Media's machines and personnel had manufactured, live, during the Summer. I watched Archimago's drama real and colorful on screen and pulsating with pop music.

"We, The People, the moviegoers, watched Life turn mythical, a place of excitement and happening and hip talk–the place to be in The Nation, the place to which it was impossible to go. . .

"Finally Kafka's first big moment in the dog run: Starlette and her lover on the park bench talking about whether they're ready for a commitment or some such nonsense but I stopped listening I just watched Kafka strain at the leash until–on cue, I remembered that cue from the Summer, The Director waving his arms–Starlette let go and Kafka ran wild before The Nation."

"Did Starlette ever show anyone your script?" asked Plantman.

"Do you think I'd be Manager of The CityPlex and not out in The Nation, writing scripts for Big Media, if she had?"

They sat in silence. The Manager of the CitiPlex molded his muffin into animal shapes.

"Who is 'Archimago,'" Plantman asked.

The Manager paused from his raisin-bran sculpture and wiped his hands on a napkin.

"Any writer in the world who is not me," he said.

XV
Tree of Knowledge Incorporated

The gold peak of the hundred-and-something-floor TKI obelisk stood five stories–base shaft tip. Office and living quarters of the Heir. TKI Technologies; TKI Systems Subsidiaries; TKI Pharmaceuticals; TKI Chemicals; TKI DDT; TKI Desktop Operating Systems; TKI PYRAMID Database. Root OS of Empire. Kit 'n caboodle. TKI Tower widest tallest hive of business in The City.

Plantman was summoned to work the indoor garden.

The Heir was forty. Nervous. So much beneath. Lawyers, advisors, accountants, managers, Vice-Presidents, researchers, workers, investors. The Business, from The Heir's vantage, ran itself. Childlike, The Heir, forty-year-old kid. Fascinated, enchanted: power, technology. His companies. His Empire. The Heir on top of all.

Preservation Project years in ferment. The Heir's great-grandfather, grandfather, father, uncle, founders the TKI Empire, frozen after death, shrunken preserved, to prove the technology ready. More than ready: now.

Indian Museum the beginning. Marketed Preservation to The Nation. Citizens must part with dearly beloved no more. Compressed preserved indefinite. Showpieces for home. Heirlooms, possessions, dolls. Family. Family. Family.

"Party!" commanded The Heir.

Gawky, bespectacled Pharaoh.

Huge bare ballroom. White walls, white floor, white ceiling. Rotating projectors. The Heir signaled. Darkness entered, obedient, to dance with light, transforming the naked ballroom to a colorful, crowded banquet. Virtual life. Celebrity holograms. Three-dimensional, electric ghosts, smoked, drank, exchanged ironic chatter with dry laughter. 3D motion graphics and design. Virtual cocktails in the bone-white ball-room, which was now bone-white no more, but a symphony of the millions of colors and gradients TKI Technologies had managed to synthesize from half a dozen dull, primary tones sucked out of the raw, earthy, antiquated rainbow.

"Go ahead, mingle," The Heir commanded.

It occurred to Plantman that that was indeed the only thing for him to do, mingle. He had arrived to a bare white ballroom and was now in the midst of rare, exotic, beautiful plants that not only didn't fall under the ownership of Topiary Techniques, but of any organic entity at all. As Horticultural Technician he was not responsible for light projections of The Heir's machine, though TKI was indeed a client of Topiary Techniques with replaceable units–somewhere–on the premises of The TKI Obelisk.

So Plantman mingled. Long dead celebrities indulged in pleasant banter, drank phantom champagne, smoked spectral cigarettes. Grand old time.

Introductions. Hands proffered. Plantman reached. Grasped nothing.

The tuxedoed "musicians" played Big Band Swing.

Plantman recognized a woman. Young. Difficult to reach. He could have sliced through the crowd. The famous "guests" were only, after all, light. Illusions. But protocol inhibited, constrained. Cleaving a crowd of even illusory celebrities would be considered rude, uppity, disrespectful.

Phantoms possess consciousness? Or one program spawning and directing scores of "character" threads on a single TKI system? Surely The Heir would know? No. He knew so little of the spidery empire below.

Close enough at last, Plantman introduced himself to The Missing Girl, for it was she. Numinous facsimile. Plain white frock, no shoes. . . like the bride in the ad for Earn Cologne. Introduced herself as The Missing Girl.

"How can you be The Missing Girl if you're here? You're no longer Missing then, are you?" he asked.

"That's the kind of question asked by people with no manners. Rude people who don't go out much, especially not to parties, because no one would invite them. Is that the problem? You've never been invited to a party?"

"Not like this one, no."

But he had. The Network. The Castle. Souls of icons. Real people behind computers, while this party was administered by one machine. No purpose but amusement of The Heir.

"I am The Missing Girl so far as knowledge of The Missing Girl exists. Just data in the party machine. 'Blips on chips.' Why delve into my ME?"

"Just curious. Like everyone else in The Nation."

"You're Plantman. You should know better. There's nothing I can say that you can't look up and find on PYRAMID."

"Then why are you here? In diaphanous flesh, so to speak?"

"A party is its atmosphere. You can't experience me in my wholeness and beauty scouring PYRAMID, squinting at a screen. Here, I'm projected in three dimensions."

"You've disappointed. I'm depressed. I thought you were really her. Here. Possibly with something new to say," said Plantman.

"I'm not here for your enjoyment, but The Heir's. He's lonely at the top. When he does have guests, and entertains them with celebrity-packed parties such as this, most of them are grateful."

"Of course they're grateful. They're projections of The Heir's machine. They're not guests, they're home movies. I'm neither. I'm here to work."

"Shhhh. The Heir must entertain."

Hush the muffled crowd. All eyes dead and living focused center-room, where The Heir stood solemnly in shirt-sleeves. A flesh-blood servant balanced a tray of drinks. The Heir downed one after another. A second flesh-blood servant held a large pyramidal case. The Heir announced he'd entertain. A special trick prepared for his guests' enlightenment and clean, salubrious thrills.

The heir "warmed up:" stretching, breathing, flexing. The Second Servant opened the case, removed the shrunken, preserved corpse of The Heir's great-grandfather, founder of TKI, and passed it to The Heir. Next, remains of The Heir's grandfather, father, uncle. Imperious somber in tiny suits. The Heir held his ancestors in his fists. The Phantom band struck up a carnival tune. The Heir juggled his uncle's, father's, father's father's, and father's father's father's shrunken remains to the wonder and amusement of nearly 100 electric ghosts. Dexterity. Élan. His celebrity guests watched, rapt. Plantman, despite his from-the-gut distaste for The Heir, was impressed that such an apparently witless man-child could possess the drive, concentration and talent to perfect such skill.

The Heir performed until the music stopped. Sweating, he bowed. Guests, the pseudo-Missing Girl, even Plantman erupted in hoots, cheers, whistles and applause. Like painted figures on the Li'l Box of Love.

The adulation ceased at the push of a button. The party vanished, guests, musicians and all. Naked light again. Bright white empty. Alone in the giant hall: Plantman, The Heir, his Servants.

The Servants wrapped The Heir's ancestors in tissue paper and returned them carefully to the red velvet floor of the miniature pyramid. The Heir offered Plantman strong drink.

"Well?" asked The Heir. "Did you enjoy?"

XVI.
The Death

Uncle Joe died. Friends, Relatives, "Strangers," came to mourn. Hundreds.

I served as pallbearer with Father, Brother-in-Law, "Relatives" barely known ("Strangers"). Metallic blue coffin. Like a shiny new car. Shame to bury such sleek merchandise. God-man Rep in vestments hoarsed his generic eulogy. Fill-in-blanks. Harped successes of Uncle Joe: Detective Novel, THE MISSING POMEGRANATE; twenty years "thought provoking" columnist for defunct radical journal "En Garde." No mention of moments spent and lost. Nothing "missing" known.

"Uncle Joe was an independent man," I delivered "family" eulogy. "Different from you and me. He left impressions."

"That was a good thing you said," said Father. "He lived a long full life. So what if he didn't have kids? He'll be remembered. All these mourners. Who would have known? I thought he was a lonely man. Poor old Uncle Joe."

Necropolis stones like dominoes stretched far as eye could see. Names. Names. Lived lives. Ended ends. Three categories of dead: forgotten, long forgotten, so forgotten as if never been.

The Forgotten shared details. Groggy mornings, work days, night snacks; television, radio, whatever devices backgrounded living at such time that living was done: entertainment; street steps into shit or gum; taste sex smell sex, consequence.

Sex Necropolis consequence. Sex. Sex.

Coffin lowered down, down. Head stone: “Here Joe Lies In Truth.”

Someone burying another, one day, will see Joe’s stone and imagine the author of THE MISSING POMEGRANATE”; Radical; Columnist; Gambler. Unofficial, unacknowledged mentor to The Missing Young, who will themselves be old or dead when new young living gaze upon Joe’s faded stone.

XVII.
The Accused

The Sentinel

Inside The City Government Complex (CGC), The Accused languished in his vault. His Last Request: to see his beloved African Violet, Rose, tended by Plantman.

This request created a host of difficulties. Officials were bound to honor the request, but none would allow Plantman to enter the CGC without tending their plants too. Long day ahead.

Plantman arrived early, before protesters gathered for and against the execution of the Accused. Rhetoric, megaphones, home-made signs.

Officials deep within the building. A lone Sentinel carrying a law book and rifle marched up and down the marble steps leading to the CGC. Member of Universal Security (US), the elite security force, a private company hired to protect High Officials, The Courts, The Senate, The Mayor, and other Important Persons (IPs) and Institutions of The City and The Nation.

Plantman brought the guard coffee and lit his cigarette.

The Sentinel sat on a stone step, leaned his automatic rifle on a pillar.

“I was a guard once. At school. The University,” Plantman said. “University Security Service. I stood sentinel over a think tank. Watching the thinkers. No intruders really. Just watching the thinkers. Truly, what would they steal at a think tank, concepts?”

Plantman nodded toward The Sentinel’s book.

“I got a lot of homework done.”

The Sentinel worked through school guarding arbiters of death against unruly activists. The murder trial lent purpose to his pay. No real reading on the job as in days past, but this was better, wasn’t it? Life experience. Something to look back on and reflect. The activists were harmless enough. But he was told The CGC was under threat of terrorist attack.

He took target practice twice a week to hear his gun blast truth at paper saboteurs. Dauntingly reliable, our young Sentinel. Stalwart, obedient, faithful.

The Sentinel smoked and imbibed mild stimulants. He answered Plantman’s questions with professional courtesy.

“Security is the bedrock of Government,” said The Sentinel. “Why have government if not to make people secure? It’s all written down in The City Charter and signed and double-signed by witnesses and lawyers. You can’t argue with that. Gotta accept it. I don’t think about the politics involved or the activists, who probably have families somewhere. I’ll shoot them down like ducks in a pond if I have to. It's my job. . . ."

"What's good for the duck is good for the lawyer," said Plantman.

Security on everyone's mind. Gotta be secure. The "sec" in security was the hard syllable of "secret." Secrets that transpire in the buildings of the CGC must be secure. True, We the People of The City and The Nation have our rights to the secrets, but we also have need of security and protection. The CGC must be protected. Therefore, We the People must be secured from the secrets that might break our hearts. We The People. Break our Citizen hearts.

Prosecutors and other Government Officials were privy to the secrets. It is the duty of U.S. Sentinels, the best in the business, to protect secrets haunting the CGC, yet unless they rise to the level of Prosecutor or Government Official, The Sentinels must not, cannot know the secrets they were hired to defend.

Don't they get curious? A teensy bit nosey? Didn't they occasionally–or maybe quite often–dream of tearing open Security Sealed envelopes, rifling files, cracking databases to actually learn something? Or was it better not to know? Not to discover the horrors that are presumed every Citizen's lot?

The Sentinel studied Law. He hoped to rise to the position of Prosecutor or Official. Then he would know what's what. Yeah, he's curious, but biding his time. The trial contains no information that he won't eventually know in time. Whether he knew now, or years later, as an Official, scanning the Database, was of little concern to The Sentinel.

Details of the murderer, the murder, did not affect him, or anyone, but the (accused) murderer, the murdered and the attorneys hired by The City to represent them. If The City's electric power shut down tomorrow, it would affect his work and studies. Whether The Accused was to be executed tomorrow, next week, or not at all, made no difference in the life of The Sentinel. He was a patient man. He had been patient in The Army, waiting for school; now he is patient in school, waiting for the day when he'll be privy to the secrets of The City.

Not an accident he chose to work in security, particularly for US Sentinels, the elite firm that provided security for The CGC. His military training was but one factor in his decision to become a Sentinel. Pious devotion to the secrets and a future as a Prosecutor were prime motivations. One day he would read the secrets; therefore, it was in his interest to make certain they were secure. How could he sleep without having a hand in this? Trust OTHERS to protect his secrets?

He couldn't be a Sentinel forever. When he left The University he would have to serve a Firm, or one of The Officials themselves. Now that he still had time, he used it constructively to protect the secrets. One day it might behoove some other young man to protect the secrets while The Sentinel, no longer a Sentinel, but a Prosecutor, pondered them day and night in service to The City, The Nation and his own curiosity.

The Defense Attorney

Plantman was welcomed to the building by a sharply dressed Official of the CGC.

"Welcome to The City Government Complex," said The Official. "Important personages wish to avail themselves of your renowned horticultural techniques before you undertake the odious task of attending that miserable little. . . specimen of Accused."

"You know secrets of The City?" asked Plantman.

"What secrets?" answered the Official.

First task to serve the lowest of all CGC officials: The Defense Attorney. Office clutter of papers, books, ashtrays overflowing. Dying Ivy lined the windowsill. The Defense Attorney drunk on cheap liquor.

"Media. Media. You make matters worse. Worse than you can imagine," said The Defense Attorney. "You pick 'alleged facts' here, 'alleged facts' there, sew them into a story. Don't know meaning of the words 'patience,' 'dignity,' 'wisdom.'"

Quite drunk, raving drunk; cheap suit soiled, ill-fitting. Plantman expended much time explaining that he, Plantman, had no association with Big Media. Finally, The City's most revered horticultural technician's notoriously phlegmatic temper blew.

"You're a caricature. Look at you," said Plantman. "You're what one might expect from a Big Media movie about a case like this. No wonder Big Media hounds you."

"You don't know. My role as Defense Attorney. I must be rumpled and I must come cheap. The City provides people like me for Defendants. Their sly way of telling the poor wretches they are doomed. That I am all that comes between a man's life and The City's wrath is indeed disturbing. It drives me to drink. The System is stacked higher than The TKI Obelisk with rickety stories, and I'm one of them. Perhaps I'm noble. Perhaps the PYRAMID itself is upside down."

"Your defense was obscene," said Plantman. "You incensed the prosecutors to excessive action. You made them furious. Why?"

"'Why,'" you ask. "'Why?' What to do? The Accused wanted me to prove. . . The only way. Convince the court of the validity of his actions and they might acquit. We pleaded for leniency. More than leniency. Understanding. Final appeal. No 'two weeks from now' two weeks from now for The Accused."

"Do you care whether The Accused lives or dies?" asked Plantman.

"Irrelevant. This is my career. How many losses can a man survive? That's their game. Drive Defense Attorneys insane. Weed out the bad ones. We're all bad ones. They're looking for the best of the bad, the ones who can outfox them. Once a Defense Attorney wins, which is rare, they make him a Prosecutor. They all, those Prosecutors, had to go through this. You can't become a Prosecutor unless you've won a case as Defense. The odds are stacked heavily against Defense. Few win. Only the cagiest, most deceitful, most obsessed prove themselves 'material' for Prosecution duty.

"I could linger in Defense forever. Don't think a future in corporate law means you step out of The Law School to work one of The City's corporations. First, unless you were born of wealth, payment for your education, which translates to at least three years service in Defense. Win a case at any time, the world is yours. You don't win a case within three years, you can auction yourself on the open market.

"They examine your record. See if, though you're not top, top notch, or even top notch, you might be just regular notch. Good enough to preside over contracts, research lawsuits, do their paperwork. How hard did you work to win for the accused? They scrutinize the nuance and oratory of your cases. If you did something interesting, say, conducted a defense with subtlety and wit, there's a chance you can go on to make real money. I've been a Defense Attorney for six years. Going on my third tour of duty. I might be here forever. Of course, if you're a Prosecutor, the world is yours. You can leave at any time to take one of the top corporate cushion spots, or run for Judge, or try for public office. 'Serve' the people of The City in a high profile position. . . "

Plantman doctored the Defense Attorney's pathetic Ivy.

"A Defense Attorney has no privileged access to The Pyramid 2.0 Database," the beleaguered man went on. "He can scan the stacks of law books, or tap into the public Pyramid databases, but he never sees the whole picture. His case is relegated to human experience and the 'facts' at hand. That is, whatever exculpatory information he can scrape together. But the Prosecutors and their numerous Officials, not to mention the Judges, have full access to Pyramid. They know what you're doing, every move you make, all the information they care to call up on anyone and everyone involved with your case.

"Tell me what genius can win against such odds? I'm beginning to believe I'll be a Defense Attorney forever. Though the high profile nature of this case, my rugged, thorough defense of The Accused, might possibly lead to a position in the private sector. Possibly."

The Defense Attorney stepped briefly from drunkenness. Wild-eyed, impassioned.

"I'm hooked. Obsessed. I cannot leave until I win. Me versus Pyramid and the golden boy Prosecutors and toady Officials with privileged access. To win a case would be a vindication, a triumph few outside The Law could understand. I might even remain a Defense Attorney of my own accord! Show them all. Beat the Pyramid a second time, a third. Exist to be a thorn in their blubbery, collective side. They'll beg me to leave. Maybe offer me a Judgeship. I'll refuse. 'A Defense Attorney I began,' I'll say, 'a Defense Attorney I'll remain.' Fuck Pyramid and all who run their grubby privileged algorithms through its data."

The Defense Attorney was less distasteful than Plantman had previously assumed. Noble, in whatever sense the word can apply to such circumstances. No starry eyed idealist faker pretending love of law and justice. Just a fighter who wanted to fight, armed with the sling of his own will and stubbornness, against the Goliath Law and its awesome armory of data. Man versus The City Law Machine (and the Pyramid Database that kept it on top of all things always).

Nobody can beat The Law, except a cunning few. But if he beat it, The Defense Attorney would spurn rewards. Stay drunk and rumpled, his only reward the ecstasy of triumph.

Proving himself the better man, the stronger man, the human man. Seen this way, his seemingly ludicrous defense based on "natural selection" not only made sense, regarding the peculiar case of The Accused, but described the Defense Attorney's own battle with The Law itself.

The Prosecutor

Plantman, working abundant foliage in the Office of the Prosecutor, suffered the Prosecutor's draft oration, which the Prosecutor practiced, without the least self-consciousness or awareness of Plantman's presence–or so it seemed–pacing back and forth before his closet mirror.

"I have data," said the Prosecutor. "I've molded this case with my own hands. Cut and dried. CUT. And. DRIED. I can't see the problem. I don't UNDERSTAND what we're waiting for. The Accused should have fried months ago. Enough, enough, I say. No more appeals! Another case of laws obstructing The Law. This 'man,' so called, killed his parents. In their home. Under the ruse of bringing them sustenance.

"He is a married man with children of his own. What message might his actions bring to The Young? What monsters will they grow to be if this man is not punished, if he is allowed to do ten, fifteen years time, then know freedom to see the weddings and graduations of his own children? This 'man,' the murderer of their grandparents. It is indeed a mad world, but not a lawless one, yet.

"What? he has a reason, a theory, JUSTIFICATION for his

heinous deeds? Why don't we abandon The Law completely, let everyone 'reason' for themselves? A tidy bit of anarchy that would be! My duty is to translate the facts into conviction and penalty. Reasons, theories, excuses from the mouths of The Accused fall upon deaf ears in this Court. You've probably spoken to some low-level official about data and Pyramid and what not. This is no longer mere data; this is my blood. The information has been fully digested. I have written my statement. Drafted my presentation. Loose bits, extraneous bytes, what have you, have merged into a coherent theme under The Law. All specifics are now general. It is whole. It fits. It is conviction. In unity there is The Law. This case is not about The Accused per se, but THE LAW DEFILED.

"Not Prosecution versus Defense; but the durability of The Law itself.

"The actions of The Accused as individual are irrelevant in and of themselves; however, they attain great relevance under light of The Law. Words, ideas, conjectures–all become meaningless in lieu of action, and meaningful only in that they have profaned The Law. If there were no Law, The Accused could very well murder his parents and get on with life. He could murder me or you or whomever he pleased.

"Because of The Law, he can murder no one without paying with his own life. Sound economics indeed. No something for nothing. No free lunch.

"Some will do anything to defy The Law. Flee. Lie. Even die in their attempt to flout The Law. Leaving debts, for instance, or killing citizens and then themselves before The City can put them to death legally. Dying to escape The Law. Mocking The

Law, mocking The City and its Citizens, and mocking ones who, like myself, defend and perpetuate The Law. The City gives me power over information so that I may obtain the knowledge to enforce The Law. The price of this privilege is my absolute fidelity to Justice, my utmost determination to keep her pristine underpants unsoiled."

The prosecutor digested ambiguous data into meaningful prosecutions for The City.

"Beautiful Law. Eternal Fiction," the Prosecutor said. "Like buildings and cars and The City herself. Creations born in the brain, birthed on paper, matured in steel and concrete. Admire The City, the fertile imaginations of her creators. Citizen Imaginations. The spirit of The Law courses through the veins and arteries of us all. Sound language constructed our collective tale, this Epic of The City. Break her and you break our universal dream. Like injecting non-sequiturs and coarse usage into a masterful novel. Breaking the linear accretion of small pleasures that is narrative."

The prosecutor would never let barbarians storm The City.

"The murderer will not interrupt our dream of The City Without End. We will not submit to his nightmare of chaos and despair."

The Lobbyist

As Plantman waited in the lobby for a CGC Official to lead him to his next task, he was approached by a Lobbyist pitching Dereliction Deterrent Technologies (DDT), a subsidiary of Tree of Knowledge Incorporated (TKI).

The Lobbyist pitched the products of DDT to The Lawmakers, who would have to choose a method of execution concomitant with the values of The City.

The Lobbyist spoke in earnest, as if Plantman were a Lawmaker himself.

"DDT has founded itself on termination technologies of the highest order," said The Lobbyist. "Cities across The Nation are using its methodologies to eliminate viral deviance in a quick, non-threatening, humane sequence."

DDT sponsored a program at Universities across The Nation called Termination Concepts (TC). TC encouraged Young Citizens (YC) to enter the debate as to how to eliminate Viral Deviance (VD) and other scourges that plagued The Nation (1N) and its Cities.

Two hallmark products of DDT were the Violent Offender Interruption Device (VOID) and Violent Anti-social Personnel Elimination Resource (VAPER).

"This is a serious and society-minded business," said The Lobbyist. "Our welfare is at stake. The greatest minds in termination technology work with DDT for the improvement of our Nation's Cities. Serious business, indeed."

Such was the technology that VAPER could eliminate a societal bug with one quick spray to the face (each can itself was guaranteed 100 or more executions, depending on the size and resilience of the Derelict, or The City received its money back) that would neutralize a Viral Deviant (VD) in a matter of seconds, while VOID used cutting edge radiation technologies to eliminate a selected VD with one millisecond blast, bursting all vessels in the manner of nuclear fallout, but leaving the body clean in its garb (rubber or latex suits were the suggested outerwear–knee-length latex dresses for females–to humanize the VD in the eyes of the squeamish observer while prohibiting the "splash effect" of air-borne particles, fluids and fleshy matter occasionally observed during radiation based terminations), veiling whatever residual ugliness such a death, one of the quickest, most humane deaths in termination technology's repertoire, might reveal. No fainting witnesses, no gory photographs.

"A nylon mask to cover the face and polyurethane plugs to prevent blood escaping from eyes nose mouth, and voilà, a clean, quick, humane termination!" crowed The Lobbyist.

The Lobbyist's mission was twofold. One, to promote the various termination technologies devised by DDT, and, two, to lobby for the televising of executions/terminations.

The Lobbyist said that large data sectors in The National Information Pyramid (NIP) suggested low crime rates in cities that have made televised executions a regular feature of daily programming.

Plantman could not help but remark that this amounted to nothing less than free television advertisement for DDT.

"Yes, but DDT benefits everyone," said The Lobbyist. "It exists for the betterment of society, so what could be wrong with advertising its good works? It would be more of a public service announcement than strict advertising for DDT."

"But DDT already has a monopoly on termination technologies Nation-wide," said Plantman.

"Can we help it if we're the best? In a matter as serious as termination technology, society can afford nothing less than the best, for the safety of its inhabitants and the moral instruction of its young. What's good for DDT. . . "

A thriving, safe city is a satisfied customer. DDT provided the ultimate VD solutions, according to The Lobbyist. Results were uploaded daily to NIP.

"This includes technical research as well as statistical results, opinion polls and more," boasted The Lobbyist. "NIP data, as well as other educational information are available directly from DDT's site on The Network. As a government contractor for various major cities, DDT has a high privilege level on NIP and is permitted to share an abundance of data with anyone who takes the time to examine the site, which includes real time videos of some of DDT's most successful products in action. DDT works closely with city administrators to ensure quality terminations. There have been few botched terminations, less than one-percent of all VD's processed across The Nation, and these have been given the full attention of DDT's quality control specialists.

"A city is like a tree. It must grow in fertile soil, under a vibrant sun. Clean, purifying water must nourish it, and fertilizer. But fungus, insects, viruses, must be destroyed immediately, lest they overcome the roots and eat into the tree, causing corruption of the leaves, rotting of the branches, and destruction of the mighty organism itself. It only takes one germ to spread a plague; it only takes one bug to spark an infestation."

"So you're The Nation's exterminators," said Plantman.

"We are The Nation's gardeners," corrected The Lobbyist.

The Senator

Lunch break. Plantman attended an open session of The City Legislature, his attention tuned to The Senator, whose office he would tend after his break.

The Senator was worse than sinister, he was suave. Younger than most of his colleagues, forty-five, trim, vigorous, concerned more with the televised discussion of the pros and cons of televised execution than with the actual subject of televised execution.

They would have to allocate money for the contract with DDT. Which option package would they select, VOID or VAPER?

The Senator desired to show himself and speak. Be seen and heard, the vicarious voice of the people. His job. He was popular. Handsome. He translated his image well to photographs and screens.

The televised session began. First order of business, procurement: VOID or VAPER?

The Senator walked calmly–confident without over-stepping his mark into what viewers might perceive as arrogance–to the podium.

"The cosmetic effect," he said. "Aesthetic termination."

The Senator had fought for The Nation in the war of his generation. National office was not out of the question. He'd played sports in college. Rugged handsome. Gray hair, stature. Eminence. He wasn't boring–a plus. Sharp wit, compassion. Spoke directly to belief. Married, two children. Played around with girls his daughter's age. Nineteen, twenty. Legal. Could have cared less whether VD's were terminated via spray to the face or blast of anti-quark.

But he was indeed concerned about the cosmetic question. Which would allow him to seem tough but humane, VOID or VAPER? He spoke extemporaneously, directly to the camera and whoever was admiring him at the outer limits of connection. He summoned conviction, spoke to persuade. His was the power to hypnotize.

Collectively, the Legislature had fiat over life and death. He wanted this power for himself. Such power would be neither neglected nor abused, should it come to him. He was not afraid to confront death, his own or the murderer's. Deliberate without passion. Decisions would be conclusive.

The Senate elected VOID. A quick, clean blast, sex appeal. Ejaculate of anti-quark. Send VD to hell. The People wanted it thus.

Having voted VOID, the Legislature's next conclusion was obvious: terminations on TV. The Citizens would learn by example. Taste the blast. Every capillary in the VD's system. Bang, you're dead. Noise of the blast was artificial. Sound effect for the instruction of witnesses. Sure, instant, violent death. Low margin of error.

The Senate was unanimous for television, a vote of confidence for DDT Inc. This pleased many.

Next on the Senator's agenda, short interview with the Eye of The City, columnist for The City's "Free Press" to demonstrate the Senator's tolerance of alternative opinions, even those, particularly the "alternatives," he openly despised.

In The Senator's office, Plantman lingered over his work, listened.

Yes the Senator believed this. No he wouldn't stand for that. Yes he had a moral obligation to something or other. No he wouldn't let politics get in the way.

Yes. No. Yes. No. Yes. No. Yes. Yes. Yes!

Always end on an "up" note. What Big Media wanted to hear. Resolution. Strength.

He was one of the few Senators to do his own data searches on Pyramid.

"No unelected official should stand between The People and

their data," he said.

What did this Eye want? Demonstration of a search?

"I don't do theater," said the Senator. "Legislation is serious business."

Yes, he'd performed his own searches even as a young Prosecutor. No, he had nothing against the Research Officials. He merely saw no need for translators when one could easily learn The Search languages himself. It brought him closer to the actual data, so important to his duty as representative of The People. Cost effective and efficient. City government was already bloated with Officials. Lawmakers must get their feet wet, dirty their hands, dive into the sea of information, sink or swim.

No, he had nothing personal against Lawmakers who used Translating Officials. In certain cases it saved time. This was just his way. He was a hands-on Senator. Blah blah blah. Bleh Bleh Bleh.

The Senator did not frighten easily, but this "Eye of The City" spooked him. Slick smile behind the deadpan. I know you, said the smile. You don't know me, retorted the Senator's grave tone. But this was only implied. No way to know whether The Eye bought it.

The Senator had thought a profile feature in the Sunday edition would do him good. But he was not relaxed for this interview; not the persona he'd spent ten years creating. Damage control. Perhaps a stellar photograph might offset possible land mines in the prose. Or invite the Newspaper Editor–better yet; the owner's representative–to lunch at the CGC. VIP treatment etc. Poke The Eye, hard.

"I feel like I'm talking to an undertaker," said The Senator.

Exactly NOT what he wanted to say to this reporter.

Ordinarily, such a comment would have made him seem spontaneous, off the cuff, not afraid to speak his mind. Interpreted by The Eye, the comment revealed The Senator in a way he did not wish to be revealed. No room for humor with this Eye of The City fellow. A light-hearted comment spawned boils, gaffes, big red blisters on the page. Too late. He would have to accept this lapse. A small mistake, yet one in his position, one with aspirations and potential, could not afford a dent, not a scratch, on the chassis. Deadpan, The Eye scribbled the Senator's blunder to glyphic accusations on his digi-pad from which they were relayed to a server (and posterity) at Free Press Headquarters in real time.

The Eye had not asked a question for several minutes. The trap had been set: let the Senator run on, for running on led to improvisation, increasing the risk of error.

The more words one released, the greater the probability one of those words would mutate into a sentence best left unheard, unquoted, forgotten. But with this scribe and his digi-pad, every word might appear on record, in the newspapers and on the network, stored, eventually, on Pyramid to be called up by The Senator's enemies when the time came to destroy him. It was not the columnist himself, but the record The Senator feared.

The Eye, whom the Senator had not reached with wit, charm,

or charisma, was a cold recorder to which The Senator dictated his own epitaph.

Only after the Eye of The City left did the Senator acknowledge the presence of Plantman. Immediately, the Senator brightened, beamed, became the familiar meta-narrative of himself again.

"Plantman. What an honor to meet you in the illustrious City Government Complex! Can I offer you a signed photograph?"

The Dissenting Judge

The Dissenting Judge, frail, old, overwhelmed, bored with data, welcomed the coming of Plantman.

"You are fortunate, Plantman. Your life is lived tending fruits of the earth. I am beset with human cares. . . "

"You look tired," Plantman said.

"Yes, tired. There comes a time when The Judge must judge himself. This is never good. Cases come and go. Input. Output. Prosecution is a fast machine. Since the Viral Deviant statutes became Law, there have been few occasions in which a judgment of innocence has been warranted, not to say legally justified. This murder, for instance. The Accused ate the fish himself. He happened to survive. If he is to be tried for murder, should he not be tried for attempted suicide as well? Under the previous statutes, attempted suicide was a ticket to the House of the Disturbed. Insanity. Hands down. The fool actually swallowed the flesh that killed his parents. But under the new Law, a VD is a VD. Extenuating circumstances, such as mental infirmity, do not apply.

"Then there is the peculiar form of masochism exhibited by The Accused. 'Standing up for his beliefs,' some might call it. 'Only the fittest survive,' according to The Accused. If he had not been meant to survive, he would have died with his parents. What would possess a man to examine this tired old theory, via live experiment, rather than relegating it to the realm of the academic, is not admissible. A VD is a VD. It is our duty only to determine whether the accused is a VD. Pyramid and the before-your-eyes facts prove undeniably that The Accused most certainly fits the legal definition of a Viral Deviant.

"Where he developed his twisted notions, what his relationship with his parents might have been–could they have long ago implanted this seed of their own destruction in his unstable mind?–is not relevant. Nor is the unfortunate fact that The Accused will leave behind a wife and children. Or that he, according to data supplied by Pyramid, has never before, in his adult life, manifested violent or deviant behavior, except for the inevitable words spoken to friends, colleagues, encounters with rivals, so on and so forth that, when taken out of context, plucked from the cold, hard-drives of Pyramid, lend proof to the contention that he is a Viral Deviant.

"We must ask ourselves: So what? Data flowing through Pyramid can mark even the most esteemed of Citizens a Viral Deviant, if presented and translated in malicious fashion–and the intent of The Prosecution is indeed malicious toward Viral Deviants–as prescribed by The Law.

"What might have been a case of a suicidal man destroying his parents, while also attempting, by all reasonable accounts, to destroy himself, is not a case we can pursue. It is now the case of a Viral Deviant who must be destroyed. Though The Accused is steadfast in his assertion that he did what he did to test the 'fitness of his bloodline,' the survivability of his children in a world grown increasingly toxic, one obvious possibility, I would even go so far as to say probability, has not been stated: This is a man of no conviction who, in accordance with the monstrous nature of his deed, has convinced himself that he acted with conviction. It is entirely possible that he poisoned himself and his parents by accident, and that, upon waking, days later, in the prison hospital, he preferred death to the horrible truth of circumstance, and convinced himself, or had himself convinced, in his confused and agonized state, that this all had some sort of, for lack of a better word, 'purpose,' that he had not accidentally poisoned his parents by feeding them the fish he caught in a local pond, a pond he and his father had fished when The Accused was a boy, but deliberately poisoned them to see if they, and he, for he did eat a large quantity of the contaminated meat, would survive the ordeal and therefore ensure the 'fitness' of his progeny. This most complicated of cases is permitted only the simplest of solutions…"

"I haven't studied the case, not in depth," said Plantman. "All I know, I know from The News."

"I had to dissent. I am too old not to dissent. In this way, perhaps, I am following the example of The Accused. For a judge, under the new Law, is permitted only a certain number of dissents before subjecting himself to review and possible impeachment. I too am testing the laws of survival. Attempting to determine if I myself, after a lifetime as a jurist, am indeed a 'survivor.'"

"I am sorry you are burdened," Plantman said.

"I am old, a man of the old statutes, which gave both judge and jury room to breathe. I did not mature under the new Law, which makes us all puppets acting according to a script while deluding ourselves that we have 'free will.' I am entering my last days as a Judge."

"You will retire?" asked Plantman.

"I will pound my gavel loud and clear," The Judge nodded. "Make a bit of noise before I go."

Natural Selection

The night before he had even committed the "crime" that was to turn him into The Accused, The Not-Yet-Accused lay awake, troubled by thoughts. His Sunday night routine. The Wife slept soundly. The pills hadn't worked–on him. Nor had the wine. He resorted to television. Disturbed. No program soothed. Until: the twenty-four-hour Hunting and Fishing channel.

Three men in a boat. Large lake, peaceful. The men spoke softly, each phrase stretched loose by long, slow diphthongs of The Nation's South. It was early morning, where they were. Foamy tongues of water lapped the boat-side. Seductively. Rhythmically.

The Host of the show, an old fisher king, geared the conversation to the day's topic: fish.

"These fish ain't dumb," he said.

"Nope," said one of his Side-Kicks.

"You gotta know your bait. Know what they're after."

"Yup. Mmm hmmm," agreed The Side-Kicks.

"Most important, you gotta know what you're after."

Again both side-kicks, opening fresh beers, agreed. Silence. Water lapping. Birds chirping. The Not-Yet-Accused soothed, calm. Alarm clock hammered him conscious.

"Morning," The Wife said.

"What time?"

"Time."

The Not-Yet-Accused and The Wife prepared breakfast wearing business attire. The Dejected Son, age eight, and The Dejected Daughter, age ten, ate cereal dejectedly at the table. The Not-Yet-Accused and The Wife drank black coffee and ate toast layered with fat-free cheese. Silent as fishermen, waiting for nothing.

The Son poured the last of the cereal and reached into the box to grab the special prize, a plastic whistle. The Daughter grabbed too. They fought. Each tugged fiercely for the toy.

"Son, you got the last prize," The Wife said. "It's Daughter's turn. Let her have it."

The Son hesitated. The Wife leaned forward.

"Let. Her. Have. It."

The Son relented. Overjoyed, The Daughter ripped the whistle from its plastic wrap and blew. Shrill and cutting, worse than the alarm clock. The Not-Yet-Accused pressed both hands to his ears.

Outside, The Wife kissed The Not-Yet-Accused. She walked the children to their private school not many blocks away. The Dejected Son waved to The Not-Yet-Accused. The Happy Daughter blew her whistle.

Beautiful Spring morning. The Not-Yet-Accused fell to reverie: youthful hours in the arms of The Missing Girl. His cellular phone yanked him back to day. Shrill cellular phone. His secretary told him some one needed something; some other needed something else.

"I'm feeling better," he said. "Not coming in today. Whatever needs to be done, or not. Pick up the pieces tomorrow. Today, I'm Missing," he said, and thought, but did not say, "Young."

He went to the garage, withdrew his car, headed for a Suburb, away from the soot and rot and steel glass towers of The City. The Suburb of his youth. The Suburb where his parents lived, still, after so many years without a green awakening of any kind (besides the occasional waxy fruit or flash-frozen, grayish vegetable).

He stopped at the Sporting Goods store to buy a fishing rod and tackle. The phone squealed like an infant when he left the car. He slammed the door to muffle its insistence.

He bought a short thin pole with a manual reel. A rod meant for a child. No buttons or levers or other such gadgetry.

He drove to the pond where he had fished as a boy. This was before he was Missed and then found, or rather, before he had left and returned.

A fence surrounded the area. PRIVATE PROPERTY NO TRESSPASSING. He found an opening someone had courteously provided, apparently with wire-cutters.

The pond, as he remembered it, was about a half mile's walk into the woods. He still wore his suit. He should have purchased a t-shirt, jeans and thick boots at the Mall. Also, he'd forgotten bait. Regardless, he was going fishing.

The pond in view, he knelt between shrubs and scratched for worms with his bare hands. He collected half a dozen sticky, writhing tubes of flesh, which he assumed the fish might find edible, and placed them and a fistful of soil in the pocket of his pin-striped jacket.

There were already fishermen at the pond. Two elderly men in loose, comfortable old-man clothes. Plaid shirts and baggy gray pants. Rubber boots. They looked at The Not-Yet-Accused and spoke to each other. The garrulous, older old man, called out to The Not-Yet-Accused.

"Playing hooky?"

"All day long," said The Not-Yet-Accused.

He had no knife. He sliced a worm over a flat rock with his house key, impaled the juicier half upon the hook, attached a float to the line, cast it in, and waited. He removed his coat and tie, rolled back his sleeves.

"Why don't you come over here and be sociable," The Garrulous Old Man called out. "We won't bite. Not like the fish."

"Didn't want to invade your turf," said The Not-Yet-Accused. "Fishermen's etiquette. You know."

"Ahhh," The Garrulous Old Man waved his hand. "There's more fish in this pond than all three of us can catch in a lifetime. Well, not in our lifetime. That ain't saying much. Your lifetime. Young guy like you can spend his life here and not empty this pond."

The Garrulous Old Man laughed heartily, nudged his mum companion.

"I didn't think there was any good fishing left in this world," said The Not-Yet-Accused. "At least, not around here."

"What're you here for, then?"

"I don't know. Just to relax. Fish. Didn't really plan on catching anything."

"Oh, you'll catch something. That's certain," said The Garrulous Old Man. "Meanwhile, let's hurry up the time."

He pulled a silver flask from his vest pocket and proffered it to The Not-Yet-Accused. The Quiet Old Man provided paper cups.

"Plenty more where that came from," said The Garrulous Old Man. "Don't be shy."

The Not-Yet-Accused drank and fished and talked with The Garrulous Old Man. The Quiet Old Man, hat low on his brow, held his pole steady and uttered not a word.

The Not-Yet-Accused felt a tug on his line. Then a hard pull. He rode the reel a few seconds, then drew in, let it ride again, and again drew in. He was not a small man–six feet, 170 pounds–but the thing on the other end of the line had a life-strength of its own. It fought him. It was not going to come easy, but it was going to come because The Not-Yet-Accused was stronger than the life on the other end of the line, the life that was hooked; snagged almost, but not yet taken. The rod bent like a blade of grass. The Not-Yet-Accused felt pain in his wrists and fingers. Not a sick, debilitating working-at-a-keyboard pain, but the buzz of muscles awakening to do what they were meant to do all along, always, from the beginning, and growing stronger despite exhaustion in his lungs.

He reeled and pulled and it, the Other Life, emerged from the water struggling, twitching, arching, but subdued. His fish. The Not-Yet-Accused was drunk with a kind of power he had never known. Or perhaps had once known, but had long ago forgotten.

He talked too much, too quickly. He talked about the office and data and fulfilling whatever his duties were supposed to be according to the job description on file at Human Resources: "Administrator of Creative Product Strategies."

He talked about endless talk at meetings where nothing ever was decided, yet every two weeks he took his paycheck, though he couldn't connect the work he did with the payment he received. Yet it was that pay, no small amount, supplemented by his Wife's sizable income, that bought insurance and the condo and the cars and food and school for the kids and gadgets, all those damned gadgets.

But he couldn't connect the work to the pay. He went to his job everyday–except this day–because that was what he did, and he possessed the goodies he possessed because that was how things were, but here he was pushing his mind and body, his will, to fight another thing, a powerful, struggling, fierce thing with a will of its own, with a will to fight The Not-Yet-Accused, a will to free itself and live. The Not-Yet-Accused was fighting for his supper. He was earning his food with his muscles, mind, senses–

"Whoa, Captain," said The Garrulous Old Man. "You don't want to eat that thing."

"What?" The Not-Yet-Accused, out of breath, was genuinely upset. "Why?"

"Because that fish is a freak. It shouldn't be alive. God knows what poison courses through its veins."

The Not-Yet-Accused held the hooked, still-struggling animal close.

"The reason we can fish here"–The Garrulous Old Man patiently explained, as if talking to an idiot or a child– "The reason there's a pond and trees rather than a school and neighborhood and shopping mall on this land is because the meadows surrounding this property are contaminated. As is the property itself."

"What? No!" exclaimed the crestfallen Not-Yet-Accused.

"Yup. Think they didn't know that when the original deal went down? Think you can bury a school and small-town like it's a fucking old shoe? They should have known it would come back to haunt them. Physics. Every dumb-assed action has an even dumber-assed opposite reaction. The Real Estate company that owns this land, on which we're trespassing by the way, is in litigation with the original owner and The State. The Real Estate people bought this property to build on. A beautiful hunk of land like this, a hunk of peace on earth, doesn't come free.

"The Hospital had been dumping here for years. This was a burial ground for the waste of generations. Why not? No one lived here. Weren't using it for anything else," he gestured ironically toward The Pond, the remaining life of which had allegedly been long extinct.

"Ever hear of leeching? Know what leeching is? The Real Estate Company hasn't been able to build on this land, to create the development they'd been planning because the property was poisoned. Somebody's gotta clean the place and somebody's gotta foot the bill. That's what all the litigation is about, and it's expected to go on for years.

"So as long as those lawsuits fly back and forth, you can come here and enjoy a good afternoon of fishing. Just don't make too much noise about it. Don't attract attention. Notice how there's no ducks in this pond? Used to be ducks. They flew off or died. Most of the animals around here disappeared or died. Listen."

They listened to nothing. No birds, no bees, no woodland creatures.

"This place used to be full of wild-life. Now there are some creatures here, mostly raccoons, they're used to garbage, and so are the little creatures they eat. But they're mutants. Freaks. They look okay, they don't have two heads or seven eyes that glow in the dark like in the movies, but they're. . . abominations. They should have been killed by the poison in the earth. The ones that survived are different. They look regular, but there's something in them, something unnatural I'd call it, that lets them live with the sickness inside them. Who knows? Maybe because they've adapted, they thrive on it. Maybe it's what gives them life. But they're not regular. They're stronger. Some gene or DNA thing or whatever you call it allowed them to survive where the others couldn't. This pond shouldn't be filled with fish and algae and mosquitoes and its own little 'bio system.' It should be dead water, like one of those pool and fountains folks pitch pennies into in The City. It was dead water for a long while. But then the fish came back. They were never really gone, of course. They just survived. A few survived, a few stronger that could live with the poison, and they repopulated the pond. It's well stocked, this water hole, but with what? Yeah, it makes for good fishing. They're probably a lot feistier than their forbears, these. . . creatures, these. . . blasphemies. That's 'natural selection.' But you don't want to eat them. They're immune to the very poison that killed their ancestors and most of the natural life around here. They're more a product of unnatural selection, I'd say. The poison in their blood probably works to their advantage somehow. Like spikes on a porcupine. Protects them against predators. Nobody wants to eat these fish. Except maybe the raccoons or whatever other characters evolved from the same spiked soup."

It occurred to The Not-Yet-Accused that The Quiet Old Man in the hat was not merely quiet, he was dumb. Retarded, perhaps severely. The Not-Yet-Accused asked The Garrulous Old Man why he and his companion kept the fish they caught in a bucket if they didn't plan on eating them.

"That's for my brother," The Garrulous Old Man pointed to The Quiet One.

"He likes to see how many we caught at the end of the day. He likes to look at them. He can count to 'four' on a good day, sometimes even 'six,' though only with his fingers. He don't speak much. Never, actually. Afterwards, I throw them back."

The Not-Yet-Accused asked if he could borrow a bucket. The Garrulous Old Man lugged over a huge plastic pail, half-filled with water, into which The Not-Yet-Accused deposited his fish of a very different breed than he'd ever caught as a boy.

The Old Men began packing their gear. The Not-Yet-Accused offered to return the bucket.

"Keep it," said The Garrulous Old Man. "Give it back next week. Remember what I told you. Whatever that fish is made of, it's not meant for stomachs such as ours."

The Garrulous Old Man led his brother by the hand. The Quiet Old Man turned longingly to the pond and uttered a long plaintive cry, an all-too-human cry, innocent, shocked, bewildered, choked with bile and blood-curdling rage.

Statement of the Accused

At last Plantman was led to the vault of The Accused. The walls and door were three feet thick, but the vault was air-conditioned, lest The Accused succumb before The City could legally VOID him. The Official punched the key-code and the door yawned open, revealing a cot, a toilet, and a small table which held The Accused's beloved African Violet, "Rose."

The Accused wore a plain white t-shirt and prison denims. Clean-shaven–perhaps a dash of EARN cologne? A pale man, shy. Not the monster depicted by The City News.

"Plantman, you've come."

"I've come," said Plantman as The Official sealed the door behind him.

"There she is," The Accused pointed to his potted plant. "Her name is 'Rose.'"

"You've taken good care of her," observed Plantman.

"I water her from my own cup," said The Accused.

Though tired from his long day at the CGS, Plantman made

a great show of tending the small plant, and listened patiently to the curious tale of the Accused:

"The fishing was a catalyst, a push in the right direction.

"All changed utterly with the poisoned fish. I never knew about the area being poisoned. I used to skim rocks and skate on that pond as a kid. All the deaths in the area. Cancer. Blood diseases. Strange infections. Mysterious dumping grounds. Connections abound. How could we have been so blind?

"My parents were probably on their way, the cancer inside them. All the memories of youth spent by the quiet pond–poisoned. I was headed for my parents just to visit. To talk about The Past.

"'Where is The Wife, The Children?' Mother asked.

"'I wanted it to be just us. Like in The Past.'

"'We were going to order in,' said Father.

"'Let me cook for you,' I said. 'It's a big fish. For three of us.'

"'God-man in heaven, it's still alive!' screamed Mother.

"I shocked them both by smashing the creature's head against the sink, several times, until its eyes dimmed; a final blow for lights-out.

"'Well, it's certainly fresh,'" Father said.

"'You're working too hard, Son,' Mother said. 'You need

rest. Maybe you should go to your room and rest.'

"'My old room,' I said. 'I must cook the fish.'

"'I'll cook the fish,' Mother said, unaware of her complicity. 'I'll fry it. With onions and potatoes. A real cook-out.'

"'We were supposed to order in,' Father said. 'Pizza. Or Chinese.'

"'Mother said, 'I'll fry the fish. A real cook-out.'

"'My room had barely changed since I moved out to attend The City University, then The Life–oh yes, almost 20 years; that is some time ago. It had been straightened and cleaned and converted to an impromptu guest room for the kids. My kids. But my old things were still there, strategically placed. Music discs on the shelf. Sports equipment in the closet. Old books and fading magazines. My past. Thoughts I had thought while being in The Past, untouchable–from where we sit now.

"I lay on the bed, pondering my old things and the Summer I left those things to became, at sixteen, one of The Missing Young. I'd slept on The City Big Park lawn and on benches. I'd held The Missing Girl in my skinny, hairless arms.

"The closet where the magazines were stacked contained cover stories of The Missing Girl. When I knew her, when I loved her, how could I have known what she'd become? A symbol. An icon. Poster-child for The Nation's Missing Young. She was, for all I knew, still Missing, and for all I dared imagine, still Young.

"These memories brought pain because I'd been a worthless bastard. A typical Summer runaway. I arrived on the street in June and left in September. I was afraid of losing myself to The Young. I had a situation to return to, and I returned to it. The contempt in The Missing Girl's eyes as I stammered my good-bye is still the featured presentation of my nightmares. I was no longer Missing, but sleepless. Always sleepless. Soon The City will end my nights of always sleepless.

"When all the newspaper and magazine stories appeared, when Big Media chose The Missing Girl to be The Missing Girl, I found myself, at age seventeen, grieving over my lost youth.

"Then The Future came.

"Sunday nights, my Wife asleep beside me, the work week breathing down my neck, those magazine covers loomed like glossy clouds above my bed. What might have been? Was there an alternative to the path I'd chosen, the path that seemed as inevitable as death itself?

"Once, I'd lain on the grass in The City Big Park with The Missing Girl. I wrote symbols on sidewalks, paper bags, rolling papers. It was a different life. A hard, miserable life, in truth, begging for beer money and food, but a life that was good for me. None of the other Missing Young knew of the knick-knacks in my room or the thoughts I'd thought at the pond.

"Fear thoughts. Anxiety thoughts.

"The pond, the trees surrounding it–I was positive there'd been chirping birds–took away some of the edge. I had always been a timid, nervous boy.

"My parents welcomed me home. After I'd bathed, of course. I loathed their teary embrace. I hated the comfort of the home I could run back to. Might I have become a poet, an artist, or at least a sort of MAN? Or would I have ended as I'd feared, begging and drinking and sleeping in The City's filthy nooks, hounded by The Authorities and Detectives of LOSD until I died of pneumonia or drug O.D. or was forcibly returned?

"I was born to live the safe life, the comfortable life, the life that kills itself before it properly begins. And the question would always haunt me: was there another way? Could I have saved myself from me?

"I smelled the fish frying downstairs. My fish. The fish I had subdued. I told myself that The Garrulous Old Man was as brain-bent as the Quiet one, that at worst, the fish would give us indigestion. But I went downstairs hoping deep that the fish would exact its revenge upon the three of us and send us straight to God-man.

"After the meal, nothing. I called The Wife to tell her I'd be spending the night at my Parents'. She'd been worried. She'd been upset. She was angry. I told her I needed to talk to my parents, and that I would explain things later. I'd drive in early to change my clothes before work. I told her I'd gone fishing.

"The fish fought back around midnight. My parents vomited side-by-side into the same lavender toilet bowl. I phoned Emergency Services.

"I awoke days later in a hospital bed with The Wife standing beside me. She told me my Parents were dead. I nodded, as if she'd told me my shirts were at the cleaners.

"A man came in to question me about the fish. Routine investigation. I could have walked away with a fine for trespassing. I told the man a story that was not quite true, but the more I talked, the truer it became. I told him I feared defective genes. I told him I deliberately sought the fish and fed it to my parents and myself to see if any of us would survive.

"If we could survive, then my own children might have a chance to actually live lives in this toxic world rather than merely maintain their bodies through seventy years of sickness, despair and medication. I told the man that since I survived, I must be fit, that is, made of stronger stuff; hence, my children had what I had, somewhere inside them. I told the man I wanted my children to be like the fish.

"The Defense Attorney urged an insanity plea, but I refused. I was going to see this through to the end. I elaborated on my story. I told Big Media, because this case was garnering a fair amount of attention, of my long-ago affair, my Summer romance, with The Missing Girl. They checked the records and concluded that I'd been Missing and in The City at the same time She had been Missing and in The City, so it could have been true. Regardless, it made great copy. The more Big Media attention I received, the firmer became my grasp on my true but not-quite-true story, and the more pressure I put on The Defense Attorney to defend the merits of my argument.

"I craved exposure. I believed, or made myself believe, that somewhere out in The Nation, perhaps within The City itself, The Missing Girl would see me on the small screen and remember."

"But now you will be put to death," said Plantman.

"Yes," The Accused said, casually. "I want you to leave here with Rose. I bequeath her to you. I'd leave her to my heirs, but she'd be dead in a month. I want the very best for her. She will thrive under the care and nurturing of Plantman."

"Where did you get this plant?" asked Plantman, accepting the last wishes of The Accused.

"She was a gift from The Wife."

"A plant of sentimental value," said Plantman.

"The Rose was the flower of my Young Summer love."

The Mayor

Plantman was surprised, but not shocked, to find The Mayor's office decorated entirely with imitation plants. He brushed the plastic leaves with his trusty feather-duster.

The Mayor sat quietly at his enormous desk, playing with a wooden sculpture of a bull with the sword of an unseen matador jutting from its side. At last the Mayor spoke.

"You've been a very naughty Plantman, Plantman."

"I? How so?"

"I know all about you."

"Everyone knows me. I'm Plantman."

"Which is precisely why you should be setting an example for The City's Young, not corrupting them."

"I'm Plantman. I tend the indoor flora of The City. I've corrupted no one."

"Your association with the so-called 'Indian,' Fire Bush, is very disappointing to me."

"Fire Bush harms no one."

"Balderdash!"

"Balderdash?"

"Fire Bush is the leader of a nefarious cult. Everywhere I turn I see young people, The Missing Young, with hair died green. They should be home with their families. They should not be dying their hair any color, at their age, much less green. I'm having him arrested."

"On what grounds?" demanded Plantman.

"He is the pied piper of The Missing Young. A cult leader. A Viral Deviant. A corrupter of Youth. I want him off the streets."

"But Fire Bush is never on the streets. He preaches in the parks."

"Yes, yes. The parks, then. I want him out of the parks. And as for you, Plantman. . . "

"Yes?"

"Watch yourself, for you are being watched."

XVIII.
Man in the Black Suit, a True-Time Defective Story

Chairman of His Own Black Suit

For the time wrote copy the Agency freelance lived alone. Had a Man in a Black Suit. A friend.

Man in the Black Suit claimed to be IMPORTANT MAN, chairman of the board, DataCo Inc. Research credit of. Research backgrounds of. Research lives of.

Database, database, government monkey work.

Man in the Black Suit said I'd been recommended highly. Who had he spoken to? The Clients whom I sent my copy? But I didn't send to clients, only The Agency.

Man in the Black Suit a liar. Chairman of nothing but his own black suit. Damn his black suit. Bizarre, a suit in that part of town. Tenements. Rats. Chickens. Dirty children. Ubiquitous workers in and out of work night and day, all-night groceries and diners.

"If you're so important, why do you live here?" I asked.

“Who said I lived here?” he said.

“That’s your apartment, directly above mine, is it not?”

“Yes,” said Man in the Black Suit. “What’s your point?”

Parable Dream Angel Gymnast

Man in the Black Suit haunted my doorway. Where could he sit but my futon, laid directly on the floor? The folding chair on which I work? But that was for me. He filled two glasses with bourbon and water, the only beverages I had.

“Why are you here in my apartment, drinking my cheap booze?

“I had a dream,” he said, told me the following:

“My flying gymnast visits from abroad. She’s beautiful. She loves me. Straps, harnesses, pulleys, cables. I fear for her safety. Bloodthirsty audience below, but she flies masterfully. She changes to furs and denim, and goes off to explore–I’d rather she didn’t, but I’m confident of her love. She’s out for the night. She’ll be back. I’m anxious.

“I hang with the boys, old high school friends, though I don’t know them. Up in The King’s hotel suite, I take conference calls; big deal brewing; they want to screw us, but we hang tough–I want to make this sale and take my flying gymnast someplace warm. . . .

“Phone calls and counter-phone calls last hours, seem like days.

Anxious drinking, smoking, nothing done–I'm mortified. I want to kill myself.

"I return to the party of old friends who are strangers: I've failed egregiously.

"My gymnast returns. Hasn't she heard the news? Has she not looked at the sky and read for herself the script of my descent? Of course! Out in the street my utter failure and ignominious defeat are common knowledge, but she could care less about the power prattle of The City–I'm not an insect, I'm a person.

"Her bronze hand leads me, step by step, to heaven. . . ."

What was one to make of such a tale? A dream he'd had? I thought not. A parable belched from his sad, lonely heart.

The Dancer

A woman came to his apartment. Flesh and blood young blood. Student Dancer, The University. Man in the Black Suit age fifty.

Hear everything in those tenements. I heard them. Afterward, music, the Dancer's bare feet slap-buffed on hard wood floor. Above my head. While I was–work. Did I mind?

On my way out for beer and cigarettes. He buzzed her in. I watched her float ghostly through the corridor, pass me on the stairs, thin as a dancer should be. She smelled of, I don't know, flowers? perfume?

Music and Cigars

Late in his apartment.

We got buzzed up there. Scotch, cigars, old Grandpa Jones LPs: "They call it that good ol' mountain dew/and them that refuse it are few. . . . "

Greatest country music selection in the world, all LP.

Fat expensive stogies. Long relaxing smokes. Nothing in MY apartment but futon, folding table, books, machine.

Man in the Black Suit said profound stuff, or sounded profound like:

"Those who can't do, leach." and

"Do not hate, but rather use THEIR bad energy against THEM."

and

"If goodness can be chewy and chocolaty, who would aspire to such sticky virtue?"

and

"Where are the people going with their heads down? They are going to work."

and

"In my youth I sowed wild words."

Shit like that.

In the Playground

Man in the Black Suit entered the playground, women's eyes upon him. Necks stiffened. Not supposed to be there; no child of his own. Sign said park was "For Children, accompanied by one or more adult. But he heard a boy on the swings chant, "I'm going to live to be a hundred and seven yeeeaaaars old!" repeatedly. He approached. "Do you love life that much, little boy?" Before the child could answer, mothers surrounded Man in the Black Suit. What kind of question was that to ask a boy? Who was this weird man? Someone call the police. Man in the Black Suit left to avoid further commotion.

Naked Lunch

Man in the Black Suit ate a sandwich. Man in the Black Suit naked, even in his black suit.

You Won't Have Man in the Black Suit to Kick Around Anymore.

He tried to speak; they wouldn't listen. "They" ghosts of erstwhile children, shells inhabiting houses, markets, offices and "commons" of The Nation. So Man in the Black Suit left public discourse. Never to return?

Identity

Get an ID. Driver's License or non-Driver's License for Being. Gray Gap-Wendy's Starbucks Duane Reade Barnes & Noble afternoon. The Bank. This bank, that one. License and Identity Bureau. Department of Self and Others. Man in the Black Suit bought identity for seven dollars. Decent photograph. Did not smile. Drank cola. Waited. Woman behind the counter called his name. Laminated card complete. Man in the Black Suit sheathed his likeness like a dagger in his wallet.

Into The Family Head

I visited my Sister and her Husband, a man of many whiskers and hard work. Within linked cubes of home, clear bounds exist. Violence and Power partitioned according to state or local custom. Morals delineated.

Children feted, fed. Pizza, pasta, cereal crunchy-sweet. Appliances break. Year is One. Family is one. Dad a blow-job every night. His due. Mother served with honor, though occasionally called in sick. Where is the God-man THEY promised? Where is money? Work hard. Study hard. Be generous, just, sincere. THEY promised feathers. THEY promised candy.

Man in the Black Suit did not concatenate his lineage. Did not extend. Whatever had begun in past times would end in the near future, with Man in the Black Suit him.

Hero

Man in the Black Suit shot a man (not in a Black Suit) outside our building. The Guy got up and ran. Three bullets in him from the tiny pistol taped to Man in the Black Suit's lower back. A gun not meant to kill but mortify.

The Guy had tried to mug us. "Gimme yer money," he said. Man in the Black Suit looked in my direction, said, "He has it." Wanna-be-would-be mugger pointed his gun at me–Bam-BangBam!–Man in the Black Suit plugged him thrice. Shoulder chest thigh. The Guy collapsed. "Lose the weapon," said Man in the Black Suit. Wanna-be-would-be mugger tossed his gun. Bleeding, gasping, ran to the hospital blocks away.

Read in the paper next morning "some Guy," wanted on many charges, admitted himself to ER and eventual police custody. Gunshot wounds. Would not say how, at whose hands. Critical but stable.

Slugs traced to Man in the Black Suit's registered weapon.

We told our story next day at the Precinct, where the assailant's gun, used in several nasty crimes of late, lay in a clear plastic bag.

Man in the Black Suit a sudden hero in the papers. He refused to be interviewed or press charges against Wanna-be-would-be mugger.

"Problems enough," Man in the Black Suit said of The Guy.

Study Hard

Man in the Black Suit studied Zen. Man in the Black Suit studied Yoga. Man in Black Suit meditated. Man in the Black Suit danced.

I Want I Need I Crave

Apartment. Studio. Six-fifty a month. Alone get work done. The Network, The Machine. No longer rise early to some cubicle, some cube. Work at "home." Such as it was. "Neighborhood changing" read newspapers. Didn't notice. Up-scaling. City shoveled out "lower-incomes" to build condominiums. Targeted my building. I didn't worry. I had work. Didn't make much, enough to get by. Grocery on the corner. Didn't go out much beyond that. Once upon Time. Once upon had women. None stuck. Alone, I worked. Watched people leave early morning en mass to offices and institutions.

Man in the Black Suit officed, I assumed, for he left morning at eight returned past six. Supposed I'd be like him at fifty. Alone as he was. As I was alone, alone, but not officed. My machines connected "work" with "home."

Sometimes, despite machines, connections, I officed, met clients. Met clients, pursued pure talk. Then home to work. The actual doing. The keyboard, screen, paper.

Newspapers, television, Network sites announced huge, unstoppable disasters, both latent and dynamic, of the scripted "real world," that few but its elite authors could ever hope to comprehend (never mind "change").

Multiple occasions of anxiety, despair stoke impetus to work, work, work it all away for good. Once. . . I don't know. Young. Would I have minded terribly if the "real world" that exhibited fewer signs of "reality" with each moment's passing, disintegrated that instant? ANY instant? Rather than prolong this terminal case. Terminal, terminal, nothing to be done (except–ho, ho–on terminals). Work, work, work. Nothing to be done? Work hard. Nothing? Nothing? Work harder.

Books of dreams. Dreaming my problem. Teachers said long ago. "Dreamer," they'd said. Read sports pages. Scores. Stats. Records. Numbers. Conversion of deeds to data. Never watched actual games. Boring.

Spoke to mother on the phone until. She died disappointed. In me, herself. She was not much older than Man in the Black Suit. Spoke to my father. Competition, deep antagonism between father and son. Natural. I needed drink. I needed cigarettes. I needed. I needed.

What time? Strange hours. Slept when workers went to Day. Showered ready for work coffee brewed when poor tired masses returned. Outside my window. Good to have a window, better than television. Watched TV when I was very young, my passive mind open. Probably why I always wanted, always wanted–SOMETHING, but never sure what. Never sure.

Wanted needed craved.

To Each His Boswell and the Nevermore

Moment of vanishing. Momentary moment. Constant. Moments passed. Man in the Black Suit would never leave. Stay moment, save moment. Perilous. Unforgiving. Forge moment, carry moment. Look back on moments, the accretion. Left that place. Gone. Forever. Left this place, eventually, too. Forever Time oblivion. Concepts cling clang clung.

Man in the Black Suit; me his Boswell. Boswell scavenged moments. Boswell and his earn machine. Connection facilitator. Living machine. Friend.

Man in the Black Suit neither work nor friend. Avocation. Subject. Not everyone an artist, you know. Starving children mouths open baby birds. Boswell nested in The City. Man in the Black Suit about town. Time. Passing. Time was. He was one of the fortunate few to be "Not unaware of." Unusually indifferent to potentialities: bills, pills, sudden disappearance in the night. Man in the Black Suit not like us. No perpetual motion to stave off stasis. No more clinging to the nevermore.

Tap, Tap, Tapping

Man in the Black Suit said, "And after we're gone and new life again as long as the earth spins, until it stops, and the sun grows dark big bloated red as a gouty toe, then where will your stories be, your poems, your wordy opinions? You're a fool."

I said, "It is pleasurable to walk the streets of The City with a buzz on, or dead drunk, for that matter. My checks from the Agency come in the mail. I must go to the bank to deposit them. I drink before going to the bank. Sometimes I linger about the shops. Stop into a deli for a beer. Sip it through a straw."

Frustration

Nothing grew. Antagonism, anomie. Peanut-butter stuff. Opinions of The Wretched. Exorcised those thoughts. Saw deep. Man in the Black suit stepped on a cupcake. Man in the Black suit polished his gun. Breathing, he claimed, was better than knowing. Suggested I take long runs in the park and breathe.

The Rift

Refuse to speak to (or of) Man in the Black Suit. Will speak (or write) to my self, of my self and for my self.

How many men in black suits? How many possible? Remember old films. Black suits abounded. Good or evil? Tailored, or rack?

What did The Poets say of men in black suits? Who cared what The Poets said?

Advertisements, marketing proposals, copy.

The Dancer danced a million years.

Loose and alone. Pedaling my exer-cycle, touched by genius.

No Omniscient Author None

They married not to be alone. They worked, were entertained. They died, one at a time, alone. Feared Life, feared Death, feared Time.
What happens, happens. What occurs.

Wouldn't know a poem from shot of Novocain.

Poets lightening inspiration Muse. That was no country for Dead Men! Peddling nowhere on recumbent exer-cycles. Questing stationary visions.

Mistuh Black Suit, He Dead

Black in the box. Color of night.

Many, many. gathered in the park to mourn Man in the Black Suit.

Me, another forty, fifty years until.

If I grow cold before machines have gleaned my teeming brain.... I want a Black Suit. I want heaven.

XIX.
The Condition

My Cubicle My Deathbed

“I am Plantman, keeper and protector of The City’s indoor flora,” screamed semi-sleep.

Thirtieth birthday.

BEING, The Bakery Girl, Muse, Music. Crowded room. Family. Happy home.

Not well. Freezing. Terrible cold. My cubicle my deathbed.

The Bakery Girl, beautiful buxom. Music’s huge shirt draped Muse’s carved diamond rare-beautiful.

“Freezing,” tried to say.

Words came Egyptian. Ancient Egypt–me. Supposing Ra. Sun god. God Sun. Father sun whole ghost. Amenhotep. Akhenaton. Nefertiti warm fragrant. Night. Ozymandias. Ramses. Cheops. John. Paul. George. Ringo.

“I’ve seen him fucked up before, but not like this,” said BEING.

“Surprised he’s not dead,” said Music.

Body fluttered chills.

“We gotta get him to a hospital,” said Muse. “There’s something wrong here. Really wrong.”

No disagree. She touched. Muse hand, my forehead.

“My god, he’s burning!”

Cab called. Music and BEING stuffed me back seat.

“City Hospital,” said The Bakery Girl to the cab driver.

Pursued pure talk. Egyptian say, Egyptian say. Nonsense.

“He’s talking like a crazy man,” said The Bakery Girl. “He’s babbling something about Egypt.”

“You okay?” asked BEING.

Explain. Explain the situation. Head Plantman. Pharaoh’s palace. Plants dying. Blame me, blame me. Danger for my life!

“Take it easy,” said BEING. “Try to sleep it off.”

Eyes closed. Sun in my head huge; sparkling Nile; glyptic peasants. Heads balanced bowls teeming snakes.

“Wheat,” I said. “Wheat not snakes.”

“He’s okay,” BEING whispered. “Drank too much or something."

"Happy birthday," muttered The Bakery Girl.

Emergency Room

Triage nurse asked I'd been drinking.

"Tremendously. A great deal," The Bakery Girl said.

"What's your name?" The Nurse asked me.

"Ra."

"Okay, Ray. Let's check your vitals," said The Nurse.

Plantman in Egypt to save Pharaoh's ailing Date Palm. Papyrus. Literature is only corrupt as its paper. Important plant priest, celebrated immortal. Statue myths. Royal garden. Scissors bucket. Ancient days, too distant to count. Moses in baby booties.

"His temperature is one hundred and six," said The Nurse.

"Holy shit," said The Bakery Girl.

"We could fry eggs on his head," said BEING.

"Has he been taking drugs?" asked The Nurse.

"I don't think so," said The Bakery Girl.

"Pink pills blue ones."

"Those are the color of the pills, Ray?" asked the nurse. "Can you name them for me? Are they prescription pills, Ray? Did you get them from a doctor?"

"Infection. Disease. Mealy bug. Pharaoh's Wandering Jew. Dead. Dead. Quarter million dollars in replacements."

"Have you been mixing drugs and alcohol, Ray?" asked The Nurse.

"Frame me, Pilate. Joseph's pink coat blue one. The Baker's fat calf must die these replacements. Reparations."

"It's the fever," said The Nurse. "He's hallucinating."

Magnificent pyramid gradients TKI sun-blast desert hues. Sphinx body. The Heir's dot head on behemoth stone shoulders.

Test-tubes to the brim with blood. Nurse's aqua scrubs. Pharaoh's Priests, Magicians, dresses like birds. . .

"How long have you been sick like this?" one asked.

"Like what?"

"Are you having trouble breathing?" one asked.

"I inhale," I said.

Tubes numbed my proboscis.

"Oxygen," one medico said.

Attractive fortyish "Nurse Mimi."

"I'm your nurse," she said.

"I'm your patient," I said.

"We're off to a good start."

"Where's BEING?"

"Your friends are in the waiting area," she said.

"I'll join them," began up.

Mimi pushed down. Powerful little hand.

"What do you do, Ray?"

"Chief gardener to Pharaoh," I said, not completely serious.

Fever subsiding.

"What? Are you trying to say you're a gardener? Is that what you are, Ray?"

"Horticultural technician. Make the desert bloom."

"We're going to send you down for tests," Mimi said.

"Number 2 pencil," I said.

Deep underground. X-ray. Tubular machines. Pharaoh in his bright beige sarcophagus. Let people go. Don't want them. Soon peace. Eternity cherished. Big empty. Burial chamber cherished nothing. Pyramid erect. Honor me with generations. Slaves. Moments stolen, lost; experience besieged. Revenge is the mother of all ghosts. History the feckless father. Man's pyramid his castle. I being of sound mind and body hereby exchange all slaves for cold beer and a reliable watch.

Time trouble. Back to Emergency Room cot in an eye-blink.

Blood results incited commotion among the scrubs.

"He has The Condition," whispered one.

"Unbelievable. He's an anaerobe," said another.

"Lowest hematocrit I've ever seen. Eleven."

"Impossible. How is he still breathing?"

"I've seen plants with higher counts."

Voices everywhere, everywhere voices manacled to opinions.

Silence. Soothing Mimi.

"You're very sick, Ray," she said. "You have The Condition. And pneumonia. But that's a secondary issue."

"Yes. The Condition. I'd better go home to bed," I said. "Not wise to fool around with these things."

"Just relax," she said, pushed down again down. "A Specialist will see you soon. Dr. Creed. He's very good."

"I tend Pharaoh's garden. Yet I am Pharaoh. Can Pharaoh and his gardener be one? What is the sound of Empire collapsing?"

"Look," Mimi said. "I know your head isn't all there because of the fever, but try not to talk about that stuff when Dr. Creed comes. He may not understand. He's strange like that. If he thinks you're strange, he'll send you away."

"I already am away. Where else could he send me?"

"You don't want to know. Just be quiet and behave yourself. Don't speak about mummies when he comes."

"Mummies? Who said anything about mummies?"

Sudden sleep, sudden dream: TKI Pyramids. Data morph. Woman. Passion sex. Information beauty girl culled PYRAMID database. Long hair sensual numbers. Oh PYRAMID sex machine sly frothing dog!

Awakened by a tall, goofy man in an ill-fitting white coat.

"Ray, this is Dr. Creed. He's going to talk to you about your blood."

Dr. Twitch Creed. Twitching Dr. Creed. Eyebrows bobbed up and down of their own accord. I laughed. Burst of hilarity, relief at last. Laugh!

"He has a very high fever, Doctor," Mimi nervously explained.

"Dr. Eyebrows" all serious business.

"When was your last transfusion?" he asked.

"I never had a transfusion," I said.

"With your Condition, you never had a transfusion?"

"I don't have a Condition," I said. "I just drank too much."

"Wanna bet?" under his breath.

Interrogation, re: The Condition. What medications? When was my last hospitalization? Was my last "drop" so precipitous? Where was my medical history on file? On, on, on. Exhausted. I craved sleep.

"I don't know what you're talking about," I said. "None of this applies."

"You're a thirty-year-old man with The Condition and you have no idea of your own history? The Condition is not something you catch like a cold, for God-man's sake. It's something you contract in childhood. Usually through exposure to toxins. You may have been in remission for quite some time, but somewhere in your past are transfusions, treatments. You can't remember anything at all?"

Hearty laugh. Cough. Composed myself. Laughed, coughed again. Creed's questions were all so serious and his eyebrows bobbed like buoys. It was all just too much. Then I broke for real. An omnipotent, unstoppable laughter of a craggy depth I'd never known. Laughter unstoppable.

"He's acting strange. I think he's high on something," somber Dr. Creed. "I might want to put him in the psych ward and treat him from there."

This blunt new development smashed the drooling post-guffaw grin directly down my throat. "Reality laugher" in its stead. Anxious nervous hiccup. You could sign into the psyche ward, but you couldn't sign out. And if an authority, a DOCTOR, no less, signed you in, there was no leaving until he was damned ready, or remembered, to sign you out. Months, maybe more. They drove you crazy in there.

"He said he's a gardener, Dr. Creed," said Mimi. "All gardeners are strange. It's not unusual for them to even talk to plants. It's what they call 'eccentric.'"

Dr. Eyebrows thought, or pretended to think, deeply. His pen hovered over the paper that could consign me to a long convalescence in a rubber room.

"Eccentric. Oh. Yes, you're right. Yes, yes, you're right, 'eccentric.' I've actually witnessed this phenomenon. Saw the man who tended my father's garden talk to plants as if they were alive."

Papers aside pen pocketed.

Assigned a "regular" room, prescribed this drug that drug and this and that other drug, all intravenous. Antibiotics for the pneumonia. He'd see me in "a day or so," after more results came in.

"Do you have any relatives I could talk to about this? Someone who's familiar with your Condition?" he asked.

"I don't know. Maybe. My father."

Gave Father's number. Creed left: rush of eye-brows, flap of coat, forehead thrum.

"That," said Mimi, "Was a seriously close call. He was ready to sign you away to psych. The burden of proof of sanity would have been entirely your responsibility."

"I'm not feeling well. I would have explained that I'm not feeling well; hence, I was not at my best."

"See what I mean? That's the kind of talk that would have kept you there for life. Only a crazy person would try to argue that he is sane. Your keepers would have become quite offended indeed were you to challenge the integrity and authority of their professional diagnoses by claiming they were incorrect."

"So once they say I'm crazy, I'm crazy? Or I really piss them off and make them crazy, in which case I'd be really crazy."

"Pretty much. Unless you can prove otherwise without offending them. But you're in the clear, and I can tell already we've brought the fever down. Why dwell on the 'what if?'"

BEING and The Bakery Girl checked in briefly.

"We're gonna get going," BEING said. "They said they're getting you a room."

"We'll be back tomorrow," The Bakery Girl said. Kissed me.

"Get some rest."

"What time is it?" I asked.

"It's almost three in the morning," BEING said.

Sad alone (boo-hoo). Good to have real friends. Real good friends.

Mimi left and returned with two burly hospital workers.

"We have a room for you," said Mimi. "These gentlemen are going to take you there now. Take care of yourself, Ray."

Wheeled labyrinth corridors hallways, another elevator more hallways. Stop. Room. Three moaning, miserable men. And Me.

"Hi, I'm Stephanie, your nurse," said my pert young nurse as the burly aides set me up.

Catheter tunneled through a vein in my right arm hooked to the squat machine from which hung bags of blood and other fluid Digital meters; flashing lights. Stephanie closed the curtains, obstructing my moribund neighbors from sight–or was it the other way around?–without my having to ask. I was unfamiliar with protocol. Was one expected to tip?

Awake. Shivering. Fever down. Clear-minded Exodus.

Should have stayed in Egypt, enjoyed chewy goodness and frosty robust less-filling virtuous dee-lites sold on gold TV (Egypt television enjoyed remarkably clear and colorful reception, which might or might not have been a by-product of solar power).

The Conditioned

Early nurse's aide collected more blood. The patient to the right of me moaned all night and begged mercy. Still dark. The usually pleasant semi-noise of pre-dawn was amplified to unpleasant by the wheeling of stretchers and machines; insistent patients buzzing the nurses' station. I was not clear enough to know exactly where I was in terms of life's journey as I waited for the sun, only that, wherever it was, it sure as hell wasn't Egypt.

Proximity made my own machine my worst enemy. Dials, bags, sound-monitored drug-infusions, blinking lights. Had to unplug myself to get up and pee and wheel machine gently lest I set off an alarm.

By actual sunrise I was wiped.

Nurse Stephanie checked my "vitals" and attached a fresh bag of something to the machine.

"What is that stuff?" I asked.

"The Solution. It's for your blood. We have to get that blood count up. You'll be receiving a unit each day. Takes about two hours to get into your system."

"Two hours. Then why am I hooked to this machine all day?"

"It's pumping antibiotics and vitamins into your system. We have to appease The Condition. I just started my shift, so I'll be here all day. You just call if you need me."

"Call" meant push the red button at bed-side.

Right-side Patient, the high-decibel moaner, put himself out of our misery. A Doctor declared him. Orderlies wheeled him far. No trace next morning. No mourning. New sheets clean blankets to absorb prayers, fluids next guy.

The replacement for the departed Right Side Patient was a pale, twig-thin, intestinal. Terminal. Shat constant. Foul yellow-brown-ooze-squirt hourly. Everywhere, everywhere, everywhere despite rubber pants and diapers. Nurses' aides, orderlies cleaned his mess, impatient despite the patient's pain–months round-the-clock fudge-squirts had burned his ass sore as a bullet wound. Each cleaning he squealed like an infant intuiting the import and finality of pain, life's inexorable "condition." Long, high-pitched, terrified.

Nicknamed "Old Faithful," such were the frequency of his eruptions. Stink deep fishy overpowered even programmatic vomiting of the chemo guys across the room.

"Look at you, a grown man messing himself like a baby," frustrated nurse's aide said one night. "Dear God-man in heaven, what a mess."

"I can't help myself. Do you think I chose this? This has been going on for months. I'm defecating myself to death. This is a terrible way to die. I'm shitting out my soul. Have you no compassion?"

Nurse's Aide softened.

"Well, the doctors will make you better. You'll see. But you should ring for us," she said, pointed the button near his bed. "Ring when you feel it coming on, so we can catch it."

Snatching motion her right hand.

"It just comes," he wept. "It just comes."

Nurse's Aid cleaned him.

"Old Faithful" groaned squealed through clenched teeth.

"It's unhealthy, that's all," she passed me. "It's not fair to the other patients."

Bad To the Bone-Marrow

Two doctors, a woman and boyish intern, came to sample my bone marrow. Worst pain experienced, this body, to date. Lay flat-belly. Intern, under doctor's direction, Novacained my pelvis. Next harpooned me with a thick needle, extracted a sample. Chips of bone, chunks of marrow. Sequence: pain, numbness, pain again.

The worst sound was that of The Student being reproached for having done the whole thing wrong.

"No, no. This sample is useless. Redo the procedure," said The Older Doctor.

Now pain numbness and anticipation of more pain numbness. Deep breath.

Repeat ordeal.

Samples me floating in a fluid-filled vial.

Doctor, Intern, chattering, gone.

Night Shades

Awake night suddenly not night four AM. Three figures my bedside. Short Man; Tall Surly Man, aka "Mr. Personality;" Thin Woman. Long white lab coats aqua scrubs. Young.

"This is him. Here's his chart," Mr. Personality.

"Amazing," Short Man.

"Freak me out," Thin Woman.

"I've never heard of anyone born with The Condition. I thought it just happens. Toxic exposure or something like that. They see it in kids on the Enemy side," Mr. Personality.

"Which Enemy? I forgot which enemy we're out to get this week," Short Man.

"Very funny, Mr. Patriot," Mr. Personality.

"Report me to the 'authorities.' I dare you," Short Man.

"I just might. Anyway, they see it after heavy-duty bombings. Something in the shit they drop, some kind of chemical in the explosives. Possibly released on impact," Mr. Personality.

"Should be a mother lode of cases after The War," The Woman.

"I'll bet," Short Man.

"Creed's going over there, you know," Thin Woman

"After it all ends. Should be a bunch of cases to exploit–uh, I mean study. Just a joke. A very unfunny joke," Mr. Personality said mocking imagine microphones imagine press conference voice not mocking, attempt to communicate message to many some ones not pretend.

"Yeah, I heard he's looking for volunteers," said Thin Woman.

"Is that right? I volunteer you," Mr. Personality poked his finger into the Short One's chest.

"No, seriously. It should be a fabulous opportunity for research," Short Man.

"Not worth it. I wouldn't go near that stuff," Mr. Personality.

"It's only toxic to kids and old folks. Anyway, by the time we get over there most of the crap'll have blown away. It's not like the intensity of the actual bombing," Short Man.

"Count me out," Mr. Personality. "They don't know what that shit does to your system years down the road."

"The National Health Clinic said it should be safe."

"That's the Military. You gonna believe the fucking Military?"

"Chicken," Thin Woman.

"That's right. You gonna volunteer to go over there?" Mr. Personality.

"If Creed asks me, yeah, why not?" The Woman. "When opportunity knocks. . . "

"Check it out, he's moving," Short One.

"Weird he's still alive. They're supposed to be dead by nineteen or twenty," Mr. Personality.

"His system adapted somehow," Thin Woman.

She poked prodded shined light my eyes.

"Who the fuck are you?" I coughed.

"We're residents. Students of Dr. Creed's," The Short One.

"Old Faithful" cried groaned gasped coughed. Shat himself. 24/7 stink splatter. Sicker. The Night Visitors paid no attention, didn't even ring nurse. Pushed red button myself.

"So 'The Mad Shitter' is still with us," Mr. Personality.

"Not for long, I don't think. Won't make the night," said The Short One.

"So, 'Mr. Condition,' how have you lived your life?" asked Thin Woman.

"Desperately. Like anybody else. Why?"

"Well, not everyone was born with The Condition. Most people develop it in early childhood, and don't last many years. Occasionally one might come across a twenty-year-old on his last legs. But a man of thirty!" Mr. Personality.

"A manual laborer, no less," Thin Woman.

"That's right. He actually went around carrying a watering can all over The City. And he said he was a runner!" The Short One.

"Amazing. I've never seen such a full remission," Thin Woman.

"Yes, truly remarkable," Mr. Personality. "But I guess that's over now. Now that the disease has taken control again, he should–"

"Fuck!" I said. "What's with you clowns? They send you in for comic relief?"

"Just students. We're studying you. Thirty years with the Condition. My, my," Mr. Personality.

"Do you throw up often?" Thin Woman.
"I'm feeling nauseous now."

Words bypassed them.

"You drink?"

"I have a few now and again."

"Wow, talk about tempting fate," The Short One.

"Well, he didn't know he had the Condition, so I suppose it helped psychologically to think he was just a normal guy with a normal life expectancy," said Mr. Personality.

"I AM a normal guy with a normal life expectancy!"

"See?" Mr. Personality, I-told-you-so grin.

"Dizziness? Shortness of breath? Must be the norm for you," Thin Woman.

"The norm for me is normal. I run ten miles a day, for God-man's sake."

New information. Freaked them out. Scribbled furiously on their pads.

"You run? As in 'exercise?'"

"Push-ups, sit-ups and pull-ups too," I said. "Easily kick any of your asses."

"Astonishing. The organism's ability to adapt. 'The Will to live' or whatever. Truly amazing," Mr. Personality.

"When was your last transfusion?" Thin Woman.

"Hell, I don't know. I already went through all this with Creed."

"You don't know? " Thin Woman incredulous.

"No."

"I told you, he knows next to nothing about The Condition," Mr. Personality. "Didn't even know he had it. Did you, Mr. Condition?"

"No, in fact. I did not."

"Well, you're here for a bone marrow transplant, aren't you?" Mr. Personality.

"Bone-marrow transplant!? Fuck no!"

"Dr. Creed has him on heavy doses of The Solution," The Short One corrected. "Dr. Creed believes that, in this case, the patient's blood might stabilize solely through application of The Solution. It's a long shot, but Dr. Creed figures we've got nothing to lose."

"'We?'" I said.

"Oh. Well. That's good, I suppose," Thin Woman.

"Why would I want a bone-marrow transplant?" I asked.

"You don't want a bone-marrow transplant. Bone-marrow transplants hurt. They have a high mortality rate. Especially if one has undergone transfusions, which you surely must have during infancy. That's why Dr. Creed has you on The Solution. State of the art medication. Produced and distributed by TKI pharmaceuticals: Longer life through chemicals," Mr. Personality, with the enthusiasm of TKI a Big Pharma hustler.

"What's wrong with me, anyway?"

"You're bad. Bad to the bone-marrow. You have bad blood," Mr. Personality. "It's all part of The Condition."

Nurse responded, finally, red button alert.

"Something wrong?" Nurse groggy, pissed off, wakened.

"My new neighbor made a mess of himself."

Concentrated yellow-brown soak-spot of "Old Faithful's" formerly crisp hospital gown soiled environs like a crashed tanker leaking crude.

"Gross!" she shrieked.

Probably inexperienced, new.

"Uh, he's been like that all night," I said. "Every hour on the hour, more or less."

"Goddam! I'll call a Nurse's Aid to clean it up. You don't worry about a thing."

"I have pneumonia. Maybe I'll get contaminated or something."

"You? With The Condition? You've got bigger things to worry about than sniffing this man's poopy-stinks, Honey."

The Night Visitors had gone. Silent slipped away.

A Second Coming

Curtains parted (dearly departed). Expected The Nurse. Hyped to complain about the Night Visitors, demand she explain. Saw Mother instead. Smoking the same cigarette. Her mortal last? Can take 'it' with you? Whatever 'it' is you love?

"Look at you, poor baby. You're a mess."

"The Condition," I said.

"Yes," she sighed. "The Condition has humbled you at last."

"What is this Condition?"

She sucked deeply on her cigarette.

"Bad blood. Bad to the bone-marrow. You almost died before you lived. I remember you, less than a year old, lying on that cold table, a needle in your tiny arm. So many transfusions. Every day another unit of blood, no bigger than a sandwich bag.

"What'd they use, a syringe?"

"Ha. Ha. Ho. Ho," she exhaled ectoplasmic smoke.

"So many transfusions? How many transfusions?"

"Twenty, twenty-five, thirty. Who remembers?"

"Shit. Why the hell didn't you tell me I had this 'Condition?'"

"You never asked. But then came the medicines and blessed remission. Those tiny pills you took every morning of your childhood. Remember? We used to call them your 'vitamins.' A regular, healthy–dare I say 'happy?–childhood. No invalid treatment for my little man. But then you stopped taking them, I assume, when you went off to The University. Why did you stop taking them?"

"I thought I was done with all that. I thought 'The Vitamins' were a childhood thing. I was strong and healthy. I was a runner for god's sake. Most of these guys with 'The Condition' don't make it past twenty. I was doing fine."

"The Condition will be with you always. You were born with it, and you will die with it. Or of it."

"When? Like. . . soon?"

"Who knows? You have a remarkable body. It adapted to The Condition like none other. Perhaps you'll go on to thirty-five, even forty!"

"Or maybe I'll go into 'blessed remission' again and pretend this nightmare never happened. Croak at a respectable age. Seventy-five, eighty. Or maybe that's greedy. Sixty-five, seventy. No?"

She smoked a bit, watched TV. I recalled small me cross-legged on her bed after school, watching celebrities of her day as she chain-smoked menthols.

Lights flashed. The machine. Battery dead. Or fluids low. Or wire tangled, or something.

“Why now? I was fine for years. What the hell happened?”

“You must have gone into remission just long enough to dapple the halcyon days of youth with music and sunshine. Playtime’s over. You’re out of remission. The Grinning Reaper knows as well as you and I that you were born to work behind a desk, not lug ‘buckets’ of water all over town.”

“Grim Reaper, not ‘grinning Reaper.’”

“My son the scholar. Have you ever met him?”

“No, thankfully. Can’t say that I have. Yet.”

“Don’t talk about things you don’t know. Listen first, then talk. But really, only if you must,” her motto.

“What about the old medicines? My ‘vitamins.’ They helped me once.”

“‘Put away those childish things,’ Mother said, pretending to quote some deep, dropped-down-from-The Ages” old grease-bard. Always quoted, rarely read. Words, phrases glommed from TV, Radio, maybe recalled college “re-released” her own.

“You’re in a new phase of The Condition. With each new phase in life we require newer, better drugs,” she said.

"What, you're a spokeswoman for TKI Pharmaceuticals now?"

"Just telling you what is and what is not," she said. Added, "Maybe you should have sent a check to the God-man when that TV show offered you the chance."

"All I need. Bounce a check on The Creator."

"I would imagine He's insured," she said.

We watched together like years ago the young me, the very young me helped Mother forget her pain.

My bed now, my pain.

No Solution

Personal visit after breakfast by The Man himself. Dr. Creed, eyebrows a-flutter, glum.

"When can I get out of here?" I asked.

"When your blood-count stabilizes, you'll be able to go home and rest."

"When can I lose this albatross," I pointed to the machine, my ball-and-chain.

"Give it a couple of days."

"You asked me about transfusions. Are you going to give me a transfusion?"

Eye brows in overdrive, he paused, sighed.

"The Solution isn't working. I'm sorry."

"What? Then what?"

"Perhaps you'll go into remission again. . . "

Will it. Will it. Will it.

"Or perhaps not. It's possible you'll slowly waste away. . . "

Wilt. Wilt. Wilt.

"Anyway, there's nothing Medical Science can do at this point. You'll have to be strong. Find something. Some kind of. . . I don't know. . . 'faith' to hang on. I'll check on you tomorrow," Creed decreed.

Will't. Will't. Will't.

Fire Bush Suppressed

Television 24/7. We moribund roommates watched old movies entertainment comedy. Cartoons.

We watched news.

Fire Bush the Featured Story. Video clips of him and assistants conducting ceremonies for large audiences (hundreds, thousands) of Missing Young, VD's, and other denizens of The Big Park. Many Missing Young now greened their hair. The Green-haired Young. No longer missing, with Fire Bush they were 'found.'

The News identified Fire Bush as a charismatic 'cult figure' with growing influence among The City's disenchanted young. The Mayor arrested Fire Bush for allegedly inciting thousands of Missing Young to be missed.

Big Media hounded Fire Bush, whose lawyer contended this Free Speech; Free Will; Freedom of Religion; Freedom to Gather Publicly, and Freedom to "Freedom to" test-case might go to the highest court in The Nation.

Fire Bush did not "instigate or instruct" Missing Young to do anything. He spoke, The Young listened. He was not responsible who listened, nor would he follow new Statutes required Missing Young be identified and turned into the police, though failure to comply with said Statutes could lead to fine and/or imprisonment. The Lawyer planned to sue The City for suppressing Fire Bush's freedom to announce and follow his own beliefs as a Free Citizen of The Nation.

Completion

Emergency Broadcast irrigation flushed through all communication networks of the Victorious Nation. The Leader announced completion of The War. The Enemy, fearing absolute and total annihilation, had desperately sued for peace. Within months, most troops would be home. Parades, Celebrity media events, and countless expressions of National congratulation would commence immediately, and continue until the last hero returned to kiss the sacred ground he/she had traveled such vast distance to defend (many, of course, would be returned to participate in various clean-up maneuvers, but not until being re-united with loved ones and photographed on their knees).

Announcements cut all channel programming. I observed my roommates' reactions. Nothing. Not even a raspberry or sarcastic cheer. That The Nation defeated The Enemy thousands of miles away meant nothing to these men who would soon leave The City and The Nation for permanent residence in Necropolis. Turning to the cheering, happy citizens screaming "We're Number One," at cameras, I realized my place was here, among the thoughtfully resigned, rather than "out there" among the mindlessly resilient.

The Summer's War had long ago grown boring. Another Big Media curiosity, another circus. Nevertheless, I was glad that Plantwoman would be safe, that she would not drop bombs on Enemy Children, nor would the friends, relatives and countrymen of Enemy Children have occasion to drop revenge on her.

Otherwise, The War meant nothing to me. I wanted nothing.

XX.
We Citizens

Blood stabilized. Still damn low; but high enough for me to escape the disinfected halls of Dr. Creed.

The Bakery Girl and BEING cabbed me home. BEING's gig ended. He got a job at "Video, Video" movie rentals, working Four PM-Midnight.

Apartment days. We watched TV, snacked creme-filled cakes till BEING had to slog off to "Video, Video." Work.

Before beginning his new life South, Father left money to feed me, shelter me, insure me another six months. Six months health insurance payments as ex-Topiary Techniques employee until cut off. Without insurance one in my "condition" was in deep shit indeed.

Free-lance work for The Ad Agency brought some small illusion of security. Gladly have me back full-time, the woman at Human Resources said. But tired, tired. I was not well. I told her I'd go full-time once I got back into condition. Good condition. Running.

I Wanted nothing. Lay there. Watch TV. Eat creme-filled cakes. Perhaps gather energy for cigars on the roof with Music and BEING. Perhaps remission again, run again, sleep peacefully again un-Conditional, no Coney Island of Egyptian Mind hot sandy beach choked bottle-neck of Nile-soaked public laundry sucking shards of broken bottle (how do they sleep on that?). To each his own, I guess, it's not my thing. . . .

Muse and The Bakery Girl were now de facto members, The Apartment. Which was a good thing. Feminine presence, feminine energy. The more the merrier. Like family. But without questions; or accusations; or ponderous opinions concerning impenetrable irrelevancies, opinions that would haunt one's days and nights.

Saturday Victory Parade, we five, US, gathered before BEING's television to watch crowds in "Don't Mess With The Nation" t-shirts chant "We're Number One" and photograph themselves waving flags on camera. Troops marched up the Valley of Heroes. Generals rode triumphant in commemorative, shiny, virgin tanks and jeeps.

Televised spectators lined streets, cheered tanks, jeeps, lorry-load missiles, troops, troops, troops.

Muse and Music banged beer cans in celebration of The Nation.

Truly the spectacle was overwhelming. The Mayor, The City Officials, The Generals; glorious speeches lauding brave men women of The Nation; the eery music of weeping and idle engines reverberating in the canyon of heroes drawn out to a ghostly moaning shiver tickling sky-scraper spines when the high tenor of the God-man rep reached high-note in the prayer/song entitled, "Cut Down So Soon oh Beautiful, Valiant, Selfless, Young," in honor of the heroes sacrificed during the Summer's fighting.

The Armed Forces Chief Staff lightened the mood when he announced the unprecedented ratio of casualties suffered by The Nation versus those of The Enemy. The Nation counted a few hundred casualties, The Enemy a quarter million souls! Enemy cities were smashed to sub-atomic particles by The Nation's warheads. Not one Enemy missile crossed the impenetrable Air Defense Network (AidNet)of The Nation.

Production value of The Parade, like that of The War itself, was superb. For those watching at home, lulls in the live action were replaced by highlight footage of one-sided tank battles and spectacular bombings.

Music and Muse were especially upbeat. Victory Night at The Apocalyptic Pancake would feature Puppets of Weltschmerz as the headline band. Representatives of several tiers of Big Media "alternative" record labels expressed interest, inviting "Puppets" to enter the "Find Next Big Band" contest. Would Puppets of Weltshmerz be the music of our Day?

Watched BEING, Music, The Bakery Girl, Muse, my self on television: reflected images among the other icons of the Nation on the enormous screen. Saw us, as we were: five young safe Citizens The City, The Nation.

Bless us, bless us, bless us, we Citizens, blessed.

XXI.
Afterture: A Para-Life Experience

See Ya

Plantman left The City to tend the Tree of Life out in The Nation and witness the appearance of The Missing Girl.

In preparation for The Journey, Fire Bush traded his trailer for an old school bus. Before he'd become Fire Bush, when he was Professor Greenman, studying the medicinal uses of plants and herbs among the few remaining indigenous peoples in jungles South of The Nation, a Healer introduced him to the Tree of Life. Greenman took fruit from the Tree of Life and planted seeds in a desert oasis way out in The Nation, where Life is. One of the seeds burgeoned and grew.

Now, out in The Nation, there thrived a genuine Tree of Life. Each year, toward the end of Summer, it bore fruit, and each year, toward the end of Summer, The Missing Girl would visit this oasis to renew herself by eating fruit of the Tree of Life. Thus she remained both Missing and Young. Perhaps she would always be Missing Young.

"I invite you to come with us on our Journey," Fire Bush said to Plantman. "Plantman must tend the Tree of Life."

"And then?" asked Plantman.

"We will wait for Her to come."

"How do you know She will come?"

"She always comes. She will remain nineteen, the age at which I introduced her to the fruit, always and forever."

On the morning of their departure, Plantman arrived carrying only his bag of equipment, his Li'l Box of Love, and the African Violet named 'Rose.'

Buffalo Gal, Chicken Killer, and the rest of Fire Bush's entourage loaded provisions onto the bus. Already seated were a dozen of the Green Haired Young. Six male, six female, all between the ages of sixteen and twenty-two. Among them were the young lovers Smashed Deer and Fidelity.

"Are you ready to leave the potted, imprisoned flora of The City to tend The Tree of Life, a tree born of wild ancestors and living wild among Life?" asked Fire Bush.

"I am," said Plantman.

"Are you ready to sleep on the wild grass of the oasis out in The Nation and wait for the coming of The Missing Girl?"

"I am ready."

Plantman boarded the bus among Fire Bush, Chicken Killer, Buffalo Gal and the dozen Green Haired Young, including that exemplary couple, Smashed Deer and Fidelity, who reminded

Plantman of the copyrighted lovers reproduced on millions of bottles of EARN cologne. The bus was driven by a giant of a man named, appropriately, 'Tree.'

But also on the bus: an older woman, familiar face known. Thirty-five thirty six. Still Missing, though not particularly young. Yet, young. Perhaps the youngest of all.

"Maybe," thought Plantman. "Maybe yes. Maybe can."

Cradling Rose, he looked back on The City shrinking, fading as the bus began its epic journey. Watching the woman he had always known, yet always missed, he had a premonition that, much as he was needed, he would never return to The City again. At least not for many years to come.

"'Beauty is truth, truth beauty. That is all ye know on earth, that is all ye need to know,' etcetera." said Fire Bush.

"Yeah, yeah; sure, sure," said Plantman. "But what is to prevent me from eating the fruit myself? Why shouldn't Plantman remain eternally young?"

"I've tried it," said Fire Bush. "I've given it to others. The Healer who introduced me to this tree warned that only certain rare, extremely rare body types respond to the fruit. The Missing Girl is one of those types. But then, so might be Plantman. Extremely rare, but possible. I'm not sure whether this is a matter of mental, perhaps extra-sensory capacity, or body chemistry. But it is something that some very few possess and the majority of us do not. The right presence or biology, of some sort. The right Condition."

OVER

www.ingramcontent.com/pod-product-compliance
Lightning Source LLC
LaVergne TN
LVHW020526100826
845148LV00010B/1362

* 9 7 8 0 9 8 1 9 8 9 1 3 6 *